**"You've go[...]**
**Jonathan v[...]**

Courtney had to smile. "Have I?"

He took hold of her hands. "Indeed you have. This notion of yours that I'm some sort of hero— it's nonsense. I'm a perfectly ordinary man caught up in, uh, some unusual circumstances. I regret getting you involved. Any reasonable woman would have had her fill of excitement and danger by now . . . her fill of me."

"I'm not a reasonable woman, Jonathan."

His smile was tender. "No, you're not, love."

"And I'll never forget you," she added softly.

Jonathan felt his control slip. "If there's anything of the hero inside me, then the only right thing to do is walk—"

She put a finger to his lips. "But you're not a hero, Jonathan, as you just pointed out.... So I won't let you walk away from me now."

## ABOUT THE AUTHOR

Elise Title is no stranger to readers of romance fiction. She's written over thirty novels under the pseudonym Alison Tyler. *Out of the Blue*, a romantic thriller with a humorous twist, marks her debut with the Superromance line. This multitalented author lives in New Hampshire with her husband and two children.

## Books by Elise Title

Don't miss any of our special offers. Write to us at the following address for information on our newest releases.

Harlequin Reader Service
901 Fuhrmann Blvd., P.O. Box 1397, Buffalo, NY 14240
Canadian address: P.O. Box 603,

# Out of the Blue

## ELISE TITLE

# Harlequin Books

TORONTO • NEW YORK • LONDON
AMSTERDAM • PARIS • SYDNEY • HAMBURG
STOCKHOLM • ATHENS • TOKYO • MILAN

FORTY YEARS OF
Romance

Published July 1989

First printing May 1989

ISBN 0-373-70363-5

To Ethel—
a very special lady.

# CHAPTER ONE

LONDON WEATHERMEN have a tendency toward optimism. The mild spring shower they'd predicted had, by four in the afternoon, blossomed into a full-fledged storm. Derek Colton scowled and pulled up the collar of his mac as the doorman at the side entrance to the Regis Hotel opened the beveled glass door with a flourish. He offered Colton the use of an umbrella, but Colton said that wouldn't be necessary. He didn't have far to go.

Colton checked his watch under the protection of the canopy and took a deep, steadying breath. The next few minutes would tell whether he'd made the right decision. For the sake of his country, never mind his own neck, he prayed he had.

The incessant beat of the rain on the pavement was almost hypnotic. The storm had swept the street clean of people. Even the little tearoom across the way had closed early. Then again, there never were many people in this part of town on a Sunday afternoon.

He remained under the canopy as he surveyed the street for any signs of life, his eyes traveling up and down the rows of parked cars. Was he being watched? But even that worry didn't disturb him as much as his worry about the irrepressible Katherine O'Malley.

He had warned her not to come. Ordered her not to come. But Katherine O'Malley rarely took orders from anyone. He remembered how her stunning emerald-colored eyes had shot daggers at him when he'd told her this was one assignment he must carry out alone. He could picture so vividly the stubborn line of her full, luscious lips, the frown marring an otherwise flawless brow. He could see her sweep her long, slender fingers through her shimmering red locks, a habit of hers when she was tense . . . or frightened. Katherine. Beautiful, vibrant, courageous Katherine. She must obey orders this time.

A sleek black Bentley limo came around the corner just as he was about to head down the street. In the front seat sat a uniformed chauffeur. Despite the dull gloom of the stormy afternoon, the headlights hadn't been flicked on. Colton watched the familiar limo pull to a stop, thirty feet from the canopied entrance to the Regis.

The chauffeur did not shut off the engine and Colton could smell the acrid petrol fumes. The rear door opened and a tall, slender woman in a tailored black mac stepped out. A chic matching wide-brimmed hat was pulled low and at an angle, partially covering one side of her face.

There was an assurance about her as she stood there staring at him, mindless of the pounding rain. No mere storm could ruffle the unflappable Katherine O'Malley.

Colton shook his head as he watched her walk toward him. Her stride bespoke grace, confidence, absolute femininity. He remained motionless as she approached, her long, untamed red tresses shining, a look of wry amusement on her face.

"You didn't really think I'd let you go bargain with the Devil on your own, my love?"

Colton's blue-green eyes narrowed. She was cool, very cool. But Colton knew her as no one else. He could see beneath that fiercely confident facade to the taut fear she contained so well. He could feel her wide-set cat-green eyes burning into his, the wind whipping at her hair as she gazed at him defiantly.

"I want you to go home, Katherine. It's too dangerous. What are you trying to do? Get yourself killed?"

"And I suppose you, my darling Colt, are immune to death?"

He sighed in frustration. "One of these days, my sweet, your stubbornness is going to be your undoing."

"Let's pray today isn't the one."

And then, because she was so brave, so beautiful, and because it was what he longed to do most, he swept her into his arms and kissed her hotly, passionately. She arched against him, his torrid kiss invading her mouth, her mind, her heart. She loved this man beyond reason, beyond life itself.

He held her against him a moment longer. "What am I going to do with you, Kate?"

Suddenly tears sprang up in her exquisite green eyes. "Whatever you do, my darling, I want you to do it forever."

"Won't you please go back? Wait for me at the café? I'll come to you, I promise."

In answer, she waved her driver off.

Colton pulled her into his arms and kissed her salty tear-stained cheek. Then he pressed his lips against her hair and breathed in the fragrant scent of jasmine.

"All right, but promise you'll stay behind in the shadows. You can keep me covered. But that's all. I mean it, Kate. You must give me your promise."

"I give you my love, Colt. Will that do?"

He smiled, even though he feared for her safety. If anything ever happened to Kate...

They kissed once more for luck and then he took off ahead of her. Giving Colt a fifty-yard head start, Katherine followed him, keeping to the shadows of the buildings, her right hand in her pocket, her slender fingers curling reassuringly around her trusty, compact .22. She would use it if anyone made a move on Colt.

The rain lashing at his face, Colton was just approaching the end of the street when the expected gray Mercedes came around the corner, its low beams illuminating the beating pellets of rain. He stiffened in anticipation as the car stopped between two streetlamps. Behind the wheel was a dark-suited driver, fedora pulled low. One lone figure sat in the shadows of the deep back seat. The obscured passenger opened his door to signal Colt, but made no move to exit.

Colton glanced behind him once more, reassured that Katherine could not be seen, then slowly he reached into the pocket of his mac and pulled out a plastic-wrapped package the size of a business envelope. He held up the packet for a moment—his signal—then tucked it safely back in his pocket. A gloved hand beckoned from the open door.

Pulsing rain mixed with sweat on Colton's face, but his expression was cool, controlled, confident.

It wasn't until he'd moved within five feet of the car door and caught a glimpse of the devilishly pale, round face in the shadow of the back seat that Derek Colton feared he'd very likely played his last card. And it wasn't an ace. His arch enemy Andres Wolfgang was holding the winning hand—not to mention a Russian-issue automatic.

At the sight of the bulky black pistol in the gloved hand of the villainous Andres Wolfgang, Colton made for the car door, straining to swing it shut, his only hope to deflect the course of the inevitable bullet.

A thunderclap exploded in his ears as he felt an incredible seering pain in his chest.

Hidden in a doorway thirty feet away, Katherine cried out in horror, her hand covering her mouth instinctively to drown out the sound. She saw a heavyset man leap out of the car and rifle Colt's pocket for the package. With cool precision, she leveled her .22 and fired. The man fell back against the open car door.

She started running down the empty street, firing faster now, wildly, recklessly, despairingly.

The wounded Wolfgang somehow managed to pull himself back into the safety of the Mercedes, and the car door flapping open, the sedan took off in a cloud of mist.

Katherine was sobbing as she reached Colt, who was sprawled on his back on the rain-drenched street. The package lay beside him. She fell to her knees and cradled his head in her arms.

Somewhere in the distance sirens wailed. Nearer was the familiar sound of the approaching Bentley limo.

Katherine held Derek's head against her breast. "It's all right, darling. You're going to be all right. You must. I love you too much to let you die."

"Katherine, you must...take the package...and make sure...it's safe."

"Yes, my darling. I promise. But first, my love, I will make sure you're safe."

She sighed with relief as the Bentley pulled up to the curb, her faithful driver leaping out. Together they got Colt into the car.

He was fast slipping into unconsciousness, but he managed a faint smile as he watched Katherine tuck the packet in her purse.

"I love you, Kate. Truly and with all my heart."

"You will make it, Colt?" Tears filled her eyes.

His smile deepened. "I'll make it."

"Take my hand, my love."

COURTNEY BLUE PRESSED the open book against her chest and sniffed loudly. Eyes closed, she whispered softly, "You will make it, Colt?"

And then, in a deeper, huskier voice, she replied, "Yes, my love, my darling Kate. Yes, I'll make it."

"Take my hand, my love. My true and only love." Slowly Courtney opened her eyes, embarrassedly looking around the bookstore to make certain it was still empty. She'd gotten so lost in *Only Fools Die* that she was afraid she might not have heard the arrival of a customer.

Vaughn's Rare and Used Books—the "Rare" having mostly been packed up and shipped off weeks earlier—was still empty. It was usually empty these days. Madison Street was the site of Boston's newest raze-and-rebuild project and half the block was already torn up. Today, what with the added hindrance of the torrential downpour, Courtney not only hadn't seen a single customer all day, she'd seen hardly a soul pass by on the street. Not that she minded in the least. In a short while she'd close up shop and go upstairs to her cozy apartment, take a leisurely bubble bath, heat up yesterday's stew and finish her latest Hilary Bennett thriller.

Courtney studied the little store with a fond smile. She'd been managing it for her uncle, Louis Vaughn, practically since graduating from Boston University eight years ago. It had proved to be a most satisfactory arrangement, allowing her uncle more time for travel and the purchase and sale of rare editions and providing Courtney with both a job she enjoyed and a place to live. Courtney had always been an avid reader. Coupled with a vivid imagination, she had, ever since childhood, secretly enjoyed slipping into Walter Mitty type fantasies. She imagined herself most often in femme fatale roles à la Hilary Bennett heroine, Katherine O'Malley. The fantasies were harmless, if somewhat addictive, but Courtney was careful to keep them under reasonable control.

Giving the musty-smelling, antiquated little shop a wistful survey, she sighed, thinking of the mammoth wrecking ball that would come swinging at her door in a few short weeks and put her not only out of a job, but a home.

Pushing aside the problem for the time being, she moved to one of the cozy, well-worn reading chairs that were as much a part of Vaughn's as the bookshelves covering every inch of wall in the shop as well as floor in between. Courtney settled in to reread the last few pages of her book. Halfway through, she paused to glance out the large, dust-streaked plate-glass window that faced the street.

How perfect, she thought. A rainy late afternoon, the street deserted just like in the novel. Courtney stared at the beading pattern the rain made on the window. She could just make out her own reflection. She tilted her head coquettishly, a soft smile on her lips. "I give you my love, Colt. Will that do?"

Setting the book down, she rose from the chair and moved closer to the window. "I can't let you bargain with the Devil all alone, my darling." She smiled seductively, her image smiling back. She laughed gaily. "I know, darling. I'm incorrigible. What? You think I'm the most beautiful, courageous, impossible woman you've ever met?" Her voice was breathy, vibrant, her smile demure now. "It isn't true. I'm a mere shop girl, darling. Rather plain, rather a stick in the mud." She sighed, taking sweeping, graceful strides back and forth in front of the window as she watched her reflection. "Oh, a marvelous disguise, you say. My darling Colt, how clever you are. And how very weary I am of the pretense. It's time to cast away illusion. I've been waiting for this moment for so long, my darling."

Courtney came to a sudden stop and inspected her reflection dolefully. She really did need to do something about her hair. It was so...boring, so...schoolmarmish. She undid the tortoiseshell barrette at her nape, shaking her shoulder-length sandy-blond hair free, deciding that was a little better. She glanced down at her plain gray sweater and black wool pleated skirt. It was a perfect shop-girl disguise, but it would never do for drinks at the Regis.

Sighing, she retrieved *Only Fools Die* and sat down on a chintz-covered armchair closer to the window. She opened to the middle of the first chapter, where the writer, Hilary Bennett, had first described the suave British secret agent Derek Colton.

*Katherine's heart quickened when she saw him for the first time. He was tall, well built, with dark, thick wavy hair, a rugged complexion that bore the remnants of a tropical tan. An altogether fine specimen, Katherine thought. And then she met his eyes. She'd never seen eyes quite that shade of blue before. They reminded her of the ocean after a special sunrise, deep, mysterious, sensual aquamarine eyes. Eyes that held a mixture of candor, sensuality and irony. Afraid of getting lost in those altogether mesmerizing eyes, Katherine dropped her gaze to the strong firm line of his nose, the passionate fullness of his lips, the sharp, angular cut of his jaw. Yes, a fine specimen, indeed.*

Courtney closed her eyes. She could picture Colt's face vividly, the laugh lines radiating from the corners of those extraordinary aquamarine eyes. Eyes that lovingly caressed her as he guided her toward the safety of the café.

The phone rang just as Derek was about to pull her into his arms.

"Damn," she muttered, reluctantly setting down her book and hurrying across the shop to answer it. Perhaps, she thought, grinning, it was Colt, telling her where their next assignation would be.

"Yes?" she said, unaware of the huskiness in her tone.

"Courtney? Is that you?"

Courtney cleared her throat and tucked the receiver in the crook of her shoulder. "Of course it's me, Uncle Lou. Who else would it be?"

"You sounded a bit . . . different." He chuckled softly.

Courtney could feel her face heat up and was glad she was all alone. Her uncle, who had raised her since she was fourteen, was forever teasing her about this habit of hers of playacting, as he called it. He'd often suggested she was a natural-born actress, but Courtney's role playing—as she called it—was for her a strictly private and personal amusement.

"I was just reading," Courtney said firmly.

"I've called to see how things are going."

"This place is a mausoleum today, what with the storm and half the street torn up. The wrecking crew was going to tear down the Claughlin Building this morning, but I guess the rain held them up."

"Yes." Uncle Lou sighed. "Progress marches on. The quaint city of Boston will soon be nothing but skyscrapers and pocket parks."

"Progress is going to be marching right into Vaughn's Rare and Used Books by the end of the month," she said in a lightly scolding voice.

"Well, I have been out looking for other locations."

"Come on, Uncle Lou. You know you'd just as soon close up shop for good. You're only worried about me. And you've absolutely no reason to worry. I've got a bit of money saved up. And there are plenty of other bookstores." She laughed. "I'll go work for the competition."

"I promised your mother on her deathbed fourteen years ago, Courtney, that I would worry after you until someone came along to pick up the slack, if you catch my drift."

Courtney grinned. "I'm perfectly capable of worrying after myself."

"But you don't worry, my girl. That's what worries me. Your head is in the clouds. You sit in that musty-smelling, cluttered shop day after day, lost in your books and your dreams. Rome burns and you fiddle away. We must live some of our dreams, Courtney. Act on them. Tell me, when was the last time you went out dancing?"

"Dancing?" Courtney laughed, taken aback by the question. "Are we talking square dancing or ballroom dancing?"

"Disco dancing. Isn't that still in vogue?"

"I'm a terrible disco dancer, Lou."

"You sell yourself short, Courtney. You're a fine woman. You're good-looking, smart as a whip..."

Courtney closed her eyes. *Beautiful, vibrant, brave, impossibly stubborn. Oh, Katherine, my love, you are the most exquisite woman I've ever beheld...*

"Courtney? Are you listening to me? Did you hear what I said?"

She laughed. "I hear you, Uncle Lou. I'm a fine specimen of a woman, right?"

"Right."

"I'd better go. I should pack up some more cartons. I'll be in touch."

She set the receiver in the cradle, her hand lingering as she glanced around the still-empty shop. The drab shop girl vanished instantly, the smile appearing on her lips—the devastating smile of Katherine O'Malley. "Yes, my darling, I'll be in touch."

She could hear Colt's voice in her head: *Promise me you won't take any foolish chances, Katherine. Your life is on the line.*

*And I suppose you, my darling, are immune to death?*

Courtney walked toward the window and stared out into the empty, rain-drenched street. "I know you're out there somewhere, my darling Colt." She stuck her hand into the pocket of her skirt. "I'll cover you, love. Wolfgang won't get another chance to harm you. I promise you, Colt."

She stared across the street at the boarded-up coffee shop, imagining she was at the door of the Regis, gazing across at the empty tearoom. The actual scene so resembled the scene from the Bennett thriller that when Courtney, à la Katherine O'Malley saw the tall, broad-shouldered, raincoated figure hurrying furtively down the other side of the street, she immediately incorporated him into her fantasy.

"Yes, there you are, my darling. Be careful. Wolfgang may well be following you."

Right on cue, Courtney spotted a large black sedan turning the corner onto Madison. Her heart quickened. "Oh, no, Colt. Wolfgang's car."

Even as she watched the man on the street quickly, nervously look back at the slowly approaching car, then break into a run, Courtney was convinced her usually vivid imagination had simply shifted into overdrive.

So did the black sedan.

Almost as if she were half in a film and half watching it, she witnessed the sedan come to a squealing stop a few feet from the man in the mac.

Then Courtney heard a pop. A barely audible sound that broke the rhythm of the storm. Nothing terribly dramatic, really. Not alarming, certainly.

Only in the same second that Courtney heard that faint pop, she saw the man in the mac, the man whom she'd fondly dubbed Derek Colton, or rather "Colt, my darling," stagger back several paces and crumble to the hard, wet pavement.

Courtney blinked several times in an attempt to erase what must have been an imaginary vision. Only it didn't erase. A sudden panic washed over her. "Come on, Blue. You're really letting your imagination get carried away this time."

No amount of blinking made the image of the fallen man or the idling black sedan vanish. And when a short, stocky figure in a navy coat leaped out of the car and dashed over to the fallen man, Courtney was finally convinced that whatever was going on out there was not a product of her imagination. The scene was real.

She raced to the door of the shop and flung it open just as the stocky man was bending over the man sprawled on the ground. The smaller man was trying to turn the larger one over onto his back when Courtney called out, "Don't! You shouldn't move him. Wait. I'll call an ambulance."

The heavyset man froze in his kneeling position as he looked across the street at the woman screaming frantically to him. Then, as he saw her start to turn, he immediately returned to his task, his efforts more feverish now.

Courtney was halfway across the shop, when she heard another car roaring down the street. Maybe a cruiser, she prayed. But when she swung around to check, the tableau was truly something out of *Only Fools Die*. The driver of the stocky man's black sedan was beeping his horn furiously. The man looked up, saw the fast-approaching silver sports car and made a beeline for his own vehicle, leaving the man in the mac on the ground. As the black sedan peeled out, the second car gave chase.

Courtney stood there dazed, smelling the pungent aroma of burned rubber mixed with automobile exhaust.

If it hadn't been for the man still lying in the street, she might have convinced herself that she had imagined the whole sequence of events. But the man was still there. Quickly Courtney pulled herself together. She had to call the police. And an ambulance. Then grab a blanket from her apartment and see what she could do for the poor man until help arrived.

Only as she was dialing 911 with trembling fingers did she clearly connect the pop she'd heard with the man in the mac falling to the ground. A gunshot. Probably a small-caliber pistol, very likely something resembling the sleek little number Katherine O'Malley used. Courtney scowled. Forget Katherine O'Malley, she chastised herself sharply as the voice came on at the other end of the line. Breathlessly, trying her best to stem her panic, she told the policeman what had happened and gave her name and address.

As soon as she hung up, Courtney rushed through to the small back room of the shop, then up the stairs to her apartment for a blanket. She also grabbed a couple of towels from the bathroom. If the man was bleeding to death...

On her way down the stairs she stumbled and nearly fell. After a second to steady herself and catch her breath, Courtney flew down the remaining steps. Her hazel eyes were as wide as saucers as she raced through the shop. Wind and rain lashed at her as she flew out the door and started across the street.

She came to an abrupt stop halfway across the road, her expression baffled. The spot where only a minute ago the man lay sprawled on the pavement was empty. The whole street was empty. Slowly, unsteadily, Courtney continued to the other side, her soaked sweater and skirt clinging unpleasantly to her body like a second skin, her leather loafers squishing with each step.

She stopped precisely where she believed the man in the mac to have fallen, and she searched the length of the street, checking the doorway of the closed-up coffee shop, thinking perhaps the poor man had managed to crawl to cover. He certainly had appeared in no condition to pick himself up and stroll away. And even if he had managed to get back on his feet, he couldn't have gotten very far in the minute or two she'd been gone.

"Where the hell did he go?" she muttered. Standing in the middle of the sidewalk, the rain beating down on her, she had a decidedly uneasy feeling in the pit of her stomach. "He was here. I...did see him. And the black sedan. And that stocky little man. I...I heard the gunshot." She continued to search the street. "Damn it. I wasn't imagining it. I couldn't have...."

It wasn't until she heard the sound of sirens wailing in the distance that Courtney remembered about the police. "Oh, God," she moaned, realizing she would have to call them back. How to explain that the wounded man in the mac had managed to vanish without a trace?

She hugged the sodden blanket and towels to her chest and started back across the street. "We're through, Colt, my love," she muttered with irritation. "I've really let things go too far this time."

# CHAPTER TWO

COURTNEY FROWNED as she hung up the phone, the angry desk sergeant's words echoing in her head. "An overactive imagination can get a person in serious trouble," he'd snapped after her muddled explanation.

She went upstairs and changed into dry clothes, then returned to the shop. She thought about those cartons she'd planned to pack, but her eyes kept drifting out the window to the deserted street. After a moment's hesitation, she walked over to the window and stared out into the late-afternoon gloom. The rain had let up a little, but the street remained silent, empty...eerie.

Courtney's frown deepened. Had it all really been her imagination? Or had she seen some of it, embellishing the rest? She went over the events in her mind, trying to make some sense of them. She pictured the man walking down the street—an ordinary man, probably on his way home to his wife and children. *He hears a car come along. He starts to run.* Courtney stopped in her musings. *Why does he start to run?* Her fingers traced a question mark on the dusty window. *He runs because it's raining hard. The car is nothing more than a coincidence.* Again she paused. *And the pop? Simple,* she decided. The car backfired. One perplexing question remained. Why did the man fall to the pavement? He was startled by the pop? He tripped over a crack?

Courtney sighed. Maybe the cop was right. Maybe she had imagined the whole thing. Because...if she did see that man and the rest of it...it was no ordinary scene. The man in the mac was no ordinary man. Of that Courtney felt convinced.

She sat down on the window seat and stared at her dirt-smudged palm. The only answer that made any sense was to forget the whole thing, go pack a few more cartons and close up shop.

A faint sound coming from the back room stopped her ruminations. She listened closely. Silence.

Oh, great, she thought. Now she was hearing things. Yes, maybe the cop was right. And Uncle Lou, as well. She really had to stop this foolish habit of daydreaming. It had gotten out of hand without her having realized it. Better to stick strictly to reality. Tomorrow, first thing, she told herself firmly, she would look for work, find a nice studio apartment, get settled.

A dull prospect, she couldn't help reflecting. A woman like Katherine O'Malley would cringe at the very thought. Adventure, excitement, danger, passion. That's what awaited a woman like Katherine O'Malley.

Another sound—a thump—from the back room, this one louder, more defined, jerked Courtney's thoughts back to the moment at hand. She listened intently. There it was again. A distinct thump. Like something falling. She stiffened. Had someone snuck down the alley next to the book-store and broken in through the back door?

Courtney felt a surge of panic. What should she do? Call the police? She grimaced. And very likely get that same desk sergeant on the line. He'd send down a squad car, all right. To cart her off to a loony bin.

She couldn't help wondering what Katherine O'Malley would do in such a situation. Whip out her trusty .22 and investigate...that's what.

Courtney didn't keep a gun in the shop. Or in her apartment, for that matter. Uncle Lou had had one in the store while the rare books were still tucked behind the locked glass cabinets. But he'd carted the weapon off with the valuable books several weeks ago.

When she heard a low, muffled moan, she sprang to her feet. Dashing over to the desk, she whipped out a letter opener from the top drawer. It hardly cut through paper, but it was the only "weapon" Courtney could think of.

Slowly, cautiously, gripping the letter opener, Courtney turned the knob on the door to the back room, praying it wouldn't squeak as she pushed it open.

She sucked in a breath as the hinges creaked loudly. Her throat was constricted as she stood to the side of the door, peering into the dimly lit room.

"Who's there?" Fear had dropped her voice a good two octaves.

Silence.

"I'm...armed." Her heart was pounding. She pushed her damp hair from her face and risked a fuller look into the room. The light switch was just inside the door on the right.

*Switch it on, Blue,* she told herself. *See for yourself that the room is empty, that once again you've let your imagination fly out of hand. Go on. Switch on the light, check behind the door, check under the rug, for heaven's sake. And then go toss that foolish Bennett thriller in the trash.*

Courtney's fingers trembled as she felt for the light switch. Her breath caught as she flicked it on.

"Turn it off, damn it."

At the sound of that harsh masculine voice, Courtney expelled her held breath in a panicked cry.

And then she saw him. Sprawled on the floor near the back wall, just behind a pile of cartons, almost in the same position she'd seen him earlier on the pavement. The man in the mac.

"Turn the light off," he ordered again.

Courtney was too stunned to think clearly. Automatically she did as the man commanded.

"That's better." He let out a pained sigh.

Gripping the letter opener, Courtney took a couple of steps into the room. The man didn't move at all. She took a few more steps. His face was turned away, so she couldn't tell if his eyes were open or if he'd slipped into unconsciousness. When she was only a few feet from him, close enough to hear his ragged breathing, he moaned again, and turned his head in her direction. It clearly took great effort. "Come closer."

He reached his hand out toward her ankle.

"Pull the shade on the window...and lock the door."

His voice was so low Courtney had to strain to hear him. His grip on her leg, however, was surprisingly strong.

"Do it." Abruptly he released her.

Why she scooted across the room and followed his command, she couldn't for the life of her say. She simply did what he'd ordered. Then, not on order, she turned on the lamp sitting atop a carton of books. The lamplight was dimmer than the overhead fixture and cast a soft glow in the room.

The man in the mac rolled onto his side and looked across at her.

Courtney emitted an involuntary gasp. *Her heart quickened when she saw him clearly for the first time. He was tall, well built, with dark, thick wavy hair, a rugged complexion that bore the remnants...*

Courtney slowly shook her head. No, she amended, there were no remnants of a tan on this man's skin. But for that, Hilary Bennett's description of Derek Colton fit the intruder perfectly. Wide-eyed, Courtney stepped closer to the man, observing *the strong, firm line of his nose, the passionate fullness of his lips, the sharp, angular cut of his jaw...*

Her hand moved to her mouth, muffling another gasp of astonishment as she noticed his eyes. The color of those eyes took her breath away. They were *the ocean after a special sunrise, deep, mysterious, sensual aquamarine eyes. Eyes that held a mixture of candor, sensuality and irony.*

She was trembling, frightened. She stared at the man as though seeing a ghost, a vision. Yes, a vision. That was it. She hugged herself tightly, convinced now that her mind truly had slipped all its gears. Oh, she'd conjured up heroes before. Many times. But never with such astounding clarity.

"Don't be afraid" she heard him whisper. "I'm not going to hurt you."

Her mouth dropped open. Even the accent was Derek's. A cultured English accent.

"No," she murmured, stepping back unsteadily. "No, this can't be happening."

She squeezed her eyes shut, then opened them very slowly. The man in the mac, the man with the incredible aquamarine eyes, hadn't vanished. In fact, he was staring at her with a bemused expression.

"I'm going mad," she whispered.

He smiled. She could see the laugh lines radiating from the corners of his eyes.

"Oh God," she muttered, "Derek..."

The man in the mac managed to push himself to a half-sitting position, using the wall for support. "Please. Don't be so alarmed. The back door was unlocked. I...I had to find someplace... Look, just give me a few minutes...to catch my breath and get my bearings." He grimaced. "Who's Derek? The owner of the shop? Is he out front?"

Courtney shook her head dumbly.

The man's raincoat had fallen open. Courtney stared at his left gray trouser leg. "You're bleeding. That's...blood. Real blood."

Despite the pain, he managed a faint smile. "Believe me, love, I'd greatly prefer it were catsup, but it isn't." He glanced down at his bloodied thigh. "I don't suppose you'd have a first-aid kit about?"

Courtney's hazel eyes narrowed as her gaze met his. "Who... who are you?"

"How rude of me." Those sensual, blue-green eyes held more than a hint of irony. "I don't often forget my manners, love. It's been a bad day, what with my apartment being ransacked, being chased through the streets, being used for bloody target practice."

Courtney came closer to him. "I saw some of it. From the shop."

She watched him pull at the bloodied cloth near his thigh and examine the wound. Then he looked up at her. "It isn't too bad. A lot of blood, but I'm fairly certain it's only a flesh wound."

"You still didn't tell me... your name." Courtney saw that the intruder was staring with faint amusement at the blunt letter opener she still gripped.

"The name's Madden. Jonathan Madden. I'm a professor at Brandeis University. And, I assure you, I'm perfectly harmless, Miss...?"

Relived beyond measure that he hadn't introduced himself as Derek Colton, Courtney couldn't help the laugh that escaped her lips. Quickly regaining her equilibrium, she introduced herself. "Blue. Courtney Blue."

Jonathan Madden took the laugh for a nervous reaction. "Please, Miss Blue, don't be frightened."

She could feel herself getting lost in those aquamarine eyes. "I'm not frightened," she stated flatly, although why she wasn't afraid was a complete mystery to her.

She knelt beside him, pulling her gaze from his eyes with effort and examining his wounded thigh. "You ought to have a doctor look at that."

Madden shook his head, a troubled expression on his face. "It isn't necessary. I just need to bandage it."

Courtney sighed. "I'll have to clean it up first so infection won't set in." She could feel his eyes fixed on her, and after a moment's hesitation she looked up. "Then I can bandage it for you, if you want."

His smile was warm and genuine. "You're very brave, Courtney Blue."

Their eyes locked. She smiled back. "Not really."

"And very beautiful," he whispered, leaning closer, his warm breath grazing her cheek.

She stared at him, transfixed. *And then, because it was what he longed to do most, he swept her roughly into his arms and kissed her hotly, passionately.*

"Are you okay, Miss Blue? Courtney?"

She gave him a startled glance and flushed. "Umm, bandages . . . and some soap and water." She glanced up at the stairs. "My apartment's up there. Can you make it?" Absently she swept her long, slender fingers through her damp windswept hair.

His smile deepened. "I'll make it."

"Take my hand . . ."

THE CHILL BREEZE bore the prickly smell of the Charles River. Dusk was falling sharply, like a shade being drawn for privacy. The rain continued to drum, softer now, on the roof of the car. The driver opened his door and exited the black sedan, cursing hotly as water splashed knee-high up his leg. He stepped out of the puddle, up onto the sidewalk.

The streetlamp illuminated his features. He was close to fifty, full faced, pasty skinned, his eyes set too closely to a broad, flattened nose. He was bulkily built, his navy coat straining at the seams as he dug his hands into his pockets. He stopped under the light. He was scowling.

The scowl deepened as he watched the tall, gaunt man approach on foot from the north. His hands dug deeper in his pockets. There'd be hell to pay now.

The gaunt man stopped to light a cigarette, then continued toward him.

*Damn,* Borofsky thought, *he knows I've failed.* Bad news traveled fast in their circle.

But it wasn't his fault. Too many events had conspired against him. If it hadn't been for that damn shop girl. And then that bloody Porsche breathing down his neck. If he'd lingered even a moment longer, he would not only have failed in his mission, he would likely have failed to take another breath. *Humph. Go explain that to Dmitri Zakharov.* Zakharov did not abide explanations.

The gaunt man, dapperly dressed in a custom-tailored tan trench coat and matching fedora, stopped three feet from Borofsky. Nothing in those bland, nondescript features indicated the slightest hint of feeling. Borofsky hated that most about Dmitri Zakharov. One never knew what he was feeling or thinking... until it was too late to do anything about it.

"A wretched evening, don't you think, Yevgenni?"

Borofsky stared nervously into Zakharov's icy blue eyes. "Wretched" was the word for it, all right. "It wasn't my fault." This time Borofsky spoke the words aloud. They lacked the same conviction as when he'd said them to himself.

Zakharov observed him with a flicker of amusement. "No, of course not. You did your best, my friend."

"Maybe he didn't even have it on him. We...can't be sure he didn't...ditch it someplace before he took off."

Zakharov took a puff of his pungent Turkish cigarette, letting the acrid smoke waft across to Borofsky's face. "Perhaps you're right."

"Maybe his apartment..." Borofsky was merely stalling for time. He'd felt the package on Madden. If he'd only had a moment longer to retrieve it...

Zakharov shook his head. "No, my friend. Not his apartment. We've already examined that possibility thoroughly." He let the lit cigarette drop. It landed on Borofsky's sodden left brown shoe. Borofsky stared down at it. He nervously watched Zakharov's right foot, clad in an expensive, highly polished black leather boot, move over his shoe and crush the cigarette out.

Borofsky shook off the dead butt from his shoe and laughed uneasily. "Allow me one more opportunity to accomplish my mission. I give you my word, Dmitri Zakharov..."

"One more opportunity?" Zakharov studied the stocky man thoughtfully. "A second chance, you mean."

Borofsky could hear the approach of footsteps behind him. He didn't turn around. He didn't have to. He saw the smile on Zakharov's face. So it was one of Zakharov's henchmen. As to why he was approaching, Zakharov's cold smile was explanation enough.

Borofsky began to tremble. "I swear...Zakharov...I won't let you down...again. I'll find Madden. I'll get the...package for you. I swear..."

The footsteps stopped. Zakharov's smile deepened. His icy blue eyes looked past Borofsky's left shoulder. He nodded faintly.

Borofsky felt his knees go weak as the large hand behind him clamped heavily down on his left shoulder.

Zakharov smiled pleasantly. "I will give you another opportunity. Yevgenni. But first my associate here, Boris Goncharov, will have a few words with you. I feel he can impress upon you the vital nature of this mission. The vital need for the matter to be settled swiftly, efficiently and with finality."

Borofsky could smell the rank, stale breath of Goncharov.

"Do I make myself clear, Yevgenni?"

Borofsky was trembling so hard his head was nodding spastically even before Zakharov finished his question.

Zakharov glanced up at the darkened sky and sighed. "Wretched evening. But perhaps it will be better tomorrow."

As Borofsky watched Zakharov turn away and walk off, he felt Goncharov's other hand clamp down on his right shoulder.

THE SLEEK, SILVER PORSCHE pulled up in front of a gas station. A disgruntled-looking attendant in a yellow slicker rose from his stool in the fluorescent-lit office and put his *Playboy* magazine down. He pulled up the hood of his slicker and went running out.

When he ducked his head at the half-opened driver's window, the disgruntled expression vanished. The woman behind the wheel made Miss April look like yesterday's news.

"Would you fill it up, please?"

Her voice had a breathy vibrato that made him forget Miss April even existed. "Yeah. Sure. How about under your hood?"

The dark-haired goddess bestowed him a ruby-lipped smile, then let her sooty-lashed bittersweet chocolate eyes cruise over his face. "No, thanks. Just the gas."

"Yeah. Sure. Lousy night, isn't it?"

"Terrible." She cast her eyes past the ogling attendant toward the white BMW parked near one of the closed bays of the garage. "I see Johnny's car is on the fritz again."

"Huh?"

"The BMW over there. It belongs to a friend of mine. Jonathan Madden."

The young man took a quick look behind him. "Oh, yeah. So, you're a friend of Professor Madden's." There was a clear note of disappointment in his voice. How did he stand a chance against a guy like Madden, with his Hollywood looks and that Prince Charlie accent?

"I told him to stick to Porsches. But he's a stubborn man." Her leather-gloved hand toyed with a stray tendril of night-black hair. "When is he picking it up? Tomorrow, I hope. We have . . . plans." Those ruby lips with their moist sheen pouted prettily. "I hate being disappointed."

"Well, uh, he said he didn't need it until Thursday. He was going to come by for it around five. Maybe he's got a buddy's car for the next couple of days." Maybe, the attendant thought, if Madden proved a disappointment, he could move in on the territory . . . Yeah, sure.

"Thursday." She showed just the barest trace of annoyance.

"Hey, I could work on it tomorrow. Give Professor Madden a call and let him know . . ."

The dark-eyed goddess smiled absently. "No. That's all right. I've got a feeling he'll be hard to track down for the next couple of days." The dark eyes flitted over the attendant's face. Her gloved fingers released the stray tendril. "Around five, you said?"

The attendant nodded.

The powered window lowered a few more inches. The gloved hand reached out, patted the young man's arm. "Well . . . thanks." She winked provocatively. "I want to surprise him."

The besotted young man grinned. "Yeah. Sure."

The electric window rose swiftly and the Porsche shot out of the station.

"Hey. What about the gas? You forgot the gas."

COURTNEY HAD EXCHANGED the blunt letter opener for a sharp pair of scissors. "I'll have to cut away a good-sized piece of your trouser."

Jonathan nodded.

Courtney carefully snipped the cloth so that the wound was fully exposed. There was a lot of blood, but she was relieved to see that it was only a flesh wound.

Jonathan let himself sink back against the couch. He closed his eyes wearily.

"It looks worse than it is. Are you all right?"

Again he nodded.

"This might hurt," she warned.

"I'll be fine." He opened his eyes again and watched her dip a clean washcloth into a basin of water. When he saw her hesitate, he managed a reassuring smile. "Go ahead."

He gritted his teeth as she gently cleaned the wound. When she applied the antiseptic he winced but remained silent.

Courtney smiled. "There. Now I can bandage it. It should heal very nicely. I doubt there'll even be much of a scar. You've been very brave, Mr. Madden."

He smiled back. "Not really. I don't suppose you'd have any brandy about the place?"

"I think I can dig some up. But I should apply the bandage first."

He put his large hand over hers for a moment. "First the brandy, love. It's been a bloody awful day."

Courtney felt a tremor of excitement shoot through her at his touch, at the sound of his voice, at the way he said "love." "Uh, right. Brandy."

"And pour one for yourself. I presume you could use a stiff drink about now."

She grinned. "Good idea." She headed for the bathroom, popping out a moment later with a reasonably decent bottle of French cognac in hand. She picked up a couple of snifters from the curio cabinet against the living-room wall.

"Pardon my curiosity, Miss Blue, but do you keep all your liquor in the bathroom?"

Courtney could feel her cheeks warm. Her entire liquor supply consisted of a bottle of cooking sherry and this cognac. She didn't drink very much, but every now and then she liked to settle into a nice hot bubble bath with a snifter of brandy. For convenience, she'd simply tucked the bottle of cognac in her medicine cabinet for those occasions when the mood struck.

Flustered by his question, she couldn't help wondering what Katherine O'Malley would say. Surely she'd come up with a witty, provocative response.

Well, now it was Courtney's chance. She smiled an alluring O'Malley-type smile. "I have a rather quirky nature, Mr. Madden. Some women believe, a place for everything, everything in its place. Personally I find such orderliness boring."

His eyebrows lifted slightly. "I see."

She poured the cognac into the two snifters, risking a quick look at her newfound hero. He was smiling. With her? Or at her?

He leaned forward and lifted one of the glasses from the table. He took a long swallow, then another, before setting the drink down. "Anytime you'd like," he said, nodding toward the tape on the coffee table.

Courtney took a fairly hefty swallow of her drink and fought back a cough. "I'm not exactly a pro at this sort of thing." She picked up the gauze pad she'd found in a kitchen drawer and the only tape she could locate—packing tape she'd been using for taping up the books. "Well, I'll do my best."

"I have the utmost confidence in you."

She worked silently, her movements quick but gentle. Never in her life had she bandaged a man's injured thigh before. Not very often had she had the opportunity to deal with a man's thigh in any condition. Really, she was quite amazed, and rather pleased with how well she was doing, all things considered.

"There, that wasn't too bad." She looked up to discover that Jonathan Madden had either fallen asleep or passed out cold. She frowned. She had wanted to pump him once she'd attended to his wound. A flurry of questions whirled in her mind—who was that stocky man, why did he shoot Madden and then hover over him like that, who was driving the silver sports car, why did the driver go racing after the black sedan? In short, what the hell was going on?

"Mr. Madden?" His eyes remained closed.

"Jonathan?" She shook him gently.

No response.

Courtney sat back on her heels on the floor and stared in silence at the stranger she'd just patched up. For all she knew he was an enemy agent who had stolen some top-secret documents. Or he could have just robbed a bank. Or...murdered his wife. "One of these days, my brave, beautiful Courtney, your foolhardiness may well be your undoing," she murmured.

Jonathan Madden stirred. Courtney pressed her hand to her lips. Oh, God, what if he'd heard her?

He heaved a deep sigh, his body sinking more fully against the sofa.

She smiled as she continued to watch his breathing deepen and grow more even. "You don't impress me as the villainous type, Mr. Madden. But I do believe you've landed yourself in a mess of trouble, love." She reached for the afghan flung over one arm of the couch and covered him. "Well, my darling Jonathan, whatever it is, I'm not going to let you face it all alone."

She rose to her feet, lifted Jonathan's discarded wet raincoat from the armchair and was about to carry it over to the hall tree, when she came to an abrupt stop. There was a bulky package in the inside pocket. A prickle of unease ran through her. She glanced nervously over at Jonathan, then furtively reached inside the pocket and pulled out a brown paper wrapped package. It was the familiar size and shape of a book.

Just as she was deciding whether to risk opening the package, she heard the bell on the shop door jingle and she jumped. In her haste to attend to Jonathan she'd completely forgotten to lock up. Of all times to have to deal with a customer. And what if it wasn't a customer?

Jonathan heard the sound, too, and was instantly awake and alert. Alert enough to spot the package in Courtney's hand before she hastily shoved it back into his coat pocket.

He was angry at himself for drifting off like that, angrier still at Courtney's prying, but he made a point of pretending not to have noticed her maneuver. He had more pressing worries at the moment, the chief one being who in bloody hell had just walked into the bookshop.

Flushed, but relieved not to have been caught snooping, Courtney quickly hung Jonathan's wet raincoat on the halltree and then turned to him, her eyes not quite meeting his. "I'll have to go see who it is."

Out of the corner of her eye she saw him nod slowly.

Briefly she met his gaze. Then she turned.

"Courtney," he whispered.

She stopped, glancing back over her shoulder.

"You won't mention to anyone that I'm here, will you?" There was urgency in his deep voice.

"I'm sure it's only a browser looking to get out of the rain for a few minutes." She hesitated. "Don't worry."

He pushed himself up to a full sitting position, noticing for the first time the afghan covering him.

"Be careful, love." She thought he eyed her as caressingly as any hero in a Bennett novel had ever eyed a heroine. Shaking her hair back from her face, Courtney felt a shiver of excitement race through her. She smiled tremulously, not the least aware of how radiant her smile looked or how strongly it affected him.

"I'll be careful. I promise." And then with a wink she couldn't resist adding, "You can't imagine how long I've been waiting for something like this."

He watched her turn quickly and exit, and felt more bemused than ever. Courtney Blue, he decided, had to be the most baffling but entrancing woman he'd ever come across. Pity about the poor timing, though.

He rolled off the sofa and rose painfully, unsteadily, to his feet. He could hear faint voices drifting up from a nearby heating vent and hobbled closer.

Sounding completely natural and amazingly at ease, Courtney was telling the customer—a woman—that no, she hadn't come across a first edition of any of the Russian Gorky's writings.

Jonathan felt a cold chill go down his spine, and leaned with heavy relief against the wall when he heard the front door jingle shut.

Courtney had done well. Perhaps, he thought with a grim smile, his chance encounter with the remarkable Miss Blue wasn't poorly timed, after all. It might in fact turn out to be the best piece of luck he'd had since this whole bloody affair had begun.

# CHAPTER THREE

COURTNEY CAME BACK UPSTAIRS and entered her apartment quietly, so as not to disturb her surprise guest in case he'd dozed off again. But Jonathan Madden was not asleep. He was standing near the window, pulling up the drawn shade a couple of inches in order to look outside. Only when Courtney softly spoke his name did he realize she was there. He turned, surprise and anger in his expression.

Courtney's expression showed equal surprise, but it combined with fear rather than anger as she stared, transfixed, at the gun in Jonathan Madden's hand. She stood paralyzed in the middle of the living room.

Only when he saw her panicked look did Jonathan remember the weapon he held in his hand.

"You shouldn't sneak up on a person like that, love." He quickly tucked the gun into his waistband.

"You handle that like a pro," Courtney responded, breathing a little easier.

He laughed lightly. "Not if you saw me try to take a shot."

Courtney arched a brow. "Is that supposed to comfort me, Mr. Madden?"

He studied her thoughtfully. "How would you know how a pro handles a weapon?"

Now it was Courtney's turn to laugh. "Oh, I've read a lot of books about spies, cops...criminals."

He leaned against the wall, taking some of the pressure off his aching thigh. "And which do you have me pegged for, Miss Blue?"

Courtney stared at him in silence for several moments. "I'm not sure yet." She slowly walked toward him. "You were checking out that woman who left my shop just now. Did you know her?"

Jonathan shrugged. "It isn't very likely that I would," he said casually. "Not that I got much of a look at her, anyway. Describe her for me." He made an effort to keep his tone mildly curious, but he could see from Courtney's expression that he hadn't been altogether successful.

Walking stiffly, he went and sat back down on the sofa, stretching his injured leg straight out, his bare heel resting on the glass-topped coffee table. Before Courtney's ministrations over his injured thigh he'd removed his soaked shoes and socks.

Courtney sat down beside him, curling her slippered feet under her. "I'd say she was very attractive, late forties or early fifties, blue eyes, short blond hair nicely styled, petite, trim figure. She has the kind of money it takes to buy designer clothes and get her hair done in a posh salon—my guess is someplace on Newberry Street. Refined, educated, didn't get her schooling on the East Coast. Probably came originally from the South. My bet is she's spent a lot of time getting rid of the drawl."

Jonathan was markedly impressed by her keen powers of observation. "Anything else?" he asked, one brow raised.

She smiled. "Yes. She's not a lover of Gorky, even though she came in asking if I had any first editions of his in the shop. Probably doesn't read very much at all. Too busy shopping at Lord and Taylor's."

Now his expression held definite awe. And something else. Wariness. Courtney Blue had to be the most observant woman he'd ever come across. She most definitely did not fit his stereotype of an ordinary shop girl. What threw him off kilter, and had from the first, was that she did not fit any stereotype at all.

"Now it's my turn," she was saying while Jonathan was ruminating.

"Huh . . . ?"

"Does her description ring a bell?"

"No," he said quickly.

Too quickly for Courtney's taste.

"What's going on, Jonathan? You've got a gun on you. Your apartment was ransacked. You've been chased through the streets, shot at . . . and my guess is it wasn't target practice by a long shot." She gave a quick smile. "Pardon the pun."

"You're very astute, Miss Blue. Brave, beautiful, intelligent . . . witty. A beguiling combination." He reached out and stroked her cheek, then let his hand move down to her shoulder, where it lingered.

Courtney was aware of her physical attraction to Jonathan Madden. That he was a total stranger and a complete enigma to her only added to his appeal. He was the stuff of which heroes were made. Courtney's heroes, at any rate. But, despite her attraction, she was quite certain that Jonathan's seductive gesture was a ploy. He was trying in typically male fashion to distract her from questioning him any further. Or demanding answers. Courtney had no doubt that he had the kind of magnetism to pull off that kind of distraction . . . most of the time. But not now. It took a lot of effort for her to fight it, but Courtney decided that she'd spent too much time fantasizing the real thing to settle for mere distraction. Besides, she was intensely curious about her guest.

She looked him in the eye. "Who are you, Jonathan?"

The fierceness in her tone made him withdraw his hand. He was a little taken aback by her less than typically female response to his advance. Had she seen through him so easily? Either he was losing his touch, or Courtney Blue was once again bringing home the point that she was unique. Very likely, he thought, some of both.

He placed his hands together, palm to palm, then cleared his throat self-consciously. "I told you. I'm a professor...."

"A professor of what?"

He hesitated, spotted a few remaining drops of cognac in his snifter and finished them off. "Russian literature." He watched her, saw the "aha" look in her eyes.

"Listen, Courtney. It's a very complicated matter. Too complicated to go into. I realize, under the circumstances, I have no right to further impose upon you. You've been... well, you've been remarkable. Most women, confronted with a bleeding man lying on their shop floor, would certainly not have responded in so calm and trusting a fashion."

She laughed softly. "You must be quite a lecturer, Professor. But don't you think you ought to bloody well get to the point, as they say in merry old England."

He grinned. "You don't beat about the bush, as they say in the good old U.S. of A."

"Beat 'around' the bush," she corrected. "Just how long have you been in the States, Professor?"

"Nearly a year. But I haven't managed an A in American idioms yet."

She cocked her head. "So, Professor, what's the favor?"

Madden sighed. "I'd very much appreciate your letting me stay the night...on the couch, of course. I'll leave in the morning. I give you my word that you would not be housing a spy, or a cop, or a criminal, Courtney. I'm a completely ordinary college professor who, through no fault of his own, has stumbled into a bit of a...problem. Strictly temporary. In fact, I hope to resolve it very soon."

"But you are in trouble."

He looked at her seriously. "Not exactly... I mean, it's not exactly trouble." He paused. "I'm not doing very well, am I?"

"I wish you'd trust me, Jonathan."

He looked closely at her. "It isn't a matter of trust. I just don't want to involve you in something that could land you in trouble, as well."

She smiled faintly. "So you *are* in trouble, Professor."

He had to laugh. "You are very persistent and very impressive, Miss Blue."

*It's true,* she thought. *I am being impressive.* She smiled inwardly. *Okay, Katherine O'Malley, move over. You've got yourself some competition.*

"So," she continued, buoyed with confidence. "Where does Gorky fit in?"

His brow knit. "Gorky?"

"There was a look of recognition in your eye when I mentioned him. Perhaps—" she paused deliberately "—I should ask you the same question that middle-aged woman whose description didn't ring a bell for you asked me. Do you happen to have a rare first edition of a Gorky work, Jonathan?"

Jonathan's expression became at once ominous. "Don't push it, Courtney. For your own sake."

She saw that she would get nowhere pursuing a headlong attack. So, as any shrewd heroine would, she switched tack.

"Where will you go when you leave here?" she asked softly.

His quick glance at her made Courtney think she hadn't altogether outsmarted him. Nor was his answer edifying.

"I'm not sure yet," he said, rubbing his hands together.

"Not back to your apartment."

"No."

"Will it be safe for you... outside?"

"I'm not sure of that, either," he admitted.

Still her gaze did not waver. "Let me help you, Jonathan."

He shook his head. "You've already done more than your share."

"I haven't done anything."

He had to smile. "I can't figure you out, Courtney Blue."

She smiled back, her eyes twinkling. "I think I like that."

He laughed briefly. "Well, I'm not sure I do."

She tilted her head, her hazel eyes sparkling. "No, I suppose you prefer the more predictable sort. They're infinitely safer."

He laughed again, in earnest. "I never knew just how transparent I was until now."

"Oh," she replied, smiling winsomely, "you're not all that transparent. I've only been able to scratch the surface, Professor. And my guess is that it's only because you've had a bloody awful day. Something tells me that under most circumstances you're quite well guarded. Which only illustrates, Professor, just how serious a fix you must be in."

"Why do you want to help me, Courtney?" His laughter was gone, as was any trace of amusement. "In your place, I'd be rather cautious of getting involved."

"Caution can be very dull, Professor."

"And you crave excitement, danger, mystery."

His tone was intentionally mocking, but Courtney eyed him evenly.

"Precisely," she said. "Besides, you need my help."

"I do?"

"I'm not convinced, Professor, that you're going to stay alive if left to your own devices."

"Perhaps I'll surprise you."

She gave him a wide, beguiling smile. "Perhaps I'll surprise you."

Their eyes met and held. Jonathan thought she was lovely, her hazel eyes flickering with wit and intelligence, her smile both sensual and mysterious, the soft blush on her cheeks radiating an innocence that her sparkling eyes belied. He let his fingers play through her hair. She closed her eyes, her smile deepening. And then, because Jonathan found her so enchanting, so brave, and because he had longed to do it from the start, he gathered her in his arms and kissed her hotly, passionately, stealing the breath from her. And, having already concluded that nothing Courtney Blue did would surprise him, he was only mildly taken aback when she responded to his kiss with an eagerness to match his own, rather than with a most understandable smack across his face.

"DAMN IT. This is no picnic for me, either. At the very most, it will take another couple of days." The dark-haired beauty nervously tapped her long, ruby-red polished nails on the side of the phone as she leaned against a glass-paned wall in the stuffy telephone booth.

"That was a bad decision, chasing after the Russian," the voice on the other end of the line said sharply.

"Jonathan was splayed out on the sidewalk, Borofsky was frisking him and then leaped in his car. I was certain he must have gotten what he was after. What would you have done under the circumstances?" Her tone was angry and defensive.

"A pointless question at this juncture, Christine."

She sighed. "Listen, I'm in the neighborhood where I last saw Jonathan. It's pretty much deserted, but I'll check around. From what I could see, he wasn't in any condition to go very far. I've got Al posted back at his apartment, and Denny will be at the university first thing in the morning. Jonathan has classes."

"Smarten up, Christine. Do you really think that Madden is going to waltz into his lecture hall tomorrow?"

"I'm just covering all bases," she retorted.

The voice on the other end of the line chuckled.

Her ruby lips formed a tight line. "I also happen to have tracked down his car at a service station. He's going to pick it up Thursday afternoon. If we don't track him down by then..."

"Yes, Christine, you just cover all bases over there. In the meantime, I'll cover some back here."

Christine's dark eyes narrowed. "You promised you wouldn't..."

"Do you have any idea, Christine, how many possible ways Madden could ditch that valuable little parcel by Thursday? The man knows he's walking around with a time bomb in his pocket, thanks to his old pal and mentor, Marcus Lloyd."

"I would never have begun this whole dirty business if you hadn't promised me that Marcus would not be harmed."

"Come, come, Christine. Your concern for your lover is quite touching. But you're talking to your oldest friend now. Someone who knows you better than you know yourself. You're like Eve in the Garden of Eden, my sweet. You long ago bit into that apple. So don't tell me after all this time you're having difficulty digesting it."

"If you were here right now, I'd slap your bloody face, you bastard," she said hotly.

He laughed in earnest now. "Ah, but the question is, my sweet, what will you do when I hand you that quarter of a million dollars? While I may be a bastard, you must admit I am a most generous bastard. A fifty-fifty split, my dear. Just remember that. You'll be able to go anywhere your little heart desires. We both know Marcus is not the sort to hold your interest for very long, love. Besides, did I say one word about harming your dear lover?"

Before she had a chance to respond, she heard a click and the line went dead. "Damn you, Daniel Emerson," she whispered. "Damn you, you bastard."

And then, taking several deep cleansing breaths and smoothing back her jet-black hair, she placed another call with the operator. The phone was picked up after the first ring.

"Hello, Marcus, darling. It's me, Christine."

"I've been worried about you. You were supposed to call hours ago."

She laughed softly. "You know how I am once I start shopping."

"How is New York?" he asked.

"As hectic and crazy as ever."

"And the weather?"

Christine stared out at the rain-swept Boston street. "A perfect spring day. Crisp and clear." That, according to the New York City AM broadcast she'd picked up on her car radio a few hours ago.

"Listen, I hope you're not still angry at how distracted I've been lately. Just some business I've had to tidy up. I shall soon be my old self again."

"Yes. Yes, darling, I'm sure you will be. I'm sorry I haven't been more understanding."

"I wondered if perhaps you, too, haven't had some worries on your mind. We shouldn't drift so far apart, Chris. We shouldn't let our personal worries interfere with what we have together. When Elizabeth died eight years ago, I immersed myself in my work. And then all that collapsed. I thought my life was finished. Until you came along. This isn't some passing fancy for me, Chris. I wish you'd believe that."

"Of course I believe that, darling."

JONATHAN'S KISS left Courtney's heart racing. Her pleasure illuminated her face, giving her a soft, vulnerable look. But the glint of daring remained in her hazel eyes. The contrast only heightened Jonathan's desire.

"Does this mean you'll let me stay the night, Courtney?" he asked in a husky voice.

It had begun raining again. Courtney could hear the steady patter on the windows. Her lips curved in a faintly comic smile. "On the couch."

His eyes lingered on her just-kissed lips. He smiled. "On the couch."

She saw the flicker of disappointment on his face. She laughed softly and stood up, trying in vain to put some order to her hair as she started across the living room in the direction of the kitchen. "I was planning to warm up some leftover stew for dinner. Would you like some? Or I could dig up something else."

"Stew sounds wonderful."

"Good." She took a couple of steadying breaths. "Let's forget about . . . what just happened, Professor."

" 'Jonathan.' "

She stared at him. "You must think I'm very reckless."

He smiled. "I think you're marvelous." He paused, his smile deepening. "And perhaps a trifle reckless. Which I must admit has proved most fortunate for me."

"Does that mean you'll let me help you?" Her hazel eyes sparkled with anticipation.

He gave a resigned laugh, then glanced down at the gaping hole in his left pant leg. "Well, you could help by finding me another pair of trousers. I have a feeling I'd look rather conspicuous ambling about town tomorrow in this costume."

Courtney crossed her arms in front of her chest. "Well . . . it's a start, anyway."

"Talking of starts, how about starting up dinner? I'm famished."

During the meal, Courtney did most of the talking. She told Jonathan she'd been managing her uncle's shop and living above it for several years. She explained that the building was due to be razed in a couple of weeks, after which she'd be footloose and fancy-free. Jonathan laughed, saying he envied her. Courtney laughed in turn, saying she envied him.

As they were finishing the meal, the phone rang. Courtney rose from the table and picked up the extension near the stove, aware that Jonathan was watching her closely.

"Hello."

"Courtney, it's me."

"Uncle Lou." She gave Jonathan a quick smile. "What's up?"

"I thought you might come to dinner tomorrow night."

"Dinner?"

"I'm not talking the frozen TV variety."

"Well, well. What's the occasion? The last time you cooked a proper dinner was to celebrate my college graduation."

"And burned most of it," he said with a chuckle. "Don't worry, Courtney. I'll be very careful this time."

"Aha. Then it is a special occasion."

"Don't be silly. Actually I'm just being a good neighbor. A very nice person just sublet an apartment in the building. She came in to use my phone a little while ago to see about getting her electricity connected, and one thing led to another and I ended up inviting her for dinner."

Courtney laughed, her gaze following Jonathan as he brought the dishes over to the sink.

"Don't tell me, Uncle Lou, that you're feeling in need of a chaperon."

"Don't be rude, girl. She's a very nice lady and I thought she'd be more comfortable... Look, if you don't want to come, I haven't actually told her you would. I could always take her to a restaurant or something."

*Why, you old devil,* she thought. *You're smitten. And you barely know the woman.* She grinned. What would her uncle think if she told him about her new houseguest?

"You don't have to take her to a restaurant, Uncle Lou. Certainly I'll come if you like."

"Good. You'll enjoy meeting her. She's got an interest in rare books."

Courtney felt a faint unease. "Oh, really."

Jonathan picked up the subtle change in her voice and looked closely at her.

"Yes," Uncle Lou said. And then he laughed a bit self-consciously. "Who knows? Maybe she'll be a good customer."

"Uncle Lou," Courtney said, her eyes meeting Jonathan's across the room, "what's the woman's name?"

"Andrea Lambert. Why?"

"Andrea Lambert," Courtney repeated, but Jonathan showed no sign of recognition. "Oh, I just wondered. Quite a coincidence, her being so interested in rare books and ending up in an apartment in your building and meeting you and all." She saw a brief flicker of tension cross Jonathan's face, but it faded quickly.

"I don't know," Uncle Lou was saying. "A lot of people have a fascination with rare books. Otherwise how do you suppose I'd have made a good living all these years?"

She laughed lightly. "True. So tell me, Uncle Lou, what does this new neighbor look like?"

"Really, Courtney, you're making far more out of this than is warranted. You'll see for yourself tomorrow night. Seven o'clock."

Courtney pursed her lips. "Right. Seven o'clock. I'll bring some wine. Oh, and possibly a friend, if that's all right." She shot a quick glance at Jonathan, who did not seem particularly keen on the idea.

"A friend," Uncle Lou echoed. "A male friend?"

Courtney sighed. "Now who's getting ideas?"

"Okay, okay. Certainly bring a friend. See you tomorrow."

Courtney placed the receiver back in its cradle. She looked over at Jonathan. "Well, what do you think?"

Jonathan smiled. "I think a cup of coffee would be nice."

She frowned. "That's not what I mean and you know it."

"Coincidences happen, Courtney." He brought the stew pot over to the sink and ran some water in it. "You'll need to let this soak for a while. It was a delicious stew."

"You can be a most frustrating man, Professor."

He glanced at her as she leaned against the counter.

"Courtney," he said, a touch of weariness in his voice, "it doesn't pay to be too much of an alarmist. It can drive one crazy. Anyway," he added, returning to the table to finish clearing it, "you'll have the opportunity to meet her tomorrow night."

"Does that mean you won't join me?"

"I can't. But I trust your judgment about whether or not she's suspicious."

She couldn't tell from his tone if he was being serious or merely humoring her. "And if she is suspicious?"

He smiled. "Why don't we cross that bridge when we come to it?"

Courtney looked at him with quickening hope. "You'll have to keep in touch, then."

He avoided her eyes. "I suppose I will."

LOU VAUGHN HEARD a soft rap on his door just after he hung up the phone. When he opened the door he was pleasantly surprised to find Andrea Lambert standing there. She really was a fine woman with her pretty blond hair, lovely blue eyes and petite slender figure. For a woman who had to be somewhere in her late forties or early fifties, she kept herself very well. And, he reflected, for a man in his early sixties, he wasn't so bad himself. No paunch, still had a full head of hair, albeit more gray than brown at this point. And he was in good health.

"Mr. Vaughn, please excuse me for troubling you again."

"No trouble at all. And please, call me 'Lou.'"

"'Lou,'" she said, smiling. "I just wanted to ask if I could have a rain check for tomorrow night's dinner. I have some business I need to attend to and it could well last until the wee hours. Would it be terribly presumptuous of me to suggest Thursday night, instead?"

"No, no, not at all . . . Andrea. Thursday night would be just fine."

She smiled warmly. "Lovely. Same time?"

He nodded. then, as he saw her start to turn, he said, "You know, it's only eight o'clock. We could have dinner together tonight—I mean as well as Thursday night. There's a nice little Italian restaurant just down the street . . ."

"It's sweet of you to invite me, Lou, but I'm exhausted and I still have some unpacking to do. But I will be looking forward to Thursday night."

"Oh." Lou smiled "I will, too." As he closed the door, his smile remained. Well, he thought, maybe a chaperon wouldn't be necessary, after all. He and Andrea Lambert would get along just fine.

He decided to phone Courtney in the morning and tell her of his change in plans. He would let her know he didn't have a date for dinner tomorrow but ask her to come, anyway. He was curious to meet this friend she'd mentioned she might bring. And if she came alone, he would use it as an opportunity to have a serious heart to heart with the girl. He was worried about his only niece, who was like a daughter to him. What Courtney needed was to add a little more spark to her mundane existence, take a few risks, live a little dangerously.

# CHAPTER FOUR

THE FAINT SOUND of footsteps woke Jonathan instantly. He sat bolt upright. He felt disoriented, but the feeling lasted for only a few moments.

He gave his hostess a groggy smile. "Oh, it's you."

Courtney smiled. "Who were you expecting?"

"What time is it?" He rubbed his eyes, then smoothed his tousled hair back from his forehead with his fingers. He felt as if he'd slept a couple of hours at best. Courtney's narrow couch left a lot to be desired. But, then, beggars couldn't be choosers.

Courtney gave him a thorough and appreciative survey. Rumpled and groggy, Jonathan Madden managed to look even more appealing than he had the night before. Perhaps it was the faint lost little boy expression in his eyes. "It's nearly eleven. You've slept a good twelve hours. How are you feeling?"

The lost little boy look vanished instantly. "Eleven?" he muttered as he threw off the covers. But when he started to rise a wave of dizziness hit him and he sat back down on the couch in a hurry.

"Steady. You need some nourishment before you leave. And I ought to rebandage that wound. But breakfast first," she said lightly. Gaily. "Technically brunch, really."

Jonathan was never in particularly great spirits in the morning. And this morning he felt more disgruntled than usual. All that sleep and he didn't even feel rested. Not to mention that he'd planned on an early start.

"No. Just coffee."

Courtney ignored his surly tone. "I make a mean omelet, Professor Madden. I'm sure you'll love it."

He sighed. "Look, Miss...Miss Blue. I don't mean to be rude. But I've got classes this morning. I've already missed one lecture. I'll have to call in. Right now all I want is a quick shower, and if you could just make me a cup of coffee, I'll get going." He rose again, this time more slowly. He was still feeling woozy, but it would pass.

Courtney folded her arms across her chest. She was dressed in a white cowl-necked sweater and jeans. Unlike her guest, she'd risen at dawn, feeling excited, invigorated, filled with expectation. She watched Jonathan limp slightly as he made his way toward the bathroom.

"Don't you think your students will find your attire a bit unusual, Professor?"

He stopped, glanced down at his mutilated trousers and his shirt that was much the worse for wear. "Right."

"Remember, I promised last night I'd go pick you up something to wear."

"It's getting so late." He paused, casting her a hopeful look. "I don't suppose you have a pair of men's trousers about? And a clean shirt."

She smiled. "Sorry. You've caught me during a dry spell."

He managed to smile back despite his aching leg and the myriad worries on his mind.

"It won't take me long," she said. "I'll just zip over to Washington Street and pick you up something suitable."

He gave her a grateful look. "I'll give you some money." He walked over to his dried-out mac, hanging on the hall tree. His wallet was in the inside breast pocket. Along with the package that was the source of all his troubles. He removed the wallet, pulling out several bills. "Here you are. A hundred ought to suffice. I have relatively simple tastes."

"Before I go off shopping," Courtney said, "I think you should have a peek out the window."

Frowning, he limped over to the living room window, being careful to stand to the side of it as he glanced down at the street.

Unlike yesterday, the street was busy today. The weather having cleared, the construction crews were back at work and they were diligently demolishing an office building down the block. There were also a few passersby, several stopping near the work site. But neither the workers nor the pedestrians drew Jonathan's attention. His gaze focused on a dark-haired woman standing in the shadows of the boarded-up coffee shop across the street. She was idly smoking a cigarette and checking her watch at intervals, as though she were waiting for someone who was late.

Courtney came up behind him. "She's been there for nearly two hours."

Jonathan scowled. The surveillance didn't surprise him. That was one of the reasons he'd wanted to get an early start, before dawn, really, hoping that under cover of darkness he could have made his escape. Now he'd have to come up with a new plan. He started to move away, but Courtney touched his arm.

"Wait. There's more. Keep watching the street. In a minute or two a dark sedan will pass slowly by. The car's been circling the street since daybreak. I imagine the driver's getting pretty dizzy by this point. Not to mention the tedium of the enterprise." She grinned. "I must say, Professor, in real life these intrigues definitely have their down sides."

Sure enough, a minute later the large sedan came cruising by. Jonathan could make out a driver and one passenger up front.

He looked over at Courtney, his face clouded. "Any others?"

She tilted her head, arching a brow. "Are you expecting anyone else?"

He gave a weary sigh. "Don't be ridiculous. Do you think something like this happens to me on a regular basis? I told you, I'm a college professor...an ordinary citizen. I've never been in this sort of situation before."

Courtney smiled. "Neither have I."

Jonathan observed her curiously. "You're sure about that? For a first timer you seem unusually calm."

"Would you feel better if I were frantic?"

He smiled, touching her lightly on the shoulder. "No. I'd feel a lot worse." She smelled of lavender soap and peppermint toothpaste. Her blond hair fell softly around her shoulders with a just-washed look. He focused on her lips, lips that were smiling back at him, lips that had, last night, returned his kiss with equal ardor. He was only faintly aware of the prickles of alarm at the edge of his emotions, signaling him to pull away from her.

Her gaze, fearless and provocative, met his and she leaned forward slightly. And Jonathan knew that for the moment he wasn't going anywhere.

As if guided by a force beyond his will, his hands found their way to her neck and he gently caressed the silken skin there. There was nothing frantic about Courtney Blue. Nothing cautious, either, he thought as his lips moved over hers in a soft, tender kiss.

"I have a plan," she whispered when he drew back.

"Courtney..."

"We need a plan, Jonathan. If someone follows me and sees me purchasing a pair of size thirty-two trousers...that is about right, isn't it?" When he nodded, she continued. "Well, they'll surely put two and two together. They're already suspicious. What we have to do is throw them off the track."

He could not argue with her logic.

"I've been busy figuring this out since dawn," she went on spiritedly. "Here's what we'll do. First, I'll make a quick phone call to a friend and then whip up that omelet for you. Cheese and tomatoes. Only you say 'tamatoes,'" she said, grinning. "Oh, and some coffee. Meanwhile, you take your shower. I'm afraid the shampoo is a bit flowery and the hot water is not absolutely reliable, but I'm sure you'll manage."

She started for the telephone, but Jonathan grabbed her arm none too gently, propelling her back to face him. "Slow down, love. I'm a bit addleminded in the morning and you aren't doing anything to improve my condition. Now let's take it one step at a time. What friend? And why are you phoning her?"

Courtney's look held a note of frustration. "Sandy Hoffman. She works at the bookstore part-time. She's about my size. She'll do perfectly."

He narrowed his gaze. "Do perfectly for what?"

She bestowed a mischievous smile on him. "For my plan, love."

"Courtney, I told you last night that I don't want you to get involved. Now, not only are you getting involved, you're taking charge." His expression hardened. "I won't have it. It's out of the question."

"Don't turn stuffy on me now, Professor. I've figured it all out. Well, not all, of course. I still don't know what kind of trouble you're in and why those people outside want to use you for target practice."

His ire up, Jonathan snapped, "You bloody well know more than you should."

Courtney blanched a little. "What is it I know?"

"Come on, love. Don't you turn coy on me now. You were prying last night. I saw your hot little hands on that parcel in my mac."

Now that the cat was out of the bag, Courtney realized there was no point in trying to deny it. "Are you going to tell me what's inside the wrapping? Does it have anything to do with the Russian novelist Maxim Gorky?"

"Courtney, believe me, we'll both be better off if you ask no further questions."

She dug her hands into her pockets. "All right, I'll skip the questions for now. We've got other worries to concentrate on. Go take your shower, Jonathan."

He eyed her cautiously. "And what are you going to do?"

"Make you that omelet for one thing."

"And for another?" He sighed.

"Give Sandy a jingle. I told you—"

"You mustn't phone that friend of yours, Courtney. I appreciate your help, honestly. But you must leave the planning to me."

She gave him a narrow look. "Your plans haven't worked that well so far, Jonathan. You're lucky to be alive."

"Perhaps I'm on a winning streak."

Her expression grew impatient. "We don't have time for new plans, Jonathan. And it isn't as though you can go skipping merrily out of the shop undetected by that reception committee out there." Her hazel eyes sparkled. "Unless we're very clever."

He grinned wryly. "Which, I presume, we are."

She gave him an affectionate pat on both shoulders. "Of course."

"But Courtney, about this friend of yours . . ."

"Don't worry. She won't know a thing about you. I promise. All I'm going to do is ask her to stop in to the shop and go over some invoices for me. And while she's doing that I shall pop over to Washington street and make my purchases. The entire operation will take less than a half hour."

"That's your plan?"

She laughed. "There's a bit more to it."

"Like what?"

"Like Sandy's poncho. Personally I'm not crazy about it. A bit gaudy for my taste. Red-and-orange stripes. But she adores it. She always wears it this time of year."

She saw that Jonathan was nodding like a man humoring a mad woman, and laughed. "It's quite simple, really. Look, a woman walks into the shop—a customer, it would appear to any observers—and she's wearing a brightly colored red-and-orange striped poncho. An item that sticks in one's mind, as it were. And then a few minutes later she leaves, a couple of book purchases tucked into a bag. And off she ambles down the street. Would our dark-haired beauty across the way or our dark sedan pair pay her any attention?"

"I take it the woman leaving the shop in the poncho is not your friend Sandy?"

She grinned. "See, you're not so addleminded, after all." She paused. "I will tell Sandy I'm off for a romantic coffee break with a new lover and I'd simply adore borrowing that glorious poncho of hers so I can knock his socks off."

"Okay, pretty good so far. But . . ."

"Several buts," she agreed. "All being attended to."

"How about your getting back into the shop? Won't our friends outside think it a bit odd that our customer is returning again after such a short time?"

"Oh, but she won't be. She being me, that is."

He looked puzzled.

"I've got that part figured out quite nicely. But—" she gave him a wink "—I want to surprise you."

He appeared wary. "I'm not terribly fond of surprises, Courtney. And I'm not terribly fond of the idea that your plan might not work."

"But it will, Jonathan. Have a little faith. I haven't let you down yet, have I?"

"I don't believe I've ever met a woman quite like you."

She touched his rough cheek with the palm of her hand, then lightly brushed her lips against his. "Are you really going to go to the university when you leave here?"

He studied her thoughtfully. "I might."

"But surely there'll be people waiting there, too."

He gave her a devilish Colton-like grin. "I've a few plans up my sleeve, too, love."

"WE ARE WASTING OUR TIME, I tell you. Driving around in circles like this, hour after hour. I tell you, Madden's not here. We'd be wise to join our comrades at the university."

An ashen Stephan Petrenko scowled at his partner. "Besides, I get carsick. And your smoking isn't helping matters any."

Borofsky turned the wheel as they approached the corner of Madison Street. He was feeling queasy with motion sickness himself, but that didn't stop him from smoking. Nor did the queasiness compare to the aches and pains in his body, compliments of Goncharov's "friendly" reminder of the imperative nature of this mission. "Look, someone's going into the shop," he said sharply as they neared Vaughn's Rare and Used Books.

Both men observed the woman in a red-and-orange striped poncho enter the bookstore. Borofsky drove a few yards past the shop, then pulled over to the curb, adjusted the rearview mirror and ostensibly began checking a street map.

Petrenko belched. "A customer, that's all." He pressed his fist against his belly. "I need one of those fizzing tablets like they show on American television. 'Pop, pop, fizz, fizz. Oh what a relief it is.'"

"Be quiet, will you? Complaints, complaints. Do you think I enjoy this any more than you? Do you think I asked for this particular assignment? Why not Florida or California? A chance to go to Disneyland just once before I am called back to Moscow. Is that asking for too much?"

"Hollywood. That's my dream." Petrenko sighed. "The land of John Wayne."

"John Wayne's dead, you idiot," Borofsky snapped.

A few minutes later, Petrenko nudged his partner. "Look, the customer's leaving. Nothing here I tell you. A waste of time. Business as usual." Petrenko belched again. "Clint Eastwood, is he dead, too?"

"No."

"Okay, him I'd like to see, too."

Ten minutes later Borofsky and Petrenko observed another young woman leave the shop and head down the street. "That must be her. The shopkeeper," Borofsky said, his spirits lifting. "Now we'll follow her. If Madden was there and passed her the package, she'll make a drop."

Petrenko's complexion was turning green. "Who cares? Just as long as she doesn't walk in circles."

THE DARK-HAIRED BEAUTY with the ruby-red lips was in a most disagreeable mood. She'd been standing in the doorway of the boarded-up coffee shop for over two hours on the faint hope that Madden had taken refuge in the bookstore and, if so, would eventually have to surface. She was none too happy that she wasn't the only one who had that idea. The same black sedan she'd given chase to last night had been circling the block since she'd been there.

When she saw the young woman in the print blouse and blue skirt exit the bookstore shortly after the customer with the poncho left, Christine assumed it must be the shopkeeper. When she saw the sedan pull out and start slowly down the street after the woman, Christine was torn between tailing the shopkeeper, too, or staying put. If Madden was hiding out in that shop, he might have sent the woman out as a decoy. Jonathan was clever. He'd count on the woman being tailed, leaving the way clear for him to make his escape. Christine decided to wait. She, too, was clever.

She did walk down the street a little ways so that if Jonathan was inside the bookstore and watching the street, he'd believe his plan had worked. When she thought she was out of his viewing range, she ducked into the doorway of a boarded-up apartment building. Her vantage point was not as good from this spot, but she'd have no trouble catching sight of a tall, dark man leaving the shop.

After about twenty minutes, Christine observed a couple of construction workers approach the bookstore. The stockier of the two was carrying a clipboard. Both men wore hard hats.

Christine lit another cigarette and watched as the workers stood outside the shop, conferring for a minute. One of them headed back down the street to where the rest of the crew was working, while the worker with the clipboard remained outside the shop, busily jotting down notes. Then he headed down the alley to the back of the shop to continue his work.

Christine frowned. She was beginning to worry that she wasn't so clever, after all. While she stood hovering in doorways, Jonathan Madden and his little parcel might be miles away. There were many things that Christine Dupré found disagreeable, but none more so than feeling the fool.

COURTNEY GRINNED at the sight of Jonathan in her terry robe. Actually, because of her height it wasn't such a bad length on him. On the other hand, he was a great deal broader than her, and the cloth hugged his muscular frame in the same places where it hung loosely on her.

"Well, what do you think of my plan now?" Courtney's hair toppled down around her shoulders as she removed the hard hat and tossed it over to Jonathan. Then she unzipped her construction worker's olive-green windbreaker, pulling out the wadded-up poncho that had accounted for much of her bulk.

Jonathan laughed. "I'm impressed."

She smiled. "You're meant to be."

She was slipping out of the jacket and unzipping the chinos to reveal her dungarees beneath. "I know they're not the most stylish garments around," she said, stepping out of the men's trousers, then quickly unbuttoning the blue workshirt.

Jonathan slipped the chinos on under the robe, turning his back to Courtney while he zipped up. Then he removed the robe and quickly donned the blue shirt, leaving it unbuttoned, his broad, muscular chest exposed, as he stuck his stockinged feet into his shoes.

Courtney tried for a studied nonchalance as her gaze trailed over his superb physical form, but she doubted she was doing a good job of it. How could she help reacting? Jonathan Madden was an exquisite specimen of a man. He put all of her fictional heroes to shame. Derek Colton be damned.

"The sedan took off after your friend," Jonathan said. "By the time they realize the error, hopefully I'll be gone. But I still have our dark-haired miss to distract. I caught her slipping into a doorway farther down the street." As he spoke he buttoned up his shirt—much to Courtney's disappointment.

"Always keep a second plan in reserve, I always say." She grinned. "Precisely for times such as this. We simply pull the same con job again. Only this time the construction worker enters and exits, instead of the customer with a poncho."

Jonathan was slipping his arms into the windbreaker. He stopped midway and caught hold of her, captivating her with a smile. "Before this is over, Miss Blue, I'm afraid I'm going to be madly in love with you."

His tone was teasing, as was his smile, but the words... Hilary Bennett couldn't have written any better.

"I must hurry." He was over at the hall tree before Courtney realized he was no longer beside her. "Listen, when I go, be sure to get rid of my old things. But don't toss them in the Dumpster in the alley. Someone might go rummaging." He removed his wallet and keys from his raincoat and slipped them into his chinos.

"Wait, Jonathan. What happens when you arrive at the university? If you're spotted and you have the parcel on you..."

"I worked on a plan or two myself while you were gone. Only..."

"Only it means involving me?"

He nodded slowly, pulling out the parcel from his mac. He extended it to her. "Here. Open it. Have a look."

Carefully she undid the plain brown wrapper, exposing a thick notebook that looked quite old. She opened to the first page. "It's in Russian. Handwritten. Gorky?"

Jonathan nodded.

"This is what they're all after? I don't understand. Even a handwritten work of Gorky's couldn't be all that valuable. Surely not valuable enough to kill for."

"Would you say a half-million dollars, might be worth killing for?"

"It's worth that much?" She looked at him, stunned. "Why?"

"How much do you know about Russian literature? Gorky in particular?"

"My uncle is something of an expert. He speaks Russian. He's been to the U.S.S.R. a few times to negotiate purchases of rare Russian books. But I don't really know that much."

"Gorky was as much a political figure as a novelist. Before his death he was working on what is often considered his masterpiece, a panoramic four-volume novel of Russian social conditions during the czarist period, the period of unrest and upheaval that lead to the Russian Revolution in 1917. Gorky supposedly died before completing the work, his death attributed to poisoning by an anti-Soviet group. What you are holding in your hands may be the finish of that Gorky masterpiece."

"Why 'may be'? Do you think it's a fraud?"

"That's what I mean to find out. If it's authentic, it's worth a small fortune. Right now the bid is up to a half-million dollars."

"How did you come to own it?"

"I don't. I'm merely a middle man, as it were. The owner is in London. I received the parcel yesterday by courier. An item as valuable as this must be authenticated before any purchaser would part with all that money."

"I see." She studied the book again. "And you were picked to authenticate it."

"Yes."

"And . . . ?"

"And?"

"Well, is it authentic?"

He sighed. "I haven't had much of a chance to find out. The process will take a good week or more of careful analysis. And it requires the utmost concentration. A difficult task when one is being chased and shot at."

"And that dark-haired woman, those men in that black sedan, they, too, want the manuscript. Only they don't want to pay for it?"

"Precisely. I believe the ones in the sedan are Russians. You can imagine they'd very much want the work of the Father of Soviet Literature to remain in Russian hands."

"And the woman?"

"I'm not sure who's sent her along."

"Oh, and let's not forget the woman who came into my shop last night."

"Yes," he admitted. "I spotted her following me yesterday afternoon."

Courtney nodded. "I think it's time you tell me about your plan."

He moved his hand to her cheek, then under her hair. "The plan involves my leaving this manuscript here with you. Just until tomorrow evening. Maybe before that."

"But is that wise? Those people outside may return. They might even break in."

"There are a thousand or more books on the shelves downstairs. We'll stick this in among them. Anyway, if my plan works, they won't be back. I'll have sent them all on a wild-goose chase."

He was still playing with her hair. "What do you say? I promise I'll return no later than tomorrow evening."

His touch was having a profound effect on her. Her limbs felt heavy, her pulse pounded and she had difficulty breathing. "Tomorrow evening," she murmured.

He kissed her lightly on the lips. A kiss that to Courtney held promise.

"How do you know you can trust me?" she whispered.

He smiled, his index finger skimming across her just-kissed lips. "Call it instinct. You haven't let me down so far. In fact, you've been positively brilliant, love."

She smiled beguilingly, a smile that would put any of Katherine O'Malley's smiles to shame. "Yes. I suppose I have, rather."

"WELL, I AM a little disappointed, Uncle Lou. I was curious to meet this new neighbor of yours."

"Come for dinner tonight, anyway, Courtney. I'm curious to meet the new friend you spoke of, as well."

"Oh, he can't make it, either. It'll only be the two of us."

"Aha, so it is a gentleman friend. Where did you meet him? What does he do?"

Courtney laughed. "You sound like a mother hen."

"I am a mother hen, you silly girl. And I expect the low-down at dinner tonight."

"There is no lowdown. I . . . hardly know him."

"That little catch in your voice tells me you'd like to get to know him better."

Courtney could not argue the point. "I'll see you at dinner, Uncle Lou." She hesitated for a moment. "Oh, and since it's going to be only the two of us, I might bring something over to show you."

"Oh?"

"It will knock your socks off. But I'll need your solemn word to keep it a secret."

"My, my, this sounds intriguing."

"It's only on temporary loan. The thing is, I'd feel better not leaving it behind while I'm gone. And I know you'll be thrilled just to have a glimpse of it."

Only after Courtney hung up the phone did she worry that she might be taking undue risks removing the Gorky work from the bookstore. What if she were followed? Accosted on the street? Then again, she'd seen no one lurking about the street for several hours now. And the thought of the rare treasure being out of sight for the evening made her nervous.

Besides, she told herself, Jonathan had been confident he could deflect suspicion from her and send everyone on a wild-goose chase. She had no idea how he meant to do that, but she was sure he would succeed. Adding to her resolve was the knowledge that her uncle might be of some assistance to Jonathan in authenticating the work.

And Courtney was quite eager to provide her hero with any assistance possible. Her eyelids fluttered closed, her mind drifting into fantasy. Only now it wasn't Derek Colton pressing his lips against her hair and breathing in the fragrant scent of jasmine. It was her real-life hero, Jonathan Madden, who was whispering, "I'll come to you, my love. I promise."

She opened her eyes, a smile on her lips. And if passion alone wouldn't bring him back to her, she had that little parcel to add greatly to her confidence in his return.

# CHAPTER FIVE

JONATHAN'S PLAN WAS WORKING just as he'd hoped. Courtney Blue wasn't the only brilliant member of this team. Team. Was that what they were now? Yes, he supposed they were. It had happened despite his better judgment, despite his protests, despite all the alarms buzzing in his head. Well, the partnership was strictly temporary, he told himself firmly. Once he took care of a couple of matters, he would return for the Gorky manuscript and then be off.

"Madden. Hold up."

Jonathan glanced over his shoulder to see his colleague from the Russian Department, Ray Silver, running across the university green.

"What happened to you this morning? I've never known you to miss a class without calling in." Silver fell into pace with Jonathan. "Good thing you made your afternoon classes. There wouldn't have been anyone to replace you."

Jonathan put his arm chummily around the small, wiry man. "I, ah, ran into something unexpected, Ray. Thanks for taking that class for me. I'm heading over to the mailbox. Walk along with me and fill me in on what you covered."

Jonathan removed a brown-paper-wrapped parcel from the inside pocket of his newly purchased tweed jacket, his construction worker's garb having been deposited several hours ago in the Dumpster behind Broderick's, a men's clothing store near the university. Once dressed like a professor, Jonathan Madden hadn't gone twenty yards from the shop before he was spotted. As planned. Within forty minutes the Russian goon who'd tried to frisk him the night before and his grubby-looking partner were on his tail. Five minutes after they fell into place, the dark-haired beauty showed up. They were all there, the whole welcoming committee. Only none of them would risk making a move on him in broad daylight with so many people around the campus. Which was precisely what Jonathan had counted on.

"What's in the package?" Ray asked.

Jonathan glanced down at the parcel in his hand. It was similar in size and shape to the one he'd left with Courtney. "Oh, just a manual a friend of mine wanted me to pick up for him."

Ray nodded and began going over the work he'd covered in Jonathan's Early Russian Literature seminar. A couple of minutes later they arrived at the mailbox. Jonathan pulled open the lid and glanced at the pickup schedule.

"What time is it, Ray?" He rubbed his empty wrist, remembering that he'd left his watch on Courtney's coffee table the previous night.

Ray squinted at his timepiece, too lazy to remove his reading glasses from this pocket. "Five-forty."

"Missed the last pickup," Jonathan said lightly, slipping the parcel rather flamboyantly into the open slot. "Oh, well." He smiled. "No hurry, really."

"Where are you heading now?" Ray asked. "Maybe we can go have a beer."

"Sorry. Another time. I've got some work to finish up at the office."

"Good thing break starts tomorrow. I need a week to get my article ready for publication. How about you, Jonathan? What are you going to do with your week off?"

Jonathan grinned. "Oh, I've got enough to keep me busy."

CIGARETTE DANGLING from the corner of his mouth, Borofsky cursed under his breath. Helplessly he watched through his binoculars as Madden dropped the coveted parcel into the mailbox. His temper boiled as he shook a fist at Petrenko.

"I told you we should have grabbed him before."

Feeling much better since he'd stopped a couple of hours ago for some of those fizzing tablets—much to this partner's irritation—Petrenko merely shrugged. "It was impossible. You cannot grab an American citizen with a crowd of people watching. It is not done. You know the rules. You, too, made study of Soviet agent's manual."

Borofsky rubbed his stubbled chin as he puffed, chimney fashion, on his cigarette. "And tell me, Comrade Petrenko, what does our manual say about breaking into American mailboxes?"

Petrenko chuckled. "Ah, now I do not recall any rules about that." He looked around. "It's a little risky, though, with so many people strolling by, no?"

Borofsky gave his partner a not-so-playful shove. "You idiot. Think. What would that movie star of yours from Hollywood...that Clint Eastwood do? He would wait until dark, no?"

Petrenko looked contrite. "After dark. Of course, after dark." Suddenly a glinty smile that exposed a row of gold teeth broke out on the stocky man's face. "I think once I saw a Clint Eastwood movie like this, Yevgenni. Only he did not bother breaking into the box. He merely ripped it off its footings and carted the whole thing off." Petrenko burst into a hearty laugh. "Or maybe it was Charles Bronson," he mused. "I love the American movies," Petrenko concluded, once again bursting into laughter.

Borofsky, however, wasn't laughing with him. His expression was thoughtful. "For once, Comrade, you do not play the idiot."

On hearing so rare a compliment, Petrenko instantly stopped laughing. "Yevgenni, you mean it?"

Borofsky nodded solemnly.

Petrenko looked puzzled. "But to what do I owe such a compliment?"

"The box, you idiot," Borofsky snapped. "The mailbox. We take it away. Before someone else gets her greedy little hands on it. Say, someone who drives a silver Porsche."

"You mean it, Yevgenni? Steal the box itself?"

"As soon as it will be dark. Meanwhile, we guard this box with our lives. You understand?"

Petrenko patted the spot on his chest where his .45 automatic was concealed. "As long as I am on duty, Yevgenni, letters and parcels go into the box, but nothing goes out."

Borofsky focused his binoculars back on the box, studying the way it was bolted to the sidewalk. "Tell me, Comrade. This American movie you saw. How did Clint Eastwood accomplish this task?"

"Accomplish what task?"

"Steal the mailbox, you idiot." He shook his head with a mixture of rage and despair. "What did I ever do to deserve such a fool for a partner?"

"Please, Yevgenni. Stop insulting me and leave me a minute for remembering...I am thinking perhaps it was Charles Bronson...."

"NOW WHAT, MISS DUPRÉ?" the young man asked after they observed Madden drop the parcel into the mailbox.

Christine smiled. "It's very simple, Dennis," she explained to the man Daniel had told her to contact if she needed assistance. "You wait until dark and break into the mailbox unless the postman comes along first. Then you simply lighten his load a bit.''

Dennis nodded.

''Meanwhile, I think, just to be on the safe side, I'll keep an eye on Madden. I want to get this business settled quickly and I don't want anything to go wrong.'' Her voice was laced with tension.

''Don't worry about a thing, Miss Dupré.''

Christine's ruby-red lips managed a smile even though his words did not exactly fill her with confidence. Nor was she as convinced as before that she'd made the wisest choice by going with greed over love. Then again, Daniel was probably right. She had little chance of holding on to a man like Marcus Lloyd on a permanent basis. Whereas money...a lot of money, even if cold comfort...was better than no comfort at all.

CHRISTINE WAS NOT the only one clever enough to cover her bases by continuing to follow Madden. Borofsky's superior, Zakharov was not about to leave the fate of that manuscript solely in the hands of two bumbling spies. He had ordered his man Goncharov on the job, as well. And like Christine Dupré, Goncharov also decided to keep an eye on Madden while his partner remained in viewing distance of the mailbox.

And so it was that both Christine and Goncharov observed their target pause at a mailbox on the other side of the campus, slip another parcel out of his inner pocket—a parcel all too familiar-looking in size and shape—and drop it down the mail slot.

Within an hour, Professor Jonathan Madden had hit six mailboxes, depositing six identical-looking parcels in each one. As he made his final drop, he turned around slowly and unbuttoned his jacket, opening it wide to show anyone who might still be watching that his deliveries had been concluded.

There, he thought as he hailed a cab, that ought to keep everyone busy for several hours and give him time to get out of sight, attend to some important business and even sneak back later that night to Courtney's bookstore to retrieve the real parcel.

"I DON'T GET IT, Uncle Lou. You seem more curious about the man who lent me this manuscript than about the item itself. I thought you'd flip when you saw this."

"I don't flip, Courtney," he said, grinning. "I'm too old to flip. But I am amazed to see this piece of work."

"Do you think it's authentic?"

Lou Vaughn stroked his chin. "It would take more than a quick study to be sure, but it certainly looks good. Which is why I'm so concerned about this man who left it in your safekeeping, Courtney. You're being damn mysterious about all this."

"Oh, stop, Uncle Lou. I'm not being mysterious at all. I told you. A perfectly reputable gentleman came in yesterday, showed me the manuscript, told me he believed it might be valuable and that he had to be out of town for the next twenty-four hours, and would I be willing to keep it at the shop for him until then."

"And he was willing to trust you with a manuscript that could be worth a king's ransom."

"Well, half a million, maybe," Courtney said, hastily adding, "I told you that, too, Uncle Lou. He's dealt in rare works on occasion and he knows through his circles about Vaughn's fine reputation. Anyway, he wasn't at all certain the manuscript was authentic. It might not be worth the paper it's printed on. Well, handwritten on, anyway."

Her attempt at humor did not remove the scowl from her uncle's face.

"Courtney, don't you realize that if this is authentic, it had to have originally surfaced someplace in the Soviet Union? That it's here now means it was smuggled out. Do you have any idea how dangerous an item such as this could be to the person holding on to it?"

Courtney had a pretty good idea, but she kept her expression bemused.

Lou continued. "The finish to a Gorky masterpiece would be considered not only a national treasure to the Russians, but there's probably millions to be made over time for the worldwide publishing rights to a work of this magnitude. My dear girl, don't think for a moment the Russians would merely sit back and let such a valuable item slip out of their hands."

Courtney sighed. "No, I suppose not. But they'd have to know where to look for it."

Lou ran his hands over his face and rubbed the back of his neck. "You can't walk around town with this, Courtney. And leaving it in the shop until this man returns makes me uneasy. With the whole of Madison Street in the throes of being torn down, there are any number of seedy characters hanging around. And there've been several reports of vandalism during the past month. No, the thing to do is leave the manuscript with me. I'll tuck it away in my wall safe and when this man returns you can bring him here to pick it up. Besides, I am flipping a little," he conceded, "old man that I am. And I'd love to examine the work more closely."

Courtney was a little uneasy about the plan, but she had to agree that it made sense. Her neighborhood wasn't the best lately. On some wild turn of bad luck the shop could be vandalized. It paid to be safe rather than sorry.

One worry remained, however. "I need a promise from you, Uncle Lou."

He furrowed his brow. "A promise?"

"That woman you were supposed to get together with tonight—that new neighbor."

Lou grinned. "We're having dinner tomorrow night, and I decided it would be just the two of us. After all, I'm a grown man—she's a grown woman. We'll spend a few hours alone, get acquainted . . . who knows, maybe it will be the start of a beautiful friendship."

That was precisely what was worrying Courtney.

"So what is this promise you want?" he asked.

"I want you to promise not to tell a soul about this manuscript, Uncle Lou. Especially not your new neighbor."

"Oh, come, Courtney, you think maybe my new neighbor is a Russian spy?" He chuckled. "Ah, such a vivid imagination. Why would a Russian spy move into my building of all places? Unless your fantasy is that she's not only a spy but a fortune teller and she looked into her crystal ball and saw that you would be coming tonight with this manuscript."

"You did say she had a particular interest in rare books. And I have a feeling she might be the same woman who came into the shop yesterday, asking if we had any Gorky first editions." Courtney's eyes narrowed. "Now you tell me if my concerns are nothing more than fantasy?"

Her uncle's face held a hint of consternation as he contemplated her. But he didn't tell her whether he thought her concerns were justified or not. He simply agreed to the promise Courtney had asked him to make.

THE BOSTON POLICE were having a busy night. And one of the crazier ones they'd had in a long time. Oh, there'd been looting of a random mailbox here and there, but six mailboxes in a ten-block radius? In one night? One of the boxes had even been heisted in its entirety. What the hell was the city coming to?

AT MIDNIGHT Jonathan put in his call to London. Marcus Lloyd answered on the first ring.

"Madden?"

"We've got even more than we bargained for, Marc. The KGB isn't the only eager beaver on the scene. A dynamite-looking brunette has been on my tail, too. And I wouldn't be surprised if there weren't more in the shadows."

"We have to move fast on this."

"Believe me, I'm moving as fast as I can." Why should mayhem and one bullet wound slow him down? he thought.

"Well, get on it, man. And, Madden, don't let that manuscript out of your hands for one moment."

Jonathan smiled sardonically. "Right. No need to worry."

"That brunette on your tail. Can you describe her?"

"I'm afraid I've only managed shadowy glimpses. Tall, dark and beautiful."

"Hmm, that doesn't narrow the field down much now, does it? My guess is she's part of the Stateside surveillance team. They're taking an active interest just in case there's more to this business than meets the eye. You're to put a call in there, anyway, so you can check on it. And Madden, after you've spoken to them, do ring me up again."

It took Jonathan a few minutes to get through on his next call.

"Yes?"

"Jonathan Madden here."

"I want a meeting. Tomorrow." The voice was brisk, irritated.

"I'll come by the office."

"Too risky. Have you any idea how much interest you've stirred up? From how many quarters?"

Jonathan laughed softly. "I've a pretty good idea."

"Grandview Restaurant, Cohasset, noon." The line went dead.

DMITRI ZAKHAROV'S narrow mouth was tight with disapproval. Borofsky's showed a dark shadow of fear hidden by a forced obsequious smile.

"I do not understand it," Borofsky muttered. "I saw him drop the parcel in the box. Petrenko... he saw him, too."

"And Goncharov saw him deposit five more identical parcels in five other boxes. Our professor had his little laugh on all of us. And managed, as well, to slip out of sight."

Zakharov's mouth loosened up a bit to smile an empty smile. It was no more comforting than his tight-lipped expression.

"You've obtained the other parcels?" Borofsky asked nervously.

"All but two. But no doubt they are the same." Zakharov flung the manual across the room, the manual whose cover read *The Clandestine Operator's Guide to Secret Terminology... what every spy always wanted to know but was too embarrassed to ask.*

Zakharov's eyes bored into Borofsky. "I shall tell you where you and Petrenko will go next, Comrade."

Borofsky was afraid his superior would say to hell, or, even worse, to Siberia.

Instead Zakharov snapped, "You will return to that bookstore, and you will search every inch of it."

"The bookstore. You think—"

"I apparently am the only one who does think, you total fool."

"What about the shop girl? She lives over the store. Should we eliminate her?"

"Not unless it proves expedient. We do not want to stir up unnecessary waves. Use temporary measures to subdue her. And make certain that neither you nor Petrenko are recognized."

JONATHAN WAS PUZZLED as he tried Marcus Lloyd's number for the third time. Blast the man. Where was he? He was expecting the call.

The phone was picked up on the fourth ring this time round. A male voice asked, "Madden?"

Jonathan hesitated. It wasn't Marcus. The voice was higher pitched and edgier.

"Who is this?" Jonathan demanded, not identifying himself.

"Never mind who this is, Professor. I have a message for you. A brief message."

"Where's Lloyd?"

"Shall we say he's being detained, Professor. Temporarily, if you cooperate. And if not . . . I'm sorry to say the detention will be permanent. Ah, perhaps you'd like to hear the message directly from Mr. Lloyd himself."

A moment later a shaken but familiar voice came on the line. "Jonathan, they want the manuscript. But don't—"

"Sorry, Professor. It would appear Mr. Lloyd has not yet gotten the message clear. But, I assure you he will. Very quickly. In the meantime, I will give you the message, instead. The manuscript in my hands, hand-delivered by you, Professor, in precisely forty-eight hours. I don't suppose I need say more about what will happen to Mr. Lloyd if that document is not here on time?"

COURTNEY CRAWLED INTO BED a little past midnight. She didn't feel tired, though. She felt alert, excited and filled with anticipation. All her life she'd dreamed of adventure, danger, dashing heroes . . . romance of the kind the Hilary Bennetts of the world created. And now it was really happening. Courtney was ecstatic. And quite certain she was in love.

For a few minutes as she lay awake in bed she considered reading a chapter or two about the daring Derek Colton and his irrepressible lover, Katherine O'Malley. But in the end Courtney opted for a fantasy strictly on her own creation. One that took the daring professor Jonathan Madden and his hopefully soon-to-be lover, the irrepressible Courtney Blue, on a breathless adventure of their own.

She was just drifting off to sleep, when she heard faint scraping sounds and then several thuds. Immediately she awoke fully, thinking it must be Jonathan arriving earlier than expected. She smoothed back her hair, grabbed her purse and dabbed on some lipstick, wiped it off a bit with a tissue so as not to be so obvious, then gracefully spread herself back on the bed, eyelids fluttering closed.

A moment later she opened her eyes and sat up with a start. Fantasy was all well and good, but how did she know it was Jonathan? *Think, Blue, think for a moment.* The shop was locked up tight. Why would Jonathan resort to breaking in, when a simple phone call would have ensured an easy entrance?

She lay down again, her muscles tense, her uncertainty mounting. She heard footsteps on the back stairs and was out of bed like a shot. Those clumsy thuds were not the light-footed steps of her dashing hero. She grabbed her robe, pulling it on hurriedly as she edged toward the front door and listened. Either the intruder was four-legged, she mused, or there were two of them. Quickly she scanned the room for a makeshift weapon, settling on her hair dryer as the only heavy object within hasty reach.

Soaring anxiety mixed with determination as she heard the lock being jimmied and the door creaking open ever so slowly.

A large head peered in. Courtney lifted the hair dryer in preparation, but as she made the downward swing, the head disappeared.

"She is not here."

"We saw her enter, idiot."

"Shh, Yevgenni. Keep your voice down." A few hoarse coughs followed. "And must you smoke even now?"

Courtney frowned. The accents were Russian, the words spoken sotto voce, the conversation almost amusing, had she been in a mood to be amused.

Poised behind the door, she clutched the hair dryer tightly, ready to strike again. Unfortunately she was unprepared for the violent shove Borofsky gave Petrenko, which sent the big lummox hurtling into the room. The front door smashed into Courtney, the doorknob ramming sharply into the pit of her stomach. A loud gasp of pain and shock escaped her lips, immediately giving her away.

The second man into the room grabbed her roughly, knocking the hair dryer from her hand. In the darkness, she was only able to make out that the man was of medium height and had a stocky build. He wore a ski mask over his face. A cigarette dangled from one corner of his mouth, the acrid smoke drifting up to Courtney's nose and making her grimace.

"Where is it?" he demanded as the man on the floor rose slowly to his feet, muttering in Russian, then in English, telling his partner to hurry because the woolen mask he was wearing greatly irritated his skin.

"I—I don't know wh-what you want," Courtney stammered, partly to carry off the role of unsuspecting innocent, partly out of real fear. "If it's money or jewels..."

Borofsky dragged Courtney over to the couch and threw her down. "It will take half the night to search. Perhaps if you save us some time your life will be spared."

"But, Yevgenni," Petrenko broke in, "our orders are not to hurt—"

"Idiot. Be quiet."

Courtney's next breath came a little easier. So, she was not to be harmed. Her fear having abated somewhat, she was able to get into the performance of the baffled and frightened shopkeeper with a great deal more gusto. With a desperate, pleading look on her face, she clutched her captor's shirt and began sobbing loudly, shaking him, swearing to him that she was a total innocent and that she had nothing of value that they could want. Borofsky had to strain to wrench her hands away. And neither he nor Petrenko had any luck whatsoever in quieting her down.

Finally, having managed to pin her hands behind her, Borofsky ordered Petrenko to put her to sleep. Courtney's struggles were real now. The fantasy had gone terribly awry. Where was her hero? If she were Katherine O'Malley, Derek Colton would be breaking down the door this very moment to rescue her from these brutes. As she riled against her fate and the utter unfairness of reality, Petrenko was pulling at the sleeve of her robe and, after some effort, jabbed her with the hypodermic. Moments later she was out cold.

"What do you think?" Petrenko asked.

"What do I think? I think the woman is a shrew. Even my wife does not have such a voice."

"Nor mine." Petrenko chuckled.

"Enough," Borofsky barked. "You search here while I start on the bookstore. If you find nothing, you will join me there. We will tear every shelf apart. If we come up empty-handed, it will not be for want of thoroughness."

Forty minutes later, the bookstore was strewn with books. Petrenko was attacking the desk in the back room. Irritated beyond measure at what he now felt certain was a fruitless task, Borofsky set his cigarette down on the last shelf as he methodically dumped book after book on the floor after a quick check with his pen light.

Petrenko finished with the desk just as Borofsky came to the last book. "Nothing," he called out.

Borofsky waded through the book-laden floor on his way to the back room. "Nothing anywhere. My only pleasure in all this, Comrade, is in knowing that our esteemed superior was wrong in his theory. Not," he added as he and Petrenko made their exit through the rear door, "that I look forward to telling him this in person."

As soon as the door shut behind the two Russians, the forgotten cigarette that Borofsky had left burning on that final bookshelf tumbled to the floor.

With all those old, dried-out books lying around, it took no time at all for the fire to grab hold.

It was only minutes later that Jonathan turned the corner of Courtney's street and saw bursts of red-orange flames and billows of smoke clouding the shopfront window. He started to run, panic and guilt flooding him. He'd known in his heart from the first that he'd been wrong to involve an innocent young woman in this dangerous affair.

There was no hope of gaining entry through the shop itself, he quickly discovered. And no time to phone for emergency help. If Courtney had returned to her apartment—he prayed she was still at her uncle's—every wasted moment might mean her death. Even now smoke was filling the upper story, and in less time than Jonathan cared to consider, the flames themselves would be thirstily rising.

Racing down the alley beside the store and rounding the corner, Jonathan located the fire escape and hoisted himself up the ladder. The climb up the rickety metal stairs took only moments, but it felt an eternity before he smashed in the window, throwing his sleeved arm across his face as protection against the rush of heat and smoke whooshing out at him.

Recklessly he climbed inside. She was sprawled out on the couch. And she wasn't moving.

For a moment Jonathan stood paralyzed, afraid he was too late, afraid she was dead. A wave of tremendous pain enveloped him with an intensity that stunned him. He had seen death before. He had felt the pain of loss. But never like this.

And then he heard a soft moan, saw a faint movement. Relief flooded him as he raced to her, gathered her in his arms. Flames leaped into the room, licking at his heels as he made his way to the window, clutching a limp Courtney against his chest.

After they'd made it safely out of the burning building and across the street far from the reach of the crumbling, fiery inferno, Jonathan could hear the sound of approaching sirens.

Slowly Courtney came to in Jonathan's arms. Her eyelids fluttered open to meet his concerned gaze. Her arms went around his neck. "My hero," she said groggily. "I knew you'd rescue me from those awful brutes."

"Brutes?"

She rested her head against his shoulder. "The Russians, darling."

Jonathan tensed. "The Russians? The Russians burned down the shop? Courtney, did they...get the manuscript?"

Still woozy, she raised her head a bit drunkenly, her smile somewhat lopsided. "Nope."

Jonathan sighed heavily as he stared across at the inferno. He had rarely suffered so ironic a defeat. "Well, then, I'm afraid it's been incinerated with all the rest. That's it, then." His thoughts flew to Marcus Lloyd. He'd managed to save Courtney from disaster, but he despaired he would not be able to do the same for his friend.

The fresh air was slowly clearing Courtney's head. She gazed up at Jonathan, touching his soot-smudged cheek. "Darling, I haven't let you down yet, have I? The book wasn't in the shop. It's perfectly safe. I promise."

Her smile was even more lopsided now. But it was the most beautiful smile Jonathan Madden had ever set eyes on.

# CHAPTER SIX

ALL IN ALL Courtney hadn't lost much in the fire. Like her uncle, she was fully insured. The value of the books that had been incinerated did not amount to much. Uncle Lou had already removed any works of significance. And as for irreplaceable personal treasures, she'd never been one to squirrel away keepsakes or valuables. The few odd bits of jewelry she owned, mostly pieces left to her by her mother, were safely stored away in a bank safe deposit box. As for the destruction of her entire wardrobe in the blaze, Courtney was not about to mourn the loss of her drab collection of serviceable ensembles. Although she would have preferred to be left with something other than her nightgown and torn robe, which she had on at the moment.

Jonathan wrapped his tweed jacket around Courtney's shoulders as she gave her report to the fire marshal while the blaze was being contained. She was careful not to mention her uninvited visitors to the shop, and she claimed she had no real idea how the fire might have started. Vandals, she supposed.

The fire under control, the fire marshal gave Courtney and Jonathan a lift in his car to her uncle's place. As the car pulled off, Courtney glanced up at the windows of her uncle's apartment from the street below.

"No lights on. He must have gone to sleep hours ago," Courtney commented.

"Will he be very upset about the fire?"

"No. We were due to be razed in a couple of weeks' time." They approached the outer door to the five-story apartment building. "Damn," she muttered. "I have a key to get inside. That is, I did have a key before it went up in smoke. Well, I'll have to buzz him."

After several buzzes with no response, Courtney looked over at Jonathan. "That's odd."

"I suppose we'll have to try the rest of the apartments," Jonathan said.

"All but the woman who just moved in. We wouldn't want to broadcast our arrival to her."

As reward for such quick thinking, Jonathan cupped her chin in his hand and kissed her lightly. Courtney returned the kiss with considerably more ardor.

"There aren't many women who can kiss like that after having been mucked about with by Russian brutes, then nearly asphyxiated in a fiery blaze," he murmured, smoothing her tangled hair back from her face.

"I read somewhere that physical danger excites the body," she said, inwardly marveling at her unabashed aplomb. How was it possible that in twenty-four hours a drab, shy shopkeeper had been transformed into this daring, flirtatious woman, ignited by danger, desire glowing and fizzing inside her? The feelings were too tenuous for Courtney to risk analyzing. For now experiencing them was quite enough.

Jonathan began pressing each buzzer methodically, skipping the one with the empty slot beside it indicating that the old tenant had moved and a name tag had not yet been made for the new one.

Out of twelve tries they got one reply, which was all they needed. Once they got inside an irritated voice called from the ground floor, "Connie, is that you?"

"No, sorry," Courtney called back hurriedly. "I must have pressed the wrong buzzer." She grinned at Jonathan as the irate tenant's front door slammed shut.

"I hope we can wake him," Courtney said when they arrived a minute later at her uncle's apartment on the fifth floor. "He's not usually a very sound sleeper, but he did have a fair amount of wine with dinner."

She rang several times, finally keeping her hand on the bell for a good twenty seconds.

Jonathan gave Courtney a puzzled look. "You don't suppose he might have gone out?"

"I can't imagine where he'd go at this hour," she said slowly, worry creeping in.

Jonathan put his hand on the doorknob and turned it, only mildly surprised at this point to feel it give.

With growing alarm Courtney watched Jonathan's other hand go for his gun.

"Courtney..."

"I'm coming inside with you," she said firmly, second-guessing him.

"Stay behind me, then," he said. There was no time to argue. And no point, he realized.

The living room looked precisely as it had when Courtney had last been there a few hours ago. Not a particularly tidy man, her uncle, things weren't any messier than earlier. They walked cautiously through the living room, Courtney forgetting about staying behind Jonathan. She was first into the kitchen, and noted the dishes now quite dry on the drainboard where she'd left them after insisting on cleaning up after their dinner.

It was a three-room apartment. After a check on the compact bathroom off the hall the only place left to look was her uncle's bedroom. Before they entered, Jonathan gripped Courtney's arm, motioning her to stay put. His expression was so fierce Courtney was not inclined to buck him. Anxiety had something to do with her cooperation, too.

She shivered despite Jonathan's jacket, her bathrobe and cotton gown. But the chill she was feeling at the moment was nothing compared to the icy sensation that raced down her spine at the cold, hard look on Jonathan's face when he stepped back into the hall.

"What . . . what is it?"

"See for yourself," he said tightly. Before she could rouse herself from the shock of Jonathan's wrathful look and biting tone, he took hold of her arm and escorted her roughly into the bedroom.

The room was empty, the bed still made. Clothes were scattered around the room in typical Uncle Lou fashion, but there was no sign of the gray slacks or the black-and-white striped jersey he'd worn that evening.

"He's . . . gone," Courtney said, casting Jonathan a puzzled look.

"Ah, but it appears he's taken some rather engrossing reading material along with him."

Courtney was not fooled by Jonathan's suddenly glib tone. She could still see the barely masked fury in his face. Her eyes moved to the wall behind her uncle's bed, coming to rest midway at the gaping and vacant steel hole that was his safe. Before she'd left the apartment earlier that night she'd witnessed her uncle tuck the manuscript into the safe and spin the lock closed. He'd said he was too tired to give the work careful study, but would spend the next morning going through it.

There was a moment's silence and then Courtney went over to the bed and sat down, a look of bafflement and worry in her eyes.

"You can't think my uncle ran off with the manuscript?"

"And for a minute I was afraid you'd lost your ability to be clever, love."

"You're wrong, Jonathan. You don't know my uncle."

"You're right. I don't know him. Therefore, I haven't one bloody reason in hell to trust him."

She could see from the seering look in his blue eyes that he wasn't at all certain at the moment that he could trust her, either.

It was a look that would have intimidated many a lass, but Courtney Blue was not about to let her fantasy-come-true end on so cruel a note.

"Listen to me, Jonathan," she said sharply, rising to her feet and striding over to him. "For one thing, if I hadn't brought your bloody manuscript here, it would be in the hands of the Russians or burned to cinders. Either way, you wouldn't have a prayer of recovering it. So you're already far ahead of the game."

Jonathan's ire matched Courtney's. "And do you bloody well think I'm any better off with the manuscript in the hands of some thief?"

In a reflex action she slapped him across the face. Tears of anger and hurt trickled down her cheeks. "My uncle is not a thief. You have no right—"

He took hold of her wrists. "Don't provoke me like that again, Courtney or—"

"Or what? Or you'll provoke me back?" she snapped, pulling away from him.

In fact, it took a great deal to provoke Jonathan, but Courtney was managing it with all too little effort.

He stormed over to the wall safe by the bed. "He's cleared it out lock, stock and barrel. What else did he keep in there?"

"I'm...not sure. Not much. He has a large vault at the bank, where he keeps most of his valuables. He just uses this safe as a temporary holding spot." She walked over to where

Jonathan was standing. "Wait...he had his—" She stopped abruptly.

Jonathan gripped her shoulder hard. "What else was in there?"

She pressed her lips tightly, stubbornly, together, certain her response would only serve to convince Jonathan even more of her uncle's duplicity.

"Courtney, you don't understand the half of this affair. For one thing, if I don't get that manuscript back, the man who sent it to me...will be murdered."

Her eyes shot open wide. "What?"

"His name is Marcus Lloyd. He's been kidnapped, and the ransom is the manuscript. Within forty-eight—damn, forty-five hours now. I'm to deliver the manuscript to London or Marcus dies."

"Oh, Jonathan, that's awful. But surely you can explain what happened—"

"Explain?" he exploded. "How the bloody hell do I explain something I can't begin to understand?"

Again she sat down on the bed—collapsed down, really. "Uncle Lou's passport was in the safe. I remember him saying he was due to renew it in a few weeks."

"Oh, terrific. He could be out of the country with the manuscript by now. On his way to heaven knows where. Russia, maybe."

Courtney gave him a sharp look, but her body sagged, her hands running nervously back and forth along the bright print bedspread. Suddenly her left hand stopped moving as it made contact with a small round metal object.

"Jonathan," she exclaimed. "Look at this."

He gazed down at the object in the palm of Courtney's hand. "It's a ring. A man's sapphire ring. It must have fallen out of the safe."

She was up on her feet, grabbing his arm, shaking him. "No. No, you don't understand. This is my uncle's favorite ring. His good luck ring he called it, because he won it years ago in an all-night poker game along with nearly seventeen thousand dollars.''

"So what?"

"He was *wearing* this ring this evening, Jonathan. He always wears the ring. Don't you see?"

"I see that he apparently decided to take it off before he pocketed his passport and absconded with the manuscript."

"No, no, no. That would be the last thing in the world he'd do. I told you. It's his good luck ring. Of all times to wear it, if he was hoping to make off safely with stolen goods he'd have worn it now. No. It's a signal. I tell you. My uncle intentionally took that ring off. He was counting on my finding it. He knew that once I saw that ring left behind like this I'd realize something was wrong." Her elated mood at having confirmed for herself her uncle's innocence immediately vanished as a new fear struck her. "Oh, my God, Jonathan. Do you realize what this means?"

"I suppose you'll tell me."

Her complexion had gone quite white. "It means he's been abducted. That's the only explanation. It's the only reason my uncle would have vanished without so much as a word to me or a goodbye note."

Jonathan's rage had ebbed, but his expression remained cautious. "Why would anyone take him? Why not just take the manuscript?"

Courtney frowned. "I haven't figured that out yet."

He smiled ruefully. "And here I thought you had all the answers, love."

Her smile was equally rueful. "I've come up with more answers than you have." The smile was replaced by a scowl. "And just as many worries."

Jonathan's expression softened. He put both hands on her shoulders and gazed down at her. "I was a bit rough on you."

She managed a more tender smile. "Even heroes have their boiling points. You should have told me about the kidnapping. It would have explained—"

"Courtney, listen to me. I'm not a hero. You've got to stop that schoolgirl notion."

But Courtney wasn't paying attention. She gripped his shirt. "Jonathan, the new neighbor. Shouldn't we check her apartment? My uncle told me she was out this evening. That's why she canceled out on dinner. But what if she wasn't? What if she saw me either come up here tonight or leave after dinner? The apartment wasn't broken into. So whoever grabbed my uncle and the manuscript had to have been invited in. My uncle would have leaped at the chance of a late-night visit from a woman he was already sorely taken with." She leaned heavily against Jonathan, whose arms automatically went around her. "The poor man. He asks her to come in, no doubt expecting a romantic tryst, and look what happens."

Gently Jonathan moved her from him. "We don't yet know what happened."

"If anything has happened to him . . ." The thought was too terrible to finish. "He's all the family I have," she whispered.

"If your theory about why your uncle is missing is correct, love, then we can assume he's all right, or we would have found him here tonight . . . in a sorry state."

She nodded, hugging herself with both arms and shivering. He slipped his arms back around her. "You've had your share of it tonight, love. Stretch out here for a bit and I'll have a look-see in the new neighbor's flat."

Courtney started to protest, but exhaustion and nerves got the better of her and she relented. When Jonathan was almost out the door, she said, "What if she's there? Alone, I mean. Will you go back to thinking my uncle—"

He pressed his finger to his lips. "There's the lucky ring he left behind." He gave her a smile. "I do believe I understand a bit more now where all that cleverness of yours stems from."

She stretched out on the bed, making a rather alluring and unique picture in his oversize jacket worn over her bedraggled night clothes. She looked over at him, met his blue-eyed gaze. Her cheeks were tinged with pink, her eyes bright.

"Until you came along, Professor Madden, I was insulated from all of life's exciting possibilities. You may argue it all you like," she said softly, "but you're as close to a hero as I've had the good fortune to come across."

SHE WAS FAST ASLEEP on her uncle's bed when Jonathan returned nearly an hour later. He'd made a couple of phone calls as well as searched the new neighbor's flat. Now he stood in the doorway of the bedroom, observing Courtney in silence.

From the moment Jonathan had received the Gorky manuscript he'd known his job wouldn't be simple, known there would be dangers and risks. But he hadn't counted on so many of them coming at him so fast. The book stolen, Marcus kidnapped, Lou Vaughn gone. All in all, more than enough problems to test the mettle of any man.

Then there was Courtney Blue. She, too, presented problems, the most unsettling one being that since he'd set eyes on her, he'd found himself beset with vivid fantasies about her. Now that kind of thought had its time and place. Unfortunately this was neither the right time nor the right place. The predicaments he faced required him to have all his wits about him. He had too much at stake to allow himself to be sidetracked, even though the detour certainly promised many untold pleasures. Besides, for all her cleverness and bravery, he was well aware that Courtney Blue had spent her life not only insulated from life's exciting possibilities but from its nasty realities, as well. She was more vulnerable than she'd ever admit. And Jonathan, usually so confident of his own tough hide, was never so uncertain as now of his own vulnerability.

Courtney awoke abruptly, springing up to a sitting position. "Well...?"

Jonathan walked over and sat down on the side of the bed. "The furniture is all there, but my bet is the place was rented furnished. No clothes in the closets, no personal papers, nothing to indicate someone living there at the moment."

"Oh, Jonathan..."

He sighed. "Your theory about what took place here tonight is looking better and better."

She bit down on her lip, shadows playing on her face. "And worse and worse."

He reached out and smoothed back her hair, trying to deny the charge of excitement touching her provoked. "Think about it this way. If she'd meant to harm your uncle, why take him with her? She'd have finished him off here and dashed away with the manuscript. No, for some reason, she needs your uncle."

Courtney's eyes widened. "To examine the work. Of course. That must be it. She must need to verify the manuscript's authenticity before she can unload it. Oh, Uncle Lou isn't an expert of your caliber, certainly, but he does know Russian, and his life has been spent in dealing in rare books. I imagine his word would be accepted."

"Well, then you can rest a bit easier. It will take several days, at least, to authenticate the manuscript. Which means that for the time being your uncle is quite safe."

"But it doesn't give us much time to track him down. Or save your friend Marcus Lloyd."

"Courtney, we can't take this kind of operation on ourselves. We'll have to leave this in the hands of professionals. I've already contacted someone. I have to meet him tomorrow down in the town of Cohasset to give him the details. You'll stay here."

"Here?"

"In your uncle's apartment. It's really the safest—"

"Oh, no, Jonathan," she stated firmly. "I'm going with you."

"But I told you, I'm putting this whole mess in the hands of people trained in such matters."

As usual, whenever he said anything she didn't want to hear, she merely went off on her own train of thought. "Did you say Cohasset?"

He frowned. "Courtney."

"That's on the way to Cape Cod. Less than forty-five minutes from Sandwich."

"Sandwich?"

"Sandwich is a little coastal town right over the Sagamore Bridge at the start of the Cape."

"And what does a town at the start of the Cape have to do with anything?"

"My uncle owns a cottage in Sandwich. We always spent summer holidays there when I was younger. Lou still goes down there quite a lot. It's a kind of getaway, a place to read, relax, study."

Jonathan looked puzzled.

"If it's true that my uncle was kidnapped so that he could authenticate the Gorky manuscript, he might very well have talked his captor into taking him down there. The area is pretty desolate this time of year, especially with the weather being so crummy."

"You're pulling at straws, Courtney. She'd have to know it's one of the first places we'd check."

"No, think about it, Jonathan. After all, you wouldn't know the place even existed. And I...I supposedly went up in smoke. She might have seen it as the ideal spot."

"You think she's with the Russians and that she was the one who set those thugs on you?"

"It makes sense, doesn't it? She sends them off to see if I have the manuscript. They don't find it, so she cleverly goes to see if I might have left it with my uncle for safekeeping. Meanwhile she orders her boys to dispose of me." A quick, quirky smile came and went. "I imagine they're busily scouting Boston for you, as well. Eliminate all players. That's the way it's done."

"It is? I see."

"Come on, Jonathan. You're not going to act naive all of a sudden. Not after all you've been through. Not after all we've been through together. Even if they have gotten the manuscript, you know too much. You're a marked man. And I'm a marked woman once they learn I'm still alive."

"Courtney, aren't you being a bit—"

"A bit what? Melodramatic? No. I may not have had a great deal of experience in these matters, Jonathan, but you might say I've studied these types of situations quite a bit. Call it a hobby. Quite frankly, Jonathan, I think I've been preparing for something like this all my life."

Jonathan wasn't one to argue the point. "A heroine in the true classic sense, love," he whispered.

An exhausted heroine, Courtney fought back a yawn as she gave him a quick smile. "We should leave for Sandwich first thing. What time do you have to meet that man in Cohasset?"

"Noon. But—"

"No problem. We'll check out the cottage first and—" This time the yawn won out.

"It's four-thirty in the morning, Courtney. We're not going anywhere right now. You need some sleep. And so do

I. We'll discuss our plans in the morning. Meanwhile, we'll stay put for what's left of the night."

She eyed him warily.

"I didn't mean it in that way," he said, reading into her look. "At least your uncle's couch looks a bit roomier than yours."

She smiled. "That wasn't what was worrying me, Jonathan. I just didn't want you to sneak off on me while I was asleep." Her smile deepened as she added, "I don't mean for you to spend the night on the couch."

"You don't?"

"Do I shock you?"

"Do I look shocked?"

Her smiled broadened. "A little."

He laughed. "Things have gotten a bit reversed, haven't they?"

"You mean, I'm supposed to wait for you to make the advance?"

"Well..."

"I had the feeling you weren't going to make it."

"Well..."

"I think you're a bit afraid of me, Professor."

"Bloody nonsense."

"I also think you're attracted to me, although I'm not sure why. A man like you must have scores of beautiful women." She paused, took a breath. "Or one beautiful woman. One special, beautiful woman. Is that it, Professor? Is there a Mrs. Professor tucked away somewhere? Or an exquisite, tempestuous lover?"

He smiled indulgently as he rose from the bed. "There is no missus and no lover. And no queues of eager young beauties awaiting my favors." He leaned over and covered her with the blankets. "As for why I find my heart pounding rapidly whenever I'm around you, the answer is quite simple. You are the loveliest, most vibrant, exciting woman

I've ever met." He kissed her on the cheek. "Now get some sleep, love."

She stared up at him with a baffled expression. "I don't understand, Jonathan. I want you. You say you want me. What . . . ?"

"Perhaps it's because it's the honorable thing to do." He smiled beguilingly, taking several steps from the bed to help him keep his mind on consequences rather than his spiraling desires. "Perhaps," he added, his smile now tender, "I'm more the hero than I ever imagined."

He walked to the door and turned to look back at her one last time. "Although to be honest, love, there are those who might disagree with that particular label. I haven't led a completely chaste life. I'm afraid I've been called a cad more often than a hero. I thought you best be warned. Just in case the time comes when I'm feeling less heroic."

# CHAPTER SEVEN

IT WAS A GOOD THING Courtney was a light sleeper. Otherwise her entry into the world of adventure would have ended at 7:19 the next morning with Jonathan Madden's stealthy departure from Lou Vaughn's apartment.

Awake at the click of the door latch, Courtney hurriedly dressed in her uncle's clothes, including his tweed sport jacket, as Jonathan had retrieved his own jacket. The borrowed shoes were a couple of sizes too big, but there wasn't much she could do about that. It was better than chasing after Jonathan in her bare feet.

On her way out the door—she was less than two minutes behind Jonathan—she grabbed one of her uncle's hats, stuffing her hair up into it in a makeshift disguise. She didn't want to run into those Russian apes or that dark-haired goddess, just in case they had somehow learned she was still alive.

Curiosity and a bit of ire kept Courtney from calling out to Jonathan as she saw him hurrying down to the corner of the block. Once there, he came to an abrupt stop, impatiently glancing up and down the street, clearly looking like a man awaiting someone.

Luck was not something Courtney considered very much in the past, be it bad luck or good luck. But as she stuck her hand absently in the pocket of her uncle's jacket and discovered a set of keys, she crossed her fingers, praying that Lady Luck would blossom for her now. Racing back inside the apartment building—her luck was already working as

one of the keys on the ring fit into the locked outer door—
Courtney exited moments later, this time through the rear
door leading to the garage. She said a silent thanks to Lady
Luck when she saw her uncle's brown Chevy parked in its
usual bay.

One of the keys on the key ring opened the locked driver's door; another key started up the engine. Courtney
pulled out of the garage, aware that her piece of luck from
the transportation gods also confirmed her uncle's decidedly bad piece of luck. The presence of his car was one more
indication that he had not left his apartment of his own volition.

Lady Luck remained with Courtney as she drove onto the
street and saw a navy sedan pull up to the curb where Jonathan was waiting. A young man in a trim tan suit stepped
out of the car, Jonathan hurriedly taking his place behind
the wheel. With a light tap of his horn, Jonathan pulled out.

Courtney set aside her simmering anger and disappointment at Jonathan's abrupt leave-taking. She needed all her
concentration to follow his car and make certain at the same
time she wouldn't be detected if Jonathan glanced in his
rearview mirror. Not that he was likely to recognize her in
her uncle's wide-brimmed fedora and the masculine garb.
Still, it paid to be careful.

Jonathan drove directly to the nearest entrance of the
Southeast Expressway heading due south. Courtney assumed he was heading for Sandwich to check out the cottage on his own, or perhaps he'd moved up his meeting in
Cohasset and would check the cottage afterward. She wondered exactly who it was Jonathan was meeting. Police?
F.B.I.? A private eye? Well, she would find out soon
enough.

Traffic was light on the route south. Jonathan's driving
was smooth and fast. Courtney wasn't an experienced
driver, so her own course was somewhat more erratic.

However, she was able to remain two to three cars back from the blue sedan for most of the trip, while still managing to keep Jonathan in view.

He signaled just before the Cohasset exit. Not used to her uncle's car, Courtney mistakenly flipped on the windshield washer instead of her right-turn flasher. Muttering as she searched for the wipers immediately after the spray exploded against the windshield, she swerved and jerked up the ramp. She grew increasingly nervous that her actions would draw Jonathan's attention, especially as theirs were the only vehicles exiting and she had no choice but to follow behind him. However, her fear that Jonathan would bring his car to a squealing halt, leap out and confront her proved unfounded. He seemed completely focused on his destination.

Courtney allowed more distance between cars as she turned left and followed Jonathan into the business section of Cohasset. So, she concluded, he was to have his meeting first. Confirmation came a minute later when he pulled into one of those quaint little New England eateries done up like an Early American coach stop. Courtney pulled her borrowed felt fedora low as she drove past Jonathan's parked car, selecting a space for her Chevy farther down the lot. She waited until he had entered the restaurant before alighting from her car.

A hostess costumed in red-and-white gingham greeted her as she walked in.

"Table for one, sir?"

Courtney fought back a chuckle as she shook her lowered head and pointed to a table off in one corner of the room where Jonathan was just sitting down across from a middle-aged man. Taking a menu from the hostess's hand, Courtney waved off escort service.

Jonathan's back was to her as she started across the half-empty dining room, headed toward his table. But the other fellow, a lanky gentleman with graying hair cut very short, seemed to stop mid-sentence when he spotted her, his attentive gaze quickly becoming cautious, then even more swiftly alarmed, as she approached. Jonathan finally turned his head in her direction, and he, too, watched her approach with a wary look.

When Courtney was about ten feet away from the table, the gray-haired fellow leaped up from his seat, his hand slipping quickly into his pocket, his alarmed expression now clearly ominous. Jonathan's own expression, on the other hand, switched from one of wariness to irritation tinged with amusement and admiration.

"Relax, Les. It's okay."

"You know this guy, Madden?"

Jonathan smirked. "Yes, you might say that."

"Well, who is he? What's he doing here?"

Jonathan narrowed his gaze on Courtney. "Good question, Les. I wouldn't mind knowing the answer to that one myself."

Courtney tipped up the fedora about an inch so that it sat at a jaunty angle on her head, a few wisps of hair escaping the band. "You might have woken me, love," she said airily, pitching her voice low as she slipped into an empty seat at the table.

The man Jonathan had called Les was still standing, still looking wary, but for an altogether different reason now. He shifted his gaze to Jonathan. "What's he mean?" he asked slowly, taking a quick glance at Courtney before refocusing on Jonathan.

Jonathan wasn't paying attention to Les's question or to the funny look the man was giving him. He leaned forward and leveled his eyes on Courtney. "I was trying to be considerate. You were sound asleep. I knew you were exhausted. There was no need for both of us to rise at the crack of dawn."

"I thought we were a team."

Jonathan sighed. "I told you last night that you were best out of it."

"That isn't the way I see it." She paused, lowering her voice even more. "I thought we had something special going, Jonathan. I thought you thought so, too. You shouldn't have walked out on me."

Still on his feet, Les had begun to attract the attention of other diners in the room, and he slunk back into his seat. He wore a deep scowl. "Look here, Madden, whatever personal stuff you've got to discuss with this guy, do it on your own time. We've got other fish to fry." A flush crept into his cheeks as he spoke.

Courtney broke into a laugh as she observed the much-discomforted Les. With a mischievous wink, she reached across and took hold of Jonathan's hand. "I do think your friend might be jealous, love."

"What...?" Les's cheeks were turning the color of beets. "You've got the wrong idea, buddy. You're in left field."

Courtney tipped her fedora a little higher, a provocative smile on her lips. "No, Les. I believe it's you who's got the wrong idea. Ideas, really. One, Jonathan and I aren't lovers." She saw poor Les's look of embarrassment and awkwardness mushroom. "And two... I'm not at all certain I want us to be lovers in the future." With a quick jerk of her head, she sent the fedora tumbling to the floor, her soft wavy hair falling down around her shoulders.

Les rubbed his jaw and stared openmouthed. "Well, I'll be damned. You really had me going there for a minute." His chuckle was filled with relief.

She gave him a faintly aggrieved look. "Well, I'm not sure I ought to be flattered by having fooled you so effectively. It doesn't say much for my femininity."

"Hey, no. Listen. I thought you were a real pretty boy." Les was beet-red again. "You know what I'm saying."

Jonathan observed Les with a mocking leer. "I know what you're saying. And I don't find it particularly flattering to my masculinity." He grinned as he shifted his gaze to Courtney. "I think I prefer the construction-worker look to that of the dapper bon vivant, love. But you pulled both off admirably."

"Thank you, darling," she said sweetly. "Now shall we carry on?"

Les enjoyed a good laugh as well as the next guy, but now wasn't the time for charades. "This is a private meeting, honey." Before Courtney could counter, he discreetly brushed his finger across his lips. A moment later the waitress approached their table. Both men ordered black coffee. Courtney ordered bacon and eggs over light with a side order of rye toast. She was staying for the duration.

As soon as the waitress left, Courtney smiled at Les. "The name's Blue. Courtney Blue."

"Oh. So you're Vaughn's niece."

"Ah, I see Jonathan's already filled you in a bit."

"Look, Courtney, do me a favor," Jonathan broke in. "Put that fedora on once again and drive back to Boston."

"What about Sandwich?"

"Last night I was so tired I couldn't think straight, so I thought perhaps Sandwich was a possibility. But this morning I remembered the passport. Your uncle took his passport, remember? Last I heard, one doesn't need a passport for a trip to Cape Cod."

Courtney had to admit Jonathan had a point. "Well, then, have you checked the airports? Has he flown out of the country?"

Les was absently shaking his head no in answer to her question, forgetting for the moment that Courtney had not been invited to his little tête-à-tête. Then again, he was impressed by her, too.

Jonathan had remained mum, so Courtney switched her focus to the more obliging Les. "I didn't catch your full name."

"Les Sharp." He chuckled. "Go on and laugh. Everyone does. But don't let the name fool you. I'm plenty sharp." His cheeks reddened again. "Most of the time." He waved a finger at her. "You're pretty sharp yourself."

"Thanks, Les. It's nice to be appreciated." She shot Jonathan an arched look.

For his part, Jonathan was beginning to feel as if he were trapped in a music hall comedy skit, and he wasn't in the mood to be amused. "I don't quite believe this."

Les cleared his throat. "Right. We'd better get on with it." He glanced from Courtney to Jonathan, giving him a questioning look.

Jonathan sighed. "Okay, okay. She's already involved up to her neck. She might as well stay."

"Thanks, Jonathan." Courtney smiled brightly. "So where are we?"

"I'll tell you where we are," Les muttered, keeping his voice low. "We're the laughingstock of the entire intelligence community."

Courtney's eyes widened. "Intelligence? You mean..."

Jonathan leaned toward her and whispered, "Les is a special agent with the CIA. Under the circumstances, I thought it wise to get professional assistance."

"We want that manuscript," Les broke in. Flushing he added, "And of course we want to help your uncle if he's in danger."

Courtney peered at Les. "Since when has the CIA taken an active interest in rare books?"

"Doesn't she—?"

"Rare Russian books," Jonathan said with import, cutting Les off.

Courtney's eyes remained on Les. "Don't I what?"

But Jonathan's pointed glare at the CIA man was quite effective. "Nothing."

Before Courtney could ask any more questions the waitress returned with the coffee and Courtney's large breakfast. As soon as the waitress was out of hearing range, Jonathan hurriedly began filling Les in. He told him about the Russians, the fire, arriving at her uncle's apartment and finding it empty and the book gone. He also shared Courtney's theory on the ring her uncle had left behind, that Lou Vaughn had been kidnapped. Courtney cut in, telling Les she was certain the woman who had abducted her uncle was the attractive middle-aged woman who called herself Andrea Lambert. She gave him a thorough description and concluded by saying she was sure the Lambert woman was a KGB agent.

Les Sharp looked impressed.

Jonathan looked doubtful. He went on to tell Les about the dark-haired beauty who'd been keeping close tabs on the bookstore yesterday morning. "She isn't one of your people by any chance?"

Les shook his head. "Langley put someone on the case as soon as we got word so many parties were interested in the parcel. Not a woman, though. A man." He dropped his voice. "Strictly a deep-cover operative. Goes by the code name Gold. I've never met him, but he's supposedly the best. If anyone can track down Lou Vaughn and the book, it's Gold. Meanwhile, I'll get that description of the Lambert woman out. We've got the airports covered, as well as the bus and train terminals. When they show, we'll have a greeting party waiting for them. Now what about this place in Sandwich?"

"No," Jonathan said. "I don't think there's much of a chance they'd head there."

Courtney disagreed. "Look, this Lambert woman might want to play it safe and stick around for a couple of days on the chance that the airports are being covered."

Jonathan shook his head. "Why would she worry? As far as she knows you're dead and no one could be wise to your uncle having been kidnapped and the book stolen from him. She wouldn't expect the airports to be watched."

Les nodded. Then he smiled awkwardly at Courtney. "The press did run a story this morning about the fire at the bookstore and the death of... Courtney Blue. As far as the Lambert woman knows—and the Russians—you're dead."

"Don't sound so apologetic, Les. That's a sharp idea." She winked. "Why the very same ploy was used by Katherine O'Malley—" She stopped abruptly.

"Who's Katherine O'Malley?" Both men asked at the same time.

Courtney smiled mysteriously. "Oh, just someone I know who dabbles in the business."

Jonathan eyed her closely. "What business?"

"Why, the spy business, love."

"A friend of yours?"

"You might say an acquaintance."

Les cleared his throat. "Forget Katherine O'Malley." His eyes narrowed. "Unless she figures into this."

Courtney smiled again. "No, not really."

"Then let's get back to the business at hand. About London. Any further word on Lloyd? Has the kidnapper contacted you again?"

Jonathan rubbed his jaw. "No. But I'm sure he will. I'll have to stall for more time, convince the bastard I'll get the manuscript back quickly. Meanwhile, I'll have to bank on this man of yours, Gold, or SIS in London, to make sure I'm able to keep my word."

"Any leads from SIS on who has Lloyd?"

Jonathan's expression was enigmatic. "I would imagine so, though they wouldn't likely confide in a private citizen."

Les nodded. "Well, I guess that's it for now. Unless there's anything you've overlooked?"

"No. I'll be in touch if anything else happens. What about this Gold fellow? Will he get directly in touch with me if he has any success?"

"Most likely."

Courtney picked up a shadow of worry on the CIA agent's face. "What is it?"

A tiny muscle tensed in Les's jaw. "I was expecting to hear from him myself by now. But he's got a reputation for running his own show. Me, I'm strictly by the book. I follow orders, not instincts."

Courtney felt a kinship with the mysterious deep-cover agent. True, she hadn't been in the spy business very long, but she, too, worked on instinct.

Les left before Courtney finished her breakfast. Jonathan stayed with her. She shoved the plate of toast across to him. "Eat something. You'll feel better."

"I feel fine."

She shrugged. "I still say we check out Sandwich. My uncle has a substantial library down there. Some reference books he might well need to help him authenticate the manuscript. It's worth a try. We're less than an hour away."

"Courtney, I'm going to fly back to London."

"Oh." She bit into a piece of toast.

"It's university break. I often go back home to visit my mother during break. And what with this business with Marcus, I feel that—"

"You think the book might surface in London, don't you? Which means you think my uncle might—"

"I don't think anything of the sort. I told you, I'm planning a visit to my mother. As for your uncle, the manuscript, even Marcus, I haven't the foggiest notion where any of them are at the moment. And those matters are now in the hands of professionals, both here and in London.''

"Les Sharp, for example." She gave Jonathan a rueful smile.

"Les is merely a collector of data. There's this man. Gold. You heard Sharp. The man's a crackerjack agent.''

"And does London have a crackerjack agent on the case?''

"I would imagine so. Marcus Lloyd is a . . . most distinguished man. I'm certain his kidnapping will take precedence over all other cases. When I return to London, I'll have to sit tight and hope that either Gold or someone from SIS tracks down the manuscript . . . or Marcus Lloyd's kidnapper.''

"And you intend to do nothing more than 'sit tight.' ''

"And have a nice visit with my mother," he answered firmly.

Courtney took another bite of toast. She didn't believe Jonathan for an instant. He was no more finished with this matter than she was. Now if real life went the way of the thrillers she so avidly read and the fantasies she so frequently played out in her mind, Jonathan would be asking her—no, imploring her—to go along. Oh, he might be looking a bit worried for her safety, but she'd easily convince him he couldn't manage without her. The question was, could Courtney convince Jonathan she should go? She certainly intended to give it her best shot.

"YEVGENNI, WHAT AM I going to do with you?" Zakharov snapped. "I tell you to search the bookstore and you burn it down. I tell you to make sure nothing happens to the shopkeeper and you incinerate her.''

Borofsky kept his head low, the scent of Zakharov's Turkish cigarette making him yearn for one of his own.

Wisely he knew this was not a good time to beg for a smoke. "But I didn't start the fire. And all we did to the woman was inject her with a little anesthetic. She was screaming, carrying on. As for the book, I give you my assurance it was not there. I swear on my mother's grave."

Zakharov's gaze was dark. "And if I ask you to swear on your own grave, Yevgenni, would you do that, as well?" He flexed his index finger in the brutish Goncharov's direction.

Goncharov strode over, ever the eager-to-serve henchman.

Calmly Zakharov put a hand on Borofsky's trembling shoulder. Indeed, the man was shaking from head to toe. In a voice filled with mock confidence, Zakharov said, "I find myself in a most disturbing dilemma, Comrade. I cannot return to Moscow without the Gorky manuscript. It would be...shall we say...a great humiliation for me. And I do not intend to be so humiliated. I will accept your word for the moment that the manuscript still exists. And so the question remains, where is it?"

"The professor," Borofsky said emphatically. "He must still have it. It is the only answer."

Zakharov glanced over at Goncharov. "Yes," he said slowly. "It does seem that way."

Borofsky's eyes didn't waver from Zakharov's. "I will find him. If it is the last thing I do."

Zakharov gave a twisted smirk. "I assure you, Comrade Borofsky, if you do not find the professor and the book, as well, it will most certainly be the last thing you do." He laughed low, the sound cold and diabolic as he gave Goncharov a sly look.

The henchman was clearly amused by his superior's remark and he laughed, too.

Only Borofsky did not laugh.

"I WANT YOUR PROMISE not to harm him," Christine demanded over the phone.

"Your concern is touching, my dear. Although I doubt Marcus would be terribly touched."

"Daniel, please..."

"Christine, get to the point of your call."

She sighed. "The shop girl is dead. Her shop burned to the ground. It was in the morning papers."

"Forget the girl. Our professor will be making his delivery shortly."

"I didn't see any mention of Marcus's disappearance in the Boston papers. How did you manage that? Where have you got him?"

"Steady on, my dear. Irrelevant questions."

"I'm flying back to London, Daniel. I'm at the airport now."

"Are you?"

"Is Marcus...is he all right?"

"Well, well, well. You truly are concerned."

"You swore this would be a simple matter, Daniel. You said nothing of kidnapping or...worse."

"Darling, once the manuscript is in my hands, the rest will be quite simple. And even more lucrative than I had hoped."

"What do you mean?"

"I have some sources who believe I can strike the best deal with the Russians. We already know how eager they are for this rare work to be returned to their country. And I've a feeling there's more there than meets the eye."

"What do you mean?"

"Don't bother your pretty head about it. All you need think about is the generous bonus I shall give you if the deal goes through."

Christine hesitated. "What guarantee do I have that you will still share the proceeds of the sale? After all, I won't be the one delivering the package now."

"Which brings me to the matter of your flight home. I prefer you hold off, Christine. I do not trust our professor. I think it best that you track him down and see to it that he does indeed make the delivery on time. That will more than earn your share of the booty for a job well done. Keep in touch, my dear."

The phone clicked and the line went dead.

Christine frowned. She knew the real reason Daniel would fork over her share. Her silence was worth at least that much. She smiled. What was that saying? Silence is golden. Indeed, how very apt.

## CHAPTER EIGHT

COURTNEY WATCHED the little roadside cottages whiz by as Jonathan drove to Sandwich. Each house they passed drew them closer to her uncle's place, closer to the end of the adventure . . . for her. But she couldn't bear the thought that it was almost over. It had only just begun. She couldn't let Jonathan walk out of her life now.

Desperate for inspiration, Courtney turned to her fantasy alter ego. *What do I do now, Katherine O'Malley? My hero's dumping me in Sandwich. I'm to twiddle my thumbs there all alone till everything is straightened out. It isn't fair. He's leaving me, Katherine. What can I do?*

The imaginary Katherine O'Malley offered a tidbit of scintillating advice: *Well darling, as a rule of thumb, do not fall apart. Which isn't to say a few tears mightn't be in order. But don't blubber. Heroes want nothing more than to flee blubbering heroines. Subtlety always. Just the touch of desperation in your eyes. And a touch of fire goes without saying. Oh, on the surface you should appear cool, resolute. But he must see the stubbornness, the fear, the yearning just beneath that brave, admirable facade.*

"I'm truly sorry about all of this, Courtney."

Jonathan's apology came as they pulled up in his sedan to the small gray weathered cottage situated on a bluff overlooking the blue Atlantic in the sleepy little Cape town of Sandwich.

The voice of Katherine O'Malley whispered in Courtney's head: *Tell him you aren't the least bit sorry. Go on. And put some heart into it.*

Courtney turned to Jonathan and forced herself to smile. "I'm not sorry about what's happened. In the past few days I've experienced more excitement and...happiness...than in my whole life. I'm only sorry it's...ending."

Jonathan turned off the ignition, gave Courtney a disconcerted glance and stepped out of the car.

Courtney leaned her head back wearily against the seat and shut her eyes. Damn the man. He was supposed to fall madly in love with her before their adventure was over. But if he ended it prematurely, how was their love supposed to blossom?

She opened her eyes slowly, watching from the window of the car as Jonathan surveyed the driveway, the house, the surrounding area. He motioned to her and she got out of the car.

"No recent tire tracks in the dirt drive. And the cottage looks undisturbed and shut up tight." He made a sweeping gesture with his arm. "Good spot for our purposes. Nicely situated. Far off the main road and not another cottage in view." He smiled. "Reminds me of our family cottage down in Devon."

When she made no response he gave a little shrug. "I'm sorry, Courtney. I know you hoped your uncle would be here."

She shook her head. "No. I realize I was just grabbing at straws to think—" She stopped. She'd been grabbing at straws, all right. And not only concerning her uncle. What a little fool to imagine that a man as handsome, as brilliant, as sophisticated as Jonathan Madden would ever fall in love with her. What would he want with an ordinary shop girl whose only attribute was a way with clever disguises?

The voice of Katherine O'Malley intruded: *Don't be mawkish, darling. It makes you decidedly unglamorous.*

"Oh, shut up," Courtney muttered. "This is all your fault."

Jonathan gave her a bemused look. "What did you say?"

She flushed. "Nothing. Skip it."

Jonathan studied her thoughtfully for a moment, then walked over to the edge of the bluff and stared down at the wild spray of water as the waves slammed against the craggy shoreline.

Courtney came over to his side.

"Beautiful spot," he said softly.

He continued to look down at the water, but she stood watching him. "Yes, it is beautiful. But lonely, too."

He looked at her then. The wind was sweeping her hair from her face, a face devoid of makeup...and artifice, he thought. She was an innocent. Sweet, tender, vulnerable. An unabashed romantic. And yet so clever. Conniving, even, when necessary. He took in the oversize man's clothes she was wearing, recalling with amusement her most recent masquerade at the restaurant. He was quite awed by her. And that made him uneasy. Perhaps that was part of the reason he felt relief mingle with his frustration now that they were parting.

Her silence was disconcerting, compelling him to speak. "I'm certain you won't have to stay here very long. I'll have Les keep in touch with you. And I'll arrange for a car so you can pick up supplies at that general store we passed a couple of miles down the road. Les will fetch your uncle's car in Cohasset and return it to its parking place in Boston so as not to arouse suspicion." Discomfort made him babble. It also made him angry. It wasn't often he was thrown off kilter by a woman. But, then, Courtney was not like any woman he'd ever met.

Courtney was too caught up in her own thoughts to pay more than passing attention to Jonathan's ramblings. *Help me, Katherine,* she implored her heroine, forgetting that she'd silenced her a moment before. *What would you do if Derek Colton was about to walk out of your life, very likely for good?*

*Play for time, darling,* Katherine responded firmly. *Something will come to you. You're more clever than you realize.*

But Courtney was feeling far from clever just then. She felt very much like Cinderella caught at the ball past midnight, her gown turned to rags, her fantasy vanishing right before her eyes. She couldn't think of a thing to say or do about her predicament. And Jonathan was turning away from the edge of the bluff.

Acting purely on impulse, Courtney caught hold of his jacket. "Jonathan..." There was desperation in her eyes, and it wasn't artificial.

"Yes? Is there something you want or need before I leave?"

Her eyelids fluttered closed, an errant tear slipping down her cheek. "Is there something I want?" she whispered tremulously. *Oh, Jonathan,* she thought, *yes, yes. I want you. I need you.*

Seeing that wayward tear trickle down her cheek made Jonathan more uneasy than ever. He was also struck by an intense desire to reach out to her, to touch her, to comfort her. Yes, even to confide fully in her. He wished he could make her see that the risks were too great, that there was too much at stake... that he wasn't the hero she so longed for him to be. In his world there were no heroes, no saints. He wished he could make her see. But he couldn't.

He hurriedly took out a pen and a scrap of paper, and scribbled down a phone number. "If you want to contact

Les..." he muttered, eager to be gone, disturbed by the way his hand trembled as he extended the paper toward her.

"Wait," she said, a note of anguish in her voice, as she saw him start to walk off.

He stopped.

She took a steadying breath. "The cottage. You haven't looked inside it."

Katherine's voice whispered, *That's the ticket, darling. Didn't I say you were clever. Keep it up now.*

Jonathan hesitated. "Well, I suppose I ought to give it a quick check."

Courtney led the way up the slate path to the barn-red front door. The key was tucked just under the cracked edge of the last piece of slate. She retrieved it and unlocked the door.

It opened onto a main room that was a modest affair, spare and functional, but with a few cozy touches such as the handmade multicolored afghan slung over the back of a mint-green upholstered armchair, the player piano atop which stood an assortment of framed photos. Two walls were covered in fully stocked bookcases, and a huge oak desk cluttered with correspondence sat under a sunny bay window.

Jonathan walked over to the desk. "Your uncle's papers?"

"Yes. I told you. He comes here a lot to catch up on work."

"What was he planning to do about his bookstore?"

"He talked about setting up shop elsewhere in town, but that's only because he's worried about me. He'd much prefer simply to travel and deal strictly in rare books." She saw that narrowed look in Jonathan's eyes as he scanned the desk once more.

"You still have your doubts about my uncle, don't you? You still think he might have run off with the manuscript.

And Andrea Lambert? Do you think the two were in cahoots? Is that what you believe, Jonathan?''

He gazed at her. "And you believe your uncle is absolutely beyond such temptations?''

She took off the sport coat, sat down on the cream-colored sofa and kicked off her oversize men's shoes. "That's exactly what I believe. He's raised me since I was fourteen. My uncle is a good man, Jonathan. He's honest and he has integrity. I wish you could have met him. Then you'd see..."

Jonathan was over at the player piano. His fingers ran lightly over the keys as he looked at the photos. He picked one up. "Is this your uncle?"

"Yes. That's me beside him. I'd just turned sixteen. It's a ghastly picture, but my uncle is fond of it. Well, he's a sentimental man. He never married, never had any children of his own. It couldn't have been an easy thing for him to suddenly be presented with a teenager to raise all by himself. But if he was distraught about the project, he never let it show. He was wonderful to me. Tender, loving. He always felt guilty about having to travel so much on business, but I never minded all that much. We had wonderful times together.'' Tears welled up in her eyes.

Jonathan came and sat down on the couch beside her. Forgetting his inner warnings, he put his arm around her and drew her against him. "We'll find him, Courtney. And if it's worth anything at all, I truly want to believe you're right about him.''

She pulled back and looked up at him. "You said 'we.'''

"Pardon?''

"You said 'we.' *We'll* find him.''

"I don't follow.''

"You're going back to London to track down my uncle. You're more involved in this whole business than you're willing to say. And what was it Les Sharp thought I knew?

Come to think about it, you never did tell me why an ordinary college professor walks around town carrying a gun. A gun you looked quite capable of using, Jonathan.''

He leaned back on the couch. "Courtney, I told you. My place was ransacked. I was being followed. It didn't take a great deal of intelligence to realize I was in danger. I knew there were certain parties after that manuscript. I knew when I received it there were a number of inherent dangers. So I purchased a gun. I did some shooting—strictly sport, mind you—back in England. There's no deep mystery.''

"I see.''

But he could tell by her tone that she did not see at all.

"As for finding your uncle and the manuscript, I include myself only in the sense that I will cooperate fully with the authorities and give them as much information as I can.''

"I see.''

"Stop it, Courtney. You don't believe a word I'm saying.'' He scowled. "Shall I tell you your problem, love? You've got too vivid an imagination.''

She had to smile. "Have I?''

"Indeed you have. And this foolish notion of yours that I'm some sort of a hero—it's nonsense, Courtney. I'm a perfectly ordinary man who's inadvertently stepped into more than I ever bargained for. I deeply regret having involved you in all this. You've risked your life. Your uncle has disappeared. Your possessions have been destroyed. Any reasonable woman would have had more than her fill of danger and excitement by now. Any reasonable woman would have been thrilled to get rid of me, forget all about me, wish she'd never laid eyes on me.''

"I'm not a reasonable woman, Jonathan.''

His smile was tender. "No, you're not, love.''

Courtney rose to her feet. "I'll never forget you, Jonathan.''

He stared up at her for several moments and then he rose, too, and stood beside her. They faced each other in silence and then he said, "If there is anything of the hero inside me, then the only right thing to do is—"

"But you're not a hero, Jonathan. That's what you keep insisting."

"Courtney..." He could feel the tremor in her body as he reached out to her. Her eyes didn't waver from his. They held such quiet expectancy.

"It doesn't matter," she whispered.

"You are incredible."

"Do you want me, Jonathan?"

"Yes." He felt a tightening in his stomach, a filament of fear entwined with a fierce desire.

His hand moved slowly to her cheek. The contact was so intense she felt a sighing in her heart, felt it spread hotly through her entire body.

Her mouth was inches from his. His blue eyes steadied on the lovely delicate shape of her lips. She had asked if he wanted her. Oh, yes, he wanted her desperately, but guilt stoked the fires of resistance in him. He was leaving. He had to leave. And when this whole sorry mess was over and he returned...? That was what was nagging at him. He wasn't certain he would return. After all these months of relative calm, months of telling himself he had never felt better, been more content, more at peace, now suddenly the question hung in the air—was he deceiving himself? Was he running from a destiny from which there was no escape?

Courtney felt him pull back before he made the physical move. She saw caution darken his eyes. His jaw tensed. She thought him never more handsome, never more desirable.

"Why, Jonathan? Why won't you make love to me?" The words escaped her lips of their own volition.

He felt a constriction in his chest. "Courtney, don't do this."

"Is it that I'm too plain, not upper crust enough, too...foolish?"

"Stop it."

"Look at me. I do look ridiculous in this getup. How stupid of me." She began clawing at the buttons of the shirt, her trembling fingers managing to undo the first two before Jonathan grabbed her hands.

She looked up into his eyes, tears sliding down her cheeks, her lips trembling. "There've hardly been any others, Jonathan. I haven't exactly been a...femme fatale. But you've no doubt guessed as much, for all my efforts. And just now I feel totally inept. I'm at a loss, Jonathan. Nothing very clever is coming to mind."

"Courtney..."

She pressed her fingers against his lips. "All I know, Jonathan, is if you walk out of my life now...if you leave me with this...empty feeling, I know that it shall never be filled. Never."

"I have so little to offer you." His words were etched with regret.

"Oh, Jonathan, you have everything."

"You may not think that tomorrow, love." His arms were pressing her against him, though he had no awareness of having made any move toward her at all.

"I don't care about tomorrow." He had given her a glimpse of unknown heights that she sensed were, for the first time, truly within her reach. What made no sense to her was that he would deny her the exquisite pleasure he alone could offer her. Once in a lifetime. Didn't he understand she would gladly settle for that rather than never to fully experience that feeling of blinding, exhilarating passion with the hero of her dreams? She clung to him, her slender body tight against the muscle and sinew of his angular frame.

Her lips were soft and yielding as his mouth found hers. He could feel a shiver of excitement run through her entire body as her tongue danced against his, her fingers light as clouds running through his dark hair.

Slowly he drew back and finished unbuttoning her shirt. The garment fell open. She wore nothing beneath, and her high, firm breasts were fully revealed.

"You're beautiful," he murmured.

His words floated around her like a whispered loving breeze, heightening the breathtaking anticipation sweeping through her.

As he guided the shirt over her shoulders, urged it down her arms until it fell to the floor, Courtney felt a sharp thrill erupt like an incendiary flame. She stared up into his deep, mysterious aquamarine eyes, every nerve ending taut, her breathing quick and shallow. This wasn't her first time, but it might as well have been. She'd never felt like this before. The room was losing shape, her own turbulent emotions creating new patterns, new forms. She felt dizzy with them.

He drew her back into his arms, his embrace aggressive, yet oddly protective. He could sense her desire as well as her inexperience. He kissed her face, her throat, her neck, then lifted her so that his mouth sought out first one firm, hard nipple, then the other. As he nuzzled and drew her deep into his mouth, the taut buds tingled and she felt a long shuddering shiver of delight. Her body surged with a fluid heat. And then her breath escaped in the softest of moans. "Oh, Jonathan, that feels so wonderful...."

Her feet touched ground again. A moment later her trousers fluttered to the floor. Courtney's pulse grew erratic, her eyes unable to move farther than Jonathan's strong, sensual mouth. She could feel the caressing warmth of his breath on her face.

He lifted her in his arms. She pressed her head to his shoulder and pointed in the direction of the bedroom. When he laid her naked on the bed moments later, Courtney felt an acute shyness overwhelm her. The light was streaming through the gauzy white curtains into the room. Jonathan's gaze traveled down her body with a stunning intensity, making her feel exposed, as if he could see every hidden flaw. Worse still, he would see her artlessness when it came to lovemaking. Jonathan Madden was probably as skilled a lover as Derek Colton. Courtney wasn't even in the same league as the confident, exquisite, unflappable Katherine O'Malley.

Courtney self-consciously covered her breasts with her hands. Jonathan was touched by her modesty and felt a disquieting, yet not altogether disturbing, sense of responsibility. The combination of guilelessness and smoldering passion emanating from her excited him more deeply, more intensely, than anything had in a long, long time.

Gently he drew her hands from her breasts, guiding them toward his shirt, urging her on as her trembling fingers unfastened each button. And then she was undressing him on her own, her nervousness forgotten as her eyes raked down his taut, firm body with its flatly muscled contours, lingering for a moment over the healing scar on his thigh, and she gave herself up to the newness of it all.

It was Courtney who reached up for Jonathan, who drew him down over her, who met his kiss as his mouth descended over hers, whose hands moved along his extraordinary body, tracing the fine, strong curves and muscles in a heated, hungry exploration.

"You're incredible, Courtney. I've never known anyone like you. You're full of surprises."

She laughed softly. "I surprise myself at times."

His tongue drew a line across her lips, his hand sliding down over her silken belly, the curve of her hips, between her legs, easing them apart. "At times like this?" he whispered, his tongue moving slowly over her chin, down her throat to her breast.

"Yes. Oh, yes," she murmured, locking her ankles around his calves.

They kissed long and deep, their tongues exploring. Beneath him, Courtney's body was soft and supple and she moved in an unconscious rhythm, her damp skin clinging to his.

Jonathan felt the desire in him like a physical ache. He could not remember feeling so aroused.

"Courtney," he whispered hot against her lips, his husky voice echoing hidden depths and promises of unimagined pleasures.

She arched up against him and he pushed down on her, frantic now to possess her fully. He hesitated for only an instant, seeking her eyes, then watching her mouth form a silent yes.

He entered her in one long, fierce, heated slide that brought a gasp of hungry delight from her lips. Their desire soared with each stroke, passion unfettered, time and space displaced. And then came joyous release, exquisite release.

Courtney slowly, unwillingly, returned from that netherworld of pure sensation. It was over too soon. But she felt an incredible sense of fulfillment, exquisitely satisfying, an experience of pure perfection.

For Jonathan, their shared intimacy offered no such easy completion. He felt incomplete, on edge. His emotions had been too strong. It was not only desire he had felt for Courtney. She touched something inside him that went beyond desire. But whatever he felt could not, must not, alter his decision.

Though she could see the effort he was making to be tender and gentle in the aftermath of their passion, Courtney sensed his inner tension.

"I'd better check in with Les," he said finally, rising, gathering up his clothes.

"I know it isn't tomorrow yet, Jonathan," she said softly as she sat up in bed, "but I have no regrets."

He gave her a sharp look. Despite her plucky smile, he'd glimpsed the flash of disappointment in her eyes, and felt a stab of guilt.

"I still want to help you, Jonathan." She saw his scowl. "I know what you're thinking. That I've stirred up more problems for you than I have helped." She stood, reaching out toward him with her hand.

He walked back to her, not taking her hand. Instead his fingers encircled her wrist.

She didn't move.

He gazed down into her face. She was such an extraordinary woman that something caught in his throat just looking at her.

Sunlight flooded the room.

Jonathan released her wrist, slowly trailing his hand up her arm. "Yes, you are making problems for me, Courtney. And I'm afraid, love, I've got more than I can handle already."

"OH, DEAR, LOU. I can call you 'Lou,' can't I? I mean...I hope there aren't hard feelings between us. I am sorry about your niece. Such a terrible thing. I know how you must be feeling. In a way, I've lost someone very dear to me, as well. My sister." Andrea Lambert wrung her hands. "Poor Denise. She always did choose the wrong men. But this last time she thought—well, I thought, too—that she had found the right man finally. She talked endlessly of Daniel Emerson's good breeding, his charm, his looks, his tenderness. From what my sister wrote me from London, he was everything a woman could ask for."

Lou Vaughn was only half listening. He must have read the newspaper article about the fire at the bookstore and

Courtney's death at least a dozen times. And still he said, "I don't believe it."

Andrea Lambert put a hand on his shoulder sympathetically. "I wish there were something I could do for you, Lou."

He shot her a dark glance.

"I mean...other than let you go."

"You have the damn manuscript."

"But I need you, as well. I have no one else to turn to. And...I can't manage this on my own. I've never been involved in anything like this before, Lou. I must find out what happened to Denise. Emerson holds the key. And I hold the manuscript. I know he wants it desperately. Denise wrote me all about his quest for it."

Lou Vaughn observed her closely. "I want one answer from you, and I want the truth. Did you have anything to do with that fire?"

The attractive, blond-haired woman blanched. "My God, Lou. No. A thousand times no. I admit I'm desperate, desperate enough to—" She stopped abruptly, a redness rising in her cheeks, the bright hue stark against her pallor as she stared at Lou's wrist handcuffed to the bedpost in the hotel room near Boston's Logan Airport. She'd purchased the cuffs along with the gun just a few days earlier. Her original plan had been to use them on Jonathan Madden. But then everything had changed and she'd been forced to improvise. If only this tragedy involving Lou Vaughn's niece hadn't occurred, she'd have been quite pleased with her quick-witted accomplishments.

Lou Vaughn sighed. She could be telling the truth. He wanted to believe her. Still he scanned the newspaper article again. There was something about it...maybe he was foolishly, stubbornly clinging to a fantasy, but he just could not believe Courtney was dead.

"Will you help me, Lou? Will you help me find my sister? And deal with Daniel Emerson?"

His eyes traveled from the handcuffs to Andrea Lambert's appealing face. "You don't exactly give me much choice."

She smiled tentatively. "I've hoped all along that once you heard the whole story you might help me without further coercion."

Lou Vaughn studied his captor with curiosity and continued interest. She was every bit as attractive as he'd initially thought. No, more so. She was daring, resourceful, clever—qualities he hadn't sensed on first meeting. And they were qualities he found very appealing. But Lou intended to stay on his guard. Those very same qualities might just be his undoing.

Finally, after a long silence, he said, "Okay, let's hear the whole story, Andrea. And then I'll decide whether I'll go along willingly for the ride."

# CHAPTER NINE

COURTNEY KNEW SOMETHING was up when Jonathan hung up the phone after a two-minute conversation with Les Sharp, Jonathan's contribution to the discussion having been little more than a few grunts mixed with a few succinct "yesses." Clearly it wasn't his end of the conversation that gave Jonathan away. It was the glint in those marvelous aquamarine eyes of his, coupled with his quickly donned enigmatic expression. *The eyes are the key to the soul,* Courtney mused, giving Jonathan a glimpse of her own.

"Come on, Jonathan, tell me what's going on." Her hazel eyes were wide, sparkling, anticipating.

He sat down on the bed next to her. "Your uncle is fine."

"My uncle's fine? That's it? That's the sum total of Sharp's report?"

"In a nutshell."

"Oh, no. No, no, no. I don't want the nutshell. Give it to me nut and all. How does Sharp know my uncle's fine? Has he seen him? Spoken to him? Arrested him? Where? When?"

"Courtney, slow down. First of all . . ."

"Yes? Yes?"

He cupped her face in his hand and kissed her tenderly. "First of all, love, get dressed. It's terribly difficult to discuss my conversation with Les when you sit here in all your naked splendor, making my mind wander to very different topics."

She smiled enticingly. "Do I really make your mind wander, Jonathan?"

He grinned. "Most assuredly, love."

"Then I wasn't all that bad? For a relative amateur, I mean."

He moved his hands to her hips, slid them up over her ribs to her breasts. "You have all the right instincts."

A warm blush highlighted her cheeks. "I'm feeling those instincts right now," she whispered. Nevertheless she drew his hands away from her breasts and tilted her head, observing him with a shrewd smile. "Now if you were the kind of hero I keep making the mistake of imagining you to be, you'd be so caught up in passion at the moment that everything else would vanish from your mind."

He quirked a brow. "And if I'm not that kind of hero?"

"Then, love, you'd be doing your utmost to get me off the topic of my uncle and your conversation with our friend Les Sharp." She slid away from him, rose from the bed and walked over to the closet. She always kept a few items of clothing at the cottage. She pulled a pair of faded dungarees and a blue-and-white striped blouse off hangers. "At the moment this is about it for what I shall amusingly call a wardrobe." Going over to the dresser, she found some underwear and socks. She even managed to dig up a pair of worn, but still serviceable sneakers stuck away on the floor of a second closet.

She dressed quickly, methodically, turning away from Jonathan's appreciative gaze so that she wouldn't be tempted to reverse the procedure, strip off every garment, Jonathan's as well as her own, pull her hero with all his faults back to the bed and once again make mad, passionate love with him.

"Okay," she said after doing up the last button of her shirt and sitting primly on the wicker rocker near the bedroom window. "Shoot."

Jonathan's jaw tightened. "There isn't much to tell."

"You need some lessons in lying, Jonathan."

He looked at her sharply and she suspected he was assessing just how much to say.

"He was spotted boarding a TWA 747 to London."

"Was he...alone?"

"A woman who fit the description of Andrea Lambert accompanied him on the flight."

Courtney ran the tip of her tongue over dry lips. After a long moment she asked, "Did it appear to whoever spotted them that he boarded...under duress? Or that he looked...drugged or something?"

Jonathan ran a hand absently over the back of his neck, his eyes fixed for a moment on her shabby sneakers. "They seemed, to all appearances, to be on cordial terms."

"Cordial?" she echoed. A cold hand squeezed at her heart. "I don't understand," she managed to say.

They regarded each other in silence for several moments. "That isn't to say..."

"No, it isn't," she agreed hastily.

"Anyway, now that they're under surveillance, you won't have to fear for his safety."

Courtney frowned. "No, just his twenty years in Sing Sing." She looked over at Jonathan. "So they aren't planning to nab them when they get off at Heathrow. What about your kidnapped friend? Don't you need that manuscript pronto?"

They were good questions. Though Jonathan hadn't exactly been supplied with the answers, he could make some solid guesses. The problem was sharing them with Courtney. After a few moments of consideration he said. "I'm hoping to play for time."

Courtney regarded him shrewdly. "I see."

He was afraid she was seeing too much. He squeezed the tense muscles in the back of his neck, then rubbed his jaw.

Finally he shook his head, a distinct look of resignation on his face. "We'll need to do a bit of shopping."

Courtney blinked. "Shopping?"

He was rubbing his jaw again. "Do let's try for something feminine this time, love."

"Feminine? What are you talking about?"

He came over to the wicker chair, where she was now sitting on the edge of the seat. He bent down, took hold of her hands. "What's become of those marvelous instincts? You're dead, remember. And, as you pointed out earlier, I'm a marked man. We can't very well go waltzing into Logan Airport and board our flight to London without some clever disguises."

He'd gotten only half his words out, when she was off the seat, falling into his arms, hugging him, kissing him. "Oh, Jonathan, then you'll let me come with you. I've always wanted to go to London. When I was a little girl my mother used to recite the poem about the child who went to London to visit the queen."

He got up, grinning, bringing Courtney up with him. "Well, love, I can't promise a visit to the queen or even to the queen mother. Will my own mother do?"

"Well . . . well, of course. That would be . . . wonderful."

He stiffened noticeably.

Courtney touched his cheek. "Relax, my elusive hero. My instincts tell me not to read anything deep into that invitation." Heroes like Jonathan Madden slipped into a heroine's life—and then out again. Her life, anyway. She'd told him—told herself, as well—that she'd accept their relationship for what it was. Strictly temporary. Her eyes sparkled nonetheless in anticipation of the time they were going to spend together in England.

Jonathan nodded awkwardly. She was doing it to him again. Making him very uncomfortable, indeed. "I don't want to deceive you, Courtney. You're an incredible, enchanting woman. It's just that I'm rather established in my ways. And it works best for me to keep the personal aspects of my life . . . simple.''

What he was telling her was that he loved his freedom the way some men loved their wives and families. Courtney wondered if she'd been gorgeous in addition to enchanting and incredible, it would have helped her cause any. She chose to doubt it.

''We should get going,'' he said, feeling a bit better for having been straight with her—on this one matter, at any rate.

Twenty minutes later they were in an expensive boutique in Hyannis, selecting Courtney's ''disguise.'' Courtney left the decision making in Jonathan's hands this time. She felt out of her element, whereas Jonathan seemed quite at ease. His taste was impeccable. And expensive.

''Jonathan, this is far too much,'' Courtney whispered as she caught a glimpse of the price tag on the smart, deceptively simple black linen dress and jacket he'd chosen for her.

''My treat, love.''

''And what kind of a bank balance do you have on a college professor's salary?''

But Jonathan didn't answer her. He was busy telling the saleswoman to remove the tags on the suit so that Courtney could wear it now.

The saleswoman's eyes drifted to Courtney's feet—to her sneakers, precisely.

Jonathan grinned. ''Do fit her with all the necessary accessories. Shoes, handbag, hat.'' He glanced over at a red hat with a wide, floppy brim. ''Something like that one over there . . . but in black.''

''Jonathan,'' Courtney began again after the saleswoman asked her shoe size, then went off to find a pair of no doubt exorbitantly priced pumps. ''Do you have any idea what this is all going to cost? And why is everything black? Am I on my way to a funeral or something?''

He ruffled her hair. ''Precisely.''

''We're going to London as mourners?''

''Well, you are, love. A wealthy, elegant mourner.''

''And you?''

''My disguise is waiting for me in Boston. It's all been arranged by our clever Les Sharp,'' he said, grinning. ''What must his mother have been thinking to give him that name?''

Courtney laughed. ''Ah, what's in a name?''

''Which reminds me, we'll need a passport for you. While you change, I'll phone Les again. I imagine he can make the necessary arrangements.''

''And what's my name going to be? I've got an idea or two.''

''We'll have to leave it up to Sharp.'' He winked. ''Anyway, what's in a name?''

The saleswoman was back, bearing gifts. Gifts with very healthy price tags, that is. Courtney took one look at the numbers after the dollar sign on the shoe box and blanched. But Jonathan insisted she take them if they fit. The expensive handbag and stylish black wide-brimmed hat with white satin band, as well. No college professor, even one who might pick up the odd dollar authenticating Russian manuscripts, could foot the bill for this little shopping spree without so much as a blink of an eye. Courtney wanted to know where the money to cover the tab was coming from. But she had no opportunity to question Jonathan further with the saleswoman hovering about, eager to please, assuredly ecstatic about the large commission she'd make on the sale.

''A bit of makeup is in order,'' Jonathan said, and the saleswoman immediately swept Courtney over to the counter adorned with designer-name cosmetics, all at designer-name prices.

This time both Courtney and Jonathan were out of their element, and relied on the saleslady to make the selections.

"I'll leave you to get ready," Jonathan said. "Meanwhile, I'll phone Les and meet you back here in about ten minutes. Will that do?"

A little overwhelmed by the quantity and quality of booty in her hands, Courtney merely nodded.

Ten minutes later she was observing herself in the dressing room mirror. The sophisticated outfit she wore was not one she would ever have chosen for herself, and she was taken aback to discover how wonderful she looked in it. The saleswoman helped with the makeup and suggested she part her hair on the right side, then pull that side back off her face with an elegant silver comb, plucked from a counter display but offered free of charge. Courtney accepted graciously, delighted with the new hairstyle.

Standing just behind Courtney, the saleswoman was clearly pleased, and more than a bit surprised, by the transformation. In a Hilary Bennett thriller she would have exclaimed, *Why darling, it's absolutely you. You look divine.* In real life Courtney had to settle for "Very nice."

Jonathan's reaction was more pronounced. "My God," he murmured, making her turn full circle, "you look magnificent. Absolutely grand. I want to ravish you on the spot."

The saleswoman busily worked on the tab, pretending not to have heard, though her blush gave her away. It increased noticeably as she handed Jonathan the total. But Jonathan hardly gave the bill a glance. He whipped out an American Express card, his eyes never straying from Courtney.

As they were leaving the boutique, Courtney caught a glimpse of herself in the freestanding full-length mirror near the door. She stopped for a moment and gazed at her new image. She hardly recognized herself. It wasn't merely the new outfit, the new hairstyle, the elegant, perfectly matched accessories. The difference was in her face, in the way her hazel eyes shone, in the shimmering glint of her sandy-blond hair. She glowed with a newfound grace and confidence. She exuded absolute femininity. Just behind her, Jonathan was looking at her spellbound, his extraordinary aquamarine eyes lovingly caressing her. Her heart quickened. For the first time in her life she felt beautiful. And special. A femme fatale to rival the best of them, fictitious or real.

LOU VAUGHN BUCKLED his seat belt as the TWA jumbo jet prepared for takeoff. He noted that Andrea Lambert's hands were steadier as she did up her belt than when she'd been holding that little semiautomatic on him. That was before their long talk, before he'd made the decision to help her. Andrea had been very convincing about her desperate worry over her much-loved sister who had disappeared. She was certain Denise's husband, Daniel Emerson, was responsible. And now Emerson, too, had vanished. She had to find out what had happened to her sister, which meant she had to find Emerson. The only thing she could think to do was to get her hands on the Gorky, which she knew from her sister's most recent letter Emerson coveted, and somehow smoke him out.

Lou had told her it was a long shot. She had agreed. But it was her only hope. When Lou had still seemed hesitant about helping her "smoke Emerson out," as an act of faith she'd even returned the manuscript to him for safekeeping. And Lou was keeping the parcel nice and safe.

The stewardess came by offering magazines, but they both shook their heads. A drink was more what Lou had in mind, and he had a feeling Andrea wanted one, too. Ten minutes later, after they had settled in for the duration, the stewardess did come by for drink orders. Lou asked for a double bourbon. Andrea ordered a sherry, then quickly changed her mind.

"I'll have a double bourbon, as well."

Lou smiled.

Andrea smiled back.

Neither of them spoke until after their drinks arrived. Andrea took a few sips in the same time the level of Lou's plastic cup had fallen by two-thirds.

"Let me have another look at that photo," Lou said.

Immediately Andrea's beautifully manicured fingers snapped open her purse. "Here. I'm afraid you can't really make him out very clearly. Denise said Daniel abhorred having his picture taken. Odd, considering how handsome she said he is."

"You've never actually met the man."

"As I told you, the one time I did visit them in London—a few months ago—Daniel was called away on business just before I arrived."

"And the business?"

"Denise was rather vague about Daniel's work. Apparently he travels a great deal and invests in various enterprises. She supposed he spent his time checking on those investments. And he occasionally purchases and resells for profit paintings, coins, manuscripts."

"And your sister felt that this particular manuscript was of special interest to Emerson?"

"Yes, I told you all this, Lou. Denise felt that Daniel was obsessed with acquiring the Gorky work. She believed he'd had a few financial setbacks and saw the manuscript as a way out of his troubles. When she questioned him further, he lost his temper and actually struck out at her."

"Had he ever...?"

"Never," Andrea said emphatically. "Until that moment they'd been very close, very happy together." She paused, her eyes downcast. "I must admit I was rather envious."

Lou frowned. "Not much to envy."

She looked over at him, nodded. "I realized that too late."

He studied her openly. "I would think a woman of your looks and style need never envy anyone."

She smiled, thanking him softly. No modest blush. No flustered denial.

He liked that. He liked her. Granted, she might be too trusting for her own good. But she had enough positive points for him to overlook that one negative. Besides, it put him in a very secure position. He leaned back against his seat, but kept his gaze on Andrea.

"You say it's been nearly three weeks since your sister disappeared?"

Andrea nodded. "Well, according to Daniel, she went on some private cruise. He's quite adept at being vague, I must say."

"What made you think he was lying?"

"You'd have to know my sister, Lou. First she was very tense after that . . . blowup with Daniel."

"All the more reason to go on a cruise. They say cruises are very relaxing."

Andrea frowned. "Not for my sister. She hates boats. She gets seasick. Only a couple of years ago I begged her to join me on a cruise down to the Bahamas. She adamantly refused. I don't think the topic ever came up between her and Daniel, so he didn't know anything about her aversion to such a holiday."

Lou nodded. "Okay, but you didn't let on to Emerson."

"No, I didn't trust him." She closed her eyes. "I didn't know what to do."

"And that's when you hired that private investigating service in London."

"Yes. With no results. Not only couldn't they get any leads on Denise, they claimed to be unable to find any sign of Daniel. The address I gave them was for a house leased to Daniel. But as far as anyone knows he gave up the lease a month ago and hasn't been seen since."

"Did the investigators find out anything about Denise?"

"Neighbors were questioned about whether anyone fitting her description was seen at the house. But the estate was very private, no neighbors close enough to observe people coming and going from the house or grounds."

"And no description of Emerson, either."

"No. The lease was handled through a legal firm. No one the investigators questioned had ever met the man. Even at the law firm. All contacts with Emerson were made over the telephone."

Lou ran his thumb thoughtfully over his bottom lip. "Let's shift to Jonathan Madden again. You say your sister wrote you that—"

"It really began after that terrible incident between her and Daniel. You see, she not only worried about his obsession over this manuscript, she feared that he had begun having an affair. She phoned me in tears late one night. Daniel hadn't come home and she was certain he was with this other woman. She went on and on, complaining, as well, about his moodiness, his secretiveness. She told me she'd discovered the key to his desk that afternoon and had riffled through some of his papers."

"And saw something about this fellow Madden?"

"A notation about Madden being the one to review the parcel, and a note about Madden living in Boston. Again, typical of Daniel, a vague reference only. But after Denise disappeared, it was the only clue I had to go on. I learned that there was a professor of Russian literature by the name of Jonathan Madden teaching at Brandeis. And on the day I began following him, I was lucky to spot that overseas parcel being delivered to his office at the college. And the rest...well, I've told you about my visit to the bookstore and my thought that Madden went there specifically to contact you. I tracked you down next, saw that For Rent sign outside your apartment building, and winged it from that point on."

Lou had listened intently to Andrea's second telling of her story. No changes, no new information. Of course, Andrea Lambert could be a top-notch actress and this could be the performance of a lifetime.

She touched his arm tentatively. "If only your niece hadn't..."

He patted her hand. "Maybe there was some mistake. Maybe she somehow escaped. I don't know why, Andrea, instinct I guess, but I just can't believe she's dead." He was a man who trusted his instincts. He was praying he could trust these particular ones.

"Oh, Lou, I hope you're right."

They finished their drinks in silence. Next came dinner and an in-flight movie that neither of them opted to watch. It was some sort of thriller and this was a case where real life had turned quite thrilling enough for them both.

Near the end of the flight Andrea turned to Lou. "You know, there's one terrible flaw to my plan. I don't know exactly how we'll let Daniel know we've got the manuscript."

"I think you had the right general idea. We have something he wants, Andrea. Something he wants very badly. I have a feeling that if we let it be known in the right places that we are in possession of the item he covets, he'll find us. And I've got a notion what those right places are."

Andrea smiled softly. "Oh, Lou, I just knew you were the perfect person to help me. I've never been one for believing in fate, but I do believe in it now. Fate brought me to you, Lou. And for that I shall always be grateful."

"So will I, Andrea. So will I."

"A FUNERAL PARLOR?"

Jonathan winked at Courtney as he pulled into the driveway of the Richardson Funeral Home on Willow Street in Charlestown, just across the river from Boston, overlooking the harbor. "I told you you were going to a funeral."

"You said the funeral was in London," Courtney corrected.

He switched off the ignition. "Yes, love. But in order to attend a funeral you need a body. Les has arranged for one to be exported from the States and transported to London for the service."

Courtney sat up straighter in her seat and looked at him. "Exactly who is this body, Jonathan?"

He leaned over and lightly kissed her lips. "I suppose this could be called a trial run for the real thing. Which I must say I hope to postpone for a number of years."

"Jonathan, you can't mean..."

He opened the door on the driver's side and stepped out. Courtney watched him come around to her side, but she was out of the car before he got to her. "You're flying to London in a coffin? You can't be serious, Jonathan."

"That's what I thought when Les Sharp proposed the idea. But actually—"

"Now I know why his mother came up with that name. She decided to raise an idiot. It's a ghastly idea, Jonathan. Morbid, dangerous. Why, you could suffocate."

He guided her inside through the back entrance to the funeral parlor. "Come on, love. It's actually quite a brilliant idea. A perfect cover, as it were." He grinned.

"That's not funny. The thought of you lying in a coffin for six or more hours isn't the least bit amusing."

"It's no doubt more comfortable than sitting in one of those cramped seats. And the coffin's been rigged to give me plenty of moving space. And breathing space. There's not a thing to worry about. But," he added, winking, "that look of despair on your face is just the ticket. After all, you are mourning the loss of your dear departed husband, Mrs. Oberchon.''

"Mrs. Oberchon?''

"Harriet Oberchon. From Braintree, Massachusetts. Widow of Alfred Oberchon of London, England.''

Courtney frowned. Harriet Oberchon. She would have preferred something with a bit more pizzazz, excitement, glamour. Something like...Katherine O'Malley.


PETRENKO STOOD just outside the phone booth, whose glass door was cracked. "What does Zakharov say?''

Borofsky waved for him to be quiet as he listened in silence to his superior's orders.

"Well?'' Petrenko said when his partner finally placed the receiver back in the cradle. "What are we to do now that we cannot find the professor?''

Borofsky scowled, giving Petrenko a not-so-gentle shove as he stepped out of the phone booth. "So we are imbeciles, are we?'' he muttered, striding fiercely down the airport terminal, Petrenko scurrying to keep up with him. "Inept, inefficient, untrained. Insults. Nothing but insults.'' He stopped abruptly, and Petrenko slammed into him from behind.

"Imbecile,'' Borofsky snapped. "Can you not even watch where you're going, you idiot?''

Petrenko scratched his head. "But, Yevgenni, that is precisely what I am trying to find out. Where are we going, Comrade?''

Borofsky shrugged. "We are to go to London. Zakharov will meet us there and give us further orders.''

A whisper of a smile fell across Petrenko's lips. "Yevgenni, maybe we will get to see the queen when we are in London. What do you think?''

Borofsky had to fight to keep his rage in check. "What do I think? I think, Petrenko, that you are lucky to still be alive. If I were in charge . . ."

"Take it easy, Yevgenni." He gave a crooked grin. "If not the queen, there is always the chance we'll catch a glimpse of that one who plays James Bond in the movies."

Borofsky grabbed Petrenko by the collar just as an elegant woman dressed in black passed by. "You had better pray that you catch a glimpse of our professor in London, you imbecile. Or the only movie stars you'll see are the ones burning with you in capitalist Hell."

# CHAPTER TEN

COURTNEY STEPPED OUT of the terminal at Heathrow wishing she'd thought to add a nice designer mac to her purchases back in Hyannis. It was raining hard, and according to the pilot's weather report during the flight, rain was predicted for the next few days. Courtney smiled, recalling that a fictional spring storm in London had been the start of this whole adventure for her.

She spotted the taxi line and walked over to wait behind a half-dozen travelers. Luckily the cabs were plentiful and her turn came quickly. Her taxi cab was one of those distinctive British vehicles with a wide, square body and the driver sitting in a separate forward compartment. Before she stepped in she glanced over at the black hearse passing slowly by. *Come to pick up Jonathan,* she thought. Taking a deep, steadying breath, she prayed his unique mode of travel had been all that he'd expected. And nothing more.

"I'm going to Brown's Funeral Parlour on Fenchurch Street in London. I believe it's off Bishopsgate," Courtney said, settling into the roomy back seat and consulting a folded section of a London street map she'd picked up back at Logan Airport in Boston.

The driver glanced back, took in his attractive passenger's somber attire and nodded. "I know where it is, ma'am," he said respectfully. "No luggage, then?"

Courtney shrugged. "No. This was...a sudden trip."

"Yes, I understand." He gave a polite nod, his eyes flickering upward for an instant, and then he pulled out into the busy morning traffic.

The trip into London took nearly an hour. Exhausted though she was, having been unable to sleep on the plane, Courtney watched the endless parade of buildings slide by her window, feeling exhilarated by it all. Westminster Abbey, the Houses of Parliament, the enormous hands of Big Ben announcing that the time was nine-twenty. She wanted to stop at every attraction, clap her hands in delight, pinch herself to make sure this wasn't all a dream. But the sights of London would have to wait. The sight Courtney was most anxious to see was Jonathan Madden rising from the "dead."

Brown's Funeral Parlour on Fenchurch was a trim white-washed two-story building with a long driveway around to the back for "deliveries." Courtney did not see a hearse in view as she asked the driver to stop in front of the main entrance to the place.

She handed the driver the required number of pounds for the fare, plus a generous tip. She hoped Les Sharp wouldn't mind her extravagance. At the funeral parlor in Charlestown, he'd supplied her with a substantial sum of British notes to cover her "travel" expenses. Courtney experienced a special thrill pocketing those notes after paying the cabbie. Not only had she managed to induce Jonathan to bring her to London—well, he hadn't actually escorted her in the literal sense—but she had even managed to get herself, however temporarily, on the payroll of the CIA. Not bad for an ordinary shop girl.

Stepping out of the taxi, she paused for a moment despite the heavy rainfall to inspect the street quickly in both directions. A few cars drove by—no furtive glances in her direction. Others were parked along the curb, all seemingly empty. And there were no pedestrians around. Not that

Courtney thought she'd been followed. Who would be following a widow by the name of Harriet Oberchon, in London to attend the funeral of her poor, departed husband, Alfred? Still, she intended to stay alert and cautious.

Courtney climbed the concrete steps to the front door, protected from the pelting rain by a black awning. She was careful to keep her pace slow, resolute, and to exhibit the decorum expected of a woman on her way to pay her last respects to her beloved Al. Not an easy pose to manage, considering the exhilaration she continued to experience.

A bell jingled softly as she opened the door and stepped into a cool, large oak-paneled hall. To the right was a staircase and to the left several closed doors. No one came out to greet her and she found herself standing in the bleak hall for several minutes, dismayed by the cloying scent of musk mingled with an unpleasant hint of evergreen. The aroma, the silence, the somber chill contributed to a mounting anxiety that tempered her excitement.

Finally she heard a door open somewhere out of sight, beneath the rise of the broad, imposing, blue carpeted stairway.

A small, gray-haired man of about sixty with rimless bifocals and a soft, soothing manner appeared alongside the staircase. Hands clasped prayerfully, he bowed to her with an air of solicitous welcome, in no way indicating concern for all the time she'd been kept waiting. "Yes? May I be of service?"

"I'm Mrs. Oberchon. Harriet Oberchon."

He smiled, introduced himself as Reginald Brown, his gray eyes flickering appraisingly from her head to her feet.

Courtney noticed then the hints of strain around that smiling mouth. And she saw that the smile did not reach his eyes.

"Well, Mr. Brown, I hope everything has been properly arranged. I mean . . . I hope there have been no complications."

Mr. Brown put a hand to his forehead and rubbed slowly. "Oh . . . no."

Neither his words nor tense look inspired confidence.

"Well, Mr. Brown, shall we proceed?" Her voice held a faint but distinct quaver.

The undertaker looked at his watch, looked at her, raised his gray-flecked eyebrows. Without another word he nodded quickly and headed down the hall, stopping at the first closed door. He opened it, stepped aside and waited for Courtney, who had followed behind, to enter first.

She'd expected to be shown into a private office. Instead Mr. Brown was bidding her enter a small chapel, where piped-in organ music softly played what Courtney assumed was an English rendition of a dirge. She hesitated at the doorway, giving Mr. Brown a baffled look.

"Perhaps you would like to take a seat in the front pew on the right, Mrs. Oberchon."

Still, she hesitated.

"Please, Mrs. Oberchon, do take a seat. It shan't be very long."

There was an edge of insistence in his voice, and having no other reasonable options at the moment, Courtney gave a disconcerted shrug and entered the chapel.

"There is a pillow beneath the seat, should you find the pew uncomfortable, Mrs. Oberchon."

She glanced over her shoulder, but Mr. Brown had already vanished. She progressed soundlessly, her footsteps muffled by the dark brown carpet, as she made her way down the center aisle to the front pew. She sat down on the far right, not bothering with the pillow, very much hoping she would not be lingering there long enough for discomfort to build.

She sat primly, hands folded on her lap in the empty chapel, doing her best to tune out the solemn sounds of the organ, the unpleasant musty scent that permeated the air, the tension pushing up her spine.

Twenty minutes later she was sitting ramrod stiff, mounting worry weighing on her nerves. Where was Jonathan? Had something terrible happened to him? She pictured him lying in a white satin-lined coffin, his handsome rugged face still, those marvelous aquamarine eyes hidden forever behind closed lids. She shivered. Her heart began to pound. A bead of sweat broke out on her brow. The waiting game might be part of the adventure, but it was a part Courtney Blue found nerve-racking.

Ten minutes. That was all she'd give him. And then... And then what?

*Go search for Mr. Brown and demand to know what was holding up the proceedings.*


"HAD A PLEASANT FLIGHT, then, Madden?" The tall, balding man with a puffy face and thick lips laughed, but there was little mirth in the laughter.

There was equally little mirth in Jonathan's responding smile. "I've had worse."

"Indeed you have."

Jonathan merely shrugged as he glanced around the parlor of the two-room flat in Bayswater. It had the appearance of having been furnished in a hurry and without much thought to style. Or even, for that matter, serviceability. The armchair Jonathan was sitting on was hard and uncomfortable, the light tan color already stained by a recent coffee spill.

"You're looking better than I'd expected, Madden. The last time I saw you you were in a sorry state."

"American air agrees with me," Jonathan said lightly, steering clear of the past.

"So it must. And teaching. It's been a long time since you'd stood in a lecture hall, Professor."

"It's rather like riding a bike. Some activities always come back to you."

The balding man smiled. "Yes, I fully believe that to be the case," he said pointedly.

Jonathan was not amused.

"Ironic, isn't it, Madden. You and I together again. Not exactly the same, to be sure, but still..." He let the sentence hang. "Poor Marcus. He's certainly had one hell of a year. But I'm sure he'll be delighted to know none of his old friends have forgotten him."

Jonathan prided himself on his coolheadedness, but he was starting to lose that well-honed control. Perhaps his escalating temper was due to having spent nearly seven hours in a coffin. Perhaps it was old memories returning to haunt him. Perhaps it was his worry over Marcus Lloyd. Or perhaps it was the irony of it all, just as Avery Noble had said.

"Get to the point of our little meeting, Avery. I'm late for a funeral."

Avery Noble laughed. "Oh, yes, your funeral. Poor form to be late for one's own funeral. But, then, with so few attending, I wouldn't fret."

Jonathan leaned forward, his expression menacing. "I'll decide when to fret or not, Avery. Let's get on with it. You always were the sort to move at a snail's pace. Funny how you still managed to tread on so many toes along the way."

"Ah, Jonathan, but my theory—well proven—is that slow and steady wins the race." Noble's upper-class British intonation got a shade more pronounced. "Whereas you, Jonathan, were always in so much of a hurry. And where has all that rushing about gotten you?"

"In one more moment, Avery, I shall show you exactly where it will get you."

Avery Noble deliberately met Jonathan's stare for nearly a minute without moving a muscle. Jonathan knew he was being pushed. He also knew that as much amusement as Avery was getting out of all this, beneath the surface he felt threatened. Slow and steady had not put Avery Noble in the driver's seat he'd coveted for so long. Cunning, deceit and disloyalty had. And Avery Noble was well aware that Jonathan knew that and was quite capable of turning it against him if provoked too far.

With a sigh meant to sound satisfied, Avery Noble slowly lifted a manila folder off the table separating him from Jonathan. He pulled out three photos and, deliberately continuing at a snail's pace, handed them over to Jonathan one at a time, saying, "Well, shall we get down to business, then?"

Jonathan studied the first one and tapped at it with his index finger. "This is the Russian goon who was taking pot shots at me in Boston." He intentionally skipped mention of the shot the Russian took at him that didn't go astray. He glanced at the next photo and nodded. "His partner. I never got a close-enough look at him to swear to it, but I'm pretty sure. If you have no objection, I'll take these along for further verification."

"Certainly."

Jonathan looked at the last photo. He let out a low whistle. Not only was the picture that of a most attractive dark-haired beauty, the pose was alluringly provocative and the costume, or lack thereof, most titillating. "Who is she?"

"Do you recognize her?"

Jonathan nodded. "A young, beautiful dark-haired woman has been keeping tabs on me in Boston for the past few days. This could be her."

"Quite, quite lovely, don't you think?"

Again Jonathan queried, "Who is she?"

"Her name is Christine Dupré. French by birth, but she's lived in London for the past year. She's an actress...of sorts. A bit of dancing, singing. She's been in three West End productions. Chorus. But with grander aspirations, I'm sure." Avery paused. "She's been Marcus Lloyd's lover for the past six months."

Jonathan looked up, his expression deliberately neutral, and then he once again studied the photo. "She is beautiful. I must compliment Marcus when I next see him." His eyes shot back over to Avery.

Avery nodded in the direction of the photos. "The two Russians are on a flight to London. And Marcus's lover is already in town. More about her momentarily. First about the couple you wired us about. Lou Vaughn and Andrea Lambert. They caught the flight before yours here. Quite a gathering of players in London town, Madden. And I understand you brought a participant of your own along, as well."

Jonathan narrowed his eyes, daring further comment. None came. He relaxed a little. "I'm here on my own time, Avery. I believe it's in both our interests, however, to cooperate with each other. But I'll make my own plans, my own decisions."

Avery shrugged. "Didn't you always, Jonathan?"

Jonathan grinned. "Some things never change, Avery."

A deliberating silence ensued before Avery Noble spoke again. "The woman, Christine Dupré, is not what one would call a devout believer in monogamy. We have reason to think she was also quite chummy with another fellow by the name of Daniel Emerson. It seems Mr. Emerson has a great interest in collecting art and other rare works. We've had our suspicions about him in the past. Middleman for black market art, that sort of thing. No conclusive evidence. Mr. Emerson is a rather elusive chap, but we've recently learned he's put a great deal of money into a new

West End show. A musical extravaganza called *Fanfare*. It's to open in the fall and tryouts have just gotten underway."

"Where does Emerson fit in?"

"We have reason to believe he was negotiating with Marcus for the Gorky work before the kidnapping. Perhaps Marcus set the price too high."

"And you think he sent the Dupré woman to get hold of the Gorky and sidestep the payment issue."

Again Avery shrugged. "It does make sense. Emerson maintained a low profile prior to Marcus's kidnapping. His contacts with Marcus were all apparently made through typed correspondence, phone calls and lawyers. We've tracked down the firm of Colby and Wittington as the one that handled Emerson's recent dealings. They claim never to have met the man personally."

Jonathan sighed. "And the Russians? Is there something more enticing about the Gorky work than its substantial literary value?"

"We are leaning more and more toward that conclusion. Of course, we shall need to study the manuscript more closely for confirmation."

"Do Vaughn and Lambert have it with them?"

"Our people in customs went through their two small overnight cases and found nothing. We felt it would arouse too much suspicion to do a strip search. We would best assume they have the item or can get their hands on it when the time comes to close negotiations. Rest assured they will be closely watched."

"And meanwhile Marcus rots?"

"I trust you'll be able to negotiate for a bit more time with his kidnapper, Jonathan. Under the circumstances."

"I still don't like your plan, Avery."

"Ah, but you do see the value of it, I'm sure. We not only want the manuscript and Marcus safe and sound. We would very much like to ferret out Emerson and every other unsavory soul involved in this affair. Especially if, as we suspect, the Russians' interest is as much political as it is literary. We may have gotten lucky at last. Those two goons in the photos are merely messenger boys, Madden. The man behind the scenes—the KGB head of operations—is the one we'd like to grab. Tag their superior and we gain entry into a tidy little network. I don't mind saying it would be quite a feather in my cap to round up so many bastards. Instinct tells me Emerson might be working with the Russians. We'll get them all. But that, my lad, takes patience. Or, as you would no doubt put it, operating at a snail's pace."

Jonathan gave Avery a seering look. "I could put it a lot more colorfully, Avery."

COURTNEY'S NERVES were coming unraveled and she nearly jumped out of her pew when she heard a disembodied voice murmur, "Have you been saying your prayers for me, love?"

She spun around to see a very much alive Jonathan smiling at her from the next pew.

Her face showed relief and irritation. "I've been out of my mind with worry. Do you realize I've been here for nearly an hour? Mr. Brown's vanished. The whole building is empty. I've been sitting in this pew for the past forty minutes, trying to decide whether to call the police, the CIA, the missing persons bureau—" She stopped, caught her breath, and only now that Jonathan was there, looking as healthy as ever, was she able to muster a winning smile. "I was rather at a loss as to how I would explain to any of them that I was looking for a perfectly healthy man in a runaway coffin."

"I was detained at customs a bit."

"At customs? You mean they wanted to open the coffin?"

"No, no. Just a bloody lot of red tape. Let's get out of here."

"Gladly," Courtney said.

Jonathan escorted her out a rear door that led directly into a garage where a plain blue Ford sedan was waiting.

"Where are we going?" she asked as they pulled onto Fenchurch Street, heading north.

"I thought you could do with a bit of rest. My mother is expecting you."

"When did you phone her? Don't tell me your coffin was outfitted with a telephone."

He grinned. "It was the deluxe model, love."

"Where were you all this time, really, Jonathan?"

He turned left onto Broad Street. "I did stop to make one or two phone calls."

"Did you make contact with Marcus's kidnappers? Did you tell them you no longer had the manuscript? You...you didn't tell them that my uncle...? If they find out about Andrea Lambert and Uncle Lou, his life could be in great danger, Jonathan."

He saw her tensed features, touched her cheek. "I promise you, your uncle is being well looked after, Courtney. No harm will come to him." He was not about to alarm her by adding, "As long as he is as loyal, honest and uninvolved, as you claim." Jonathan could not forget the hungry, greedy look in Avery Noble's face. The man was ready to devour every suspect he could get his hands on then ask questions.

Courtney studied his profile, her worries rising despite Jonathan's assurances. He was very enigmatic, this hero of hers, she mused. There was so much going on beneath the surface of that irresistibly handsome facade. He gave little away. Oh, perhaps at first it had all been fantasy, her drawing so many similarities between Jonathan and the fictional Derek Colton. But now she was beginning to believe there was more fact to the similarities than fiction. Both men were

# PLAY THE "LUCKY 7" SLOT MACHINE GAME!

# NO COST! NO OBLIGATION TO BUY! NO PURCHASE NECESSARY!

## PLAY "LUCKY 7"
## AND GET AS MANY AS SIX FREE GIFTS . . .

## HOW TO PLAY:

1. With a coin, carefully scratch off the silver box at the right. This makes you eligible to receive one or more free books, and possibly other gifts, depending on what is revealed beneath the scratch-off area.

2. You'll receive brand-new Harlequin Superromance® novels. When you return this card, we'll send you the books and gifts you qualify for *absolutely free!*

3. If we don't hear from you, every month we'll send you 4 additional novels to read and enjoy. You can return them and owe nothing, but if you decide to keep them, you'll pay only $2.74* per book, a savings of 21¢ each off the cover price! There is *no* extra charge for postage and handling. There are no hidden extras.

4. When you join the Harlequin Reader Service®, you'll also get our monthly newsletter, as well as additional free gifts from time to time just for being a member.

5. You must be completely satisfied. You may cancel at any time simply by sending us a note or a shipping statement marked "cancel" or by returning any unopened shipment to us by parcel post at our expense.

*In the future, prices and terms may change, but you always have the opportunity to cancel your subscription. Sales taxes applicable in N.Y. and Iowa.

secretive, clever about avoiding issues they chose not to discuss. Both men gave away little about their pasts. Both men were keenly passionate, yet determined to maintain control and safe distance in personal relationships that threatened to become too intimate. Even as Derek Colton adored Katherine O'Malley, he was adamant about remaining fancy-free. And if Katherine O'Malley with all her beauty, charm and wealth could not win her hero's commitment, Courtney felt she herself didn't stand a chance.

As they drove, the weather remained wet and blustery. Jonathan was quiet, and Courtney, no longer drawn to the passing scenery, was suspended in inner thought. So it was that a shock of surprise escaped her lips when she looked up after Jonathan announced they had arrived.

She felt breathless as she stared at the enormous, stately, gray stone Elizabethan mansion in its devotedly groomed setting of formal gardens, lush lawn, shrubbery and trees in varying stages of bloom. The manse itself, which sat like a huge jewel on a knoll, managed to be at once formidable and entrancing.

Courtney gave Jonathan a narrow glance. "Are we visiting the queen, after all?"

He grinned. "Hardly."

"Hardly? My God, Jonathan, this is the grandest home I've ever seen."

Courtney's feeling of intimidation obscured any notice of Jonathan's rise of discomfort. Bringing female houseguests to the family manse was something he hadn't done in a very long time. "It's really rather gone to seed over the past twenty years. Mother's getting on, and what with the economy and all, she's cut back on staff. She's even begun considering throwing the place open to the public to raise some additional income."

Courtney said nothing. She was feeling too overwhelmed.

He came around and helped her out of the car. "I should warn you, my mother's a bit of a . . ." He paused, in search of the right word.

"A bit of a snob?"

"Not at all," he said. "She's just very . . . British. And I should mention I'm her only son, a fact that she rarely allows me to forget. I'm afraid I've been a bit of a disappointment to her, though she's very good about not displaying that feeling openly."

Courtney took a steadying breath. Almost simultaneously the front door to the stately mansion opened. A tall, distinguished-looking gentleman in a black suit came out and hurried down the steps under an open umbrella, a second umbrella in hand.

"Thanks, Donald," Jonathan said, taking the extra umbrella from the man.

"Yes, sir. Lady Edith is expecting you. She's in the morning room."

Jonathan nodded. "There's no luggage, Donald. You can go ahead."

Donald quickly concealed his brief expression of surprise as he turned and went back up the steps to the house, pausing at the open front door to await their arrival.

"'Lady Edith,'" Courtney murmured. "So I *am* going to be the guest of royalty."

"Nonsense. Mother's last husband happened to be a ne'er-do-well whose only claim to fame, but most assuredly not fortune, was his inherited title. And being 'Lady' Edith was just about the only thing Mother obtained from the divorce settlement."

He could feel the tension in Courtney as her fingers gripped his.

"Don't be nervous, Courtney. Think of everything you've pulled off thus far. Contending with my mother will be the least of it, I guarantee you."

Courtney wasn't so sure. And she was even less confident as she faced Lady Edith for the first time.

Dressed in a chic soft apricot silk dress, Lady Edith was a tall, imposing woman who exuded poise, elegance and glamour, if not exactly beauty. Her hair was dark like Jonathan's, though Lady Edith's coif was lightly sprinkled with silver threads that were most becoming. Her eyes were blue, not the brilliant aquamarine of Jonathan's, but as clear, shrewd and intelligent.

After the formal introduction, Jonathan engaged his mother in idle chitchat, leaving Courtney to gaze about the lovely circular morning room, a spacious, multiwindowed room decorated with as much attention to detail as the grand entrance she'd walked through and the enormous parlor she'd managed a glimpse of.

Only after several minutes passed was Courtney aware that Lady Edith was observing her closely, even as she filled her son in animatedly on the local news. Flustered, Courtney gave a brief, nervous smile and looked over at Jonathan.

He smiled back, but the smile was laced with tension. Apparently he was not all that more comfortable around his mother than she was. Courtney had an inkling why a moment later.

"Well, Jonathan, I assume this is not a social call," Lady Edith said bluntly, but not entirely without warmth. "Which I further assume means you've gotten yourself involved in something nasty again."

Jonathan shot his mother a frigid look, which he hastily camouflaged with a quick laugh. "Of course this is a social visit." Quickly he turned back to Courtney, who was now regarding him attentively. He raised his eyebrows as if to say *Don't take mother seriously.*

But Courtney was taking her very seriously, indeed. Just what kinds of nasty things had Jonathan Madden done in the past? And why did Lady Edith assume this visit meant he was once again into something nasty? Courtney didn't have the answers to those questions, but she had every intention of finding them out. From the closed-off look Jonathan was giving her, she also knew that getting them was not going to be easy. But, then, nothing inspired Courtney more than a good challenge.

## CHAPTER ELEVEN

EXHAUSTION FINALLY CAUGHT up with Courtney that afternoon. Intending to take a twenty-minute rest at most, she ended up sleeping a good five hours and would have slept through the night had Lady Edith's butler, Jeeves, not rapped softly on her bedroom door, announcing that dinner would be served shortly.

Well, his name wasn't Jeeves, really. It was Donald. But ever since Courtney's arrival at the Maddens' magnificent manse, she'd been having more than her usual difficulty separating fantasy from reality. The fairy-tale setting, meeting the regal Lady Edith and her staff, seeing Jonathan for the first time in the role of landed gentry, finding herself at the heart of an adventure that might have been plucked from a Hilary Bennett best-seller, all seemed quite fantastic. And Courtney was loving every moment of it.

Rising from her sumptuous four-poster in the elegant guest bedchamber, done in warming shades of mint green and cream, Courtney went over to the huge walnut armoire, where she'd carefully hung up her widow's weeds. It was a good thing black was so versatile. The outfit would see her through what she guessed would be a formal dinner.

She blinked several times upon opening the closet. The black dress and jacket were still there, but they'd been moved to one side to make room for a half-dozen other outfits, all new and none of which had been hanging there earlier.

The costumes, three daytime outfits, two evening dresses and one tennis set, were all simple, elegant and clearly expensive. And they all bore the mark of a man with taste and breeding. In short, Jonathan Madden.

As Courtney dressed for dinner, having chosen without hesitation the aquamarine satin evening dress that fell softly to mid-calf from the waist and had a simple scooped neck and capped sleeves, she felt very much like Cinderella getting ready for the ball. And she had no complaint whatsoever that instead of a fairy godmother, she'd been blessed with a six-foot-two, ruggedly handsome, suave, charming albeit enigmatic hero, who was doing a wonderful job of making her dreams come true.

Lady Edith was having her traditional gin and tonic in the library when Courtney arrived. After Courtney received a firm nod of approval, Lady Edith had Jeeves—that is, Donald—prepare a cocktail for Courtney. A Booth gin and tonic was suggested, and Courtney, still caught up in the fantasy of glitz and glamour, merely nodded.

"Where's Jonathan?" Courtney asked after a few awkward minutes of polite chatter about the "simply dreadful weather."

"Oh, he left hours ago," Lady Edith said. "He never does stay put for very long when he comes to visit."

Courtney frowned. "Did he say where he was going?"

Lady Edith gestured vaguely as she gave Courtney an indulgent smile. "Does he ever?"

Courtney frowned. "Well, did he say what time he would be getting back?"

Lady Edith motioned to her to sit beside her on a tapestry sofa. "Are you and my son close friends, Courtney?"

Courtney took a sip of gin and tonic. "We've been through a lot together in a relatively short time."

Lady Edith observed Courtney with a shrewd, bold study. "Are you in some sort of trouble?"

Trouble? Courtney shook her head. "Not exactly."

"I imagine whatever is going on, it's likely to be rather complicated. Am I correct?"

Courtney had to smile. "Absolutely correct."

Lady Edith nodded. "Yes, it always is."

"Always?" Courtney prodded.

"An intriguing man, my son. Very much a loner. Oh, he's very charming, handsome to a fault, and quite, quite clever. But he's never been one to share a great deal of himself. Even as a schoolboy he seemed to hold himself apart. And ever since he's been, shall we say, all grown up, he's been impossibly mysterious about his personal and business affairs."

"When Jonathan and I first arrived you made some mention about him no doubt being involved in another 'nasty' piece of business. Has Jonathan been in trouble in the past?" Courtney couldn't keep the burning curiosity from her voice, nor did she try. She hoped Lady Edith would be more forthcoming than her son.

But Courtney's hopes were quickly dashed. Lady Edith merely shrugged. "As I said, Jonathan has never been one to confide his troubles. Not to me, anyway. However, I needn't be the most insightful woman to realize that any man who carries a gun, receives phone calls at all hours of the night and has on more than one occasion shown up here in the wee hours of the morning bruised and battered, claiming he's walked into a streetlamp... well, my dear, I'd have to say he's had his share of troubles in the past. And I've developed a sixth sense about my adventure-prone son. Little inner signals that tell me when he's mucking about in murky waters. I felt those signals go off when the two of you arrived early this afternoon."

Lady Edith paused. "Actually I was hoping you would tell me what is going on. I had thought when Jonathan left for the States that he was putting trouble behind him."

Courtney sighed. "I doubted from the start that he was merely an ordinary college professor."

A faint smile curved Lady Edith's lips. "There's nothing ordinary about my son. Sometimes, I must admit I wish he were more...prosaic. But that would be rather dull. I do adore Jonathan, but he can be most secretive at times. To this day, I've no firm idea why he left London the way he did six months ago and returned to teaching. He hadn't taught in years."

"What was he doing in London then? For a living?"

Lady Edith smiled indulgently. "It hasn't exactly been necessary for Jonathan to...earn 'a living,' as you put it."

Courtney felt a little foolish. Earning a living would not be a concern for a man of the landed gentry.

"But Jonathan has never been one to sit about idly," Lady Edith went on. "He's always had a fascination with languages, especially Russian. And literature. He did do some lecturing early on, and over the years he's done some government work, authenticating documents, translating certain papers and such. I do know he had a security clearance, so he must have dealt with rather delicate material at times."

"And then six months ago, Jonathan just packed up and left for Boston?" Courtney asked. "He gave you no reason?"

There was a long pause before Lady Edith continued, her regal expression tinged with concern.

"There was a rumor going about shortly before Jonathan left for the States that he might be involved in a most distasteful piece of business with a close acquaintance of his...in government."

Courtney's eyes widened. "Who was that?"

Lady Edith hesitated. "Perhaps I oughtn't to stir up muddy waters again. And Jonathan might not want me to—"

"Please, Lady Edith. I...I care about Jonathan very much. And...I know so little about him. I want to understand him. I want...to help him."

Lady Edith retrieved a lace-bordered linen handkerchief from the pocket of her lilac evening dress and dabbed at her brow. "I really know so little myself. Other than all the rumors floating about at the time, very little was mentioned in the more reputable papers. Rumor had it that this older, distinguished gentleman by the name of Marcus Lloyd was involved in a scandal. He held a rather high government position, but I was never quite clear what it was precisely. I do know that Jonathan on occasion met with him socially, as well as professionally."

"Did you know him, as well?" Courtney asked.

"No. I never met the man. Anyway, a little over six months ago this Mr. Lloyd was accused of misappropriation of government funds. Before any formal charges were pressed, he announced his retirement from public service. I imagine certain pressures were brought to bear on Mr. Lloyd, encouraging him to avoid scandal and embarrassment to himself and Her Majesty's government. That was the end of the incident."

"And Jonathan told you nothing more about it?"

"Jonathan was clearly upset by the affair. And quite angry. He insisted Mr. Lloyd was as honest as the day was long, and that the charges were trumped up to push the gentleman out. At the time I was worried because Jonathan's name had also been mentioned in the papers. No direct accusations or anything, but I know that he was briefly under investigation. Some government investigators came here one day and asked me what they referred to as routine questions. Jonathan was livid about that." Lady Edith hesitated. "And then when he took off for the States so...abruptly...I must admit I was worried about what he might have gotten himself into." The troubled expression on

Lady Edith's face remained as she gave Courtney a careful study. "And now he's back, and I'm afraid he may land in some trouble once again."

Courtney's heart went out to Jonathan's mother. "Your son hasn't done anything wrong, Lady Edith. I'm afraid he's not confided in me a great deal more than he has in you. But I do know he's come home to help a friend in trouble. I have every confidence in Jonathan. I'm sure everything will turn out well in the end...for everyone concerned." Didn't all adventures have happy endings? Or was she simply banking on fantasy to see them through?

Lady Edith seemed momentarily satisfied with Courtney's response. Consulting her jeweled watch, she said, "Shall we dine?"

"Shouldn't we wait for Jonathan?"

Lady Edith rose gracefully from the sofa. "Didn't I say? Jonathan won't be back for dinner, my dear. He's unlikely to be back for several days."

"Several days? But—"

"Oh, I'm sure he'll be in touch. Don't fret, please. I'm delighted to have some company. Especially a friend of Jonathan's. He hasn't brought many around in the past. And he did seem eager for you to enjoy your stay with me. He suggested I might show you around London. We can take in the museums and some shows if you like. And of course there's the club. Golf, tennis. Most of the guests are a bit stodgy, I'm afraid, but there are a few whom I'm sure you'll enjoy getting to know."

Courtney was stunned. Devastated. Furious. "He can't. He can't have walked out on me like this."

"Oh, dear," Lady Edith said with a sigh. "I'd assumed you realized he had some matters to attend to."

"We. *We* have matters to attend to. He can't simply discard me like an old shoe. I won't have it."

Lady Edith smiled brightly. "Ah, a woman with spirit. I like that."

Courtney took hold of Lady Edith's wrist. "You must have some idea where he went. Some clue."

"I'm afraid he didn't say a word." She paused, a conspiratorial smile lighting her attractive face. "Well, shall we have a look in his room? Perhaps he's left some clue behind without realizing it."

Courtney smiled. "A woman with spirit. I like that."


"WHAT DO YOU MEAN, she's left?" Jonathan demanded.

"She's a rather headstrong girl, isn't she?" Lady Edith said with a trace of a smile on her lips. Fortunately she was having this conversation with her son via the telephone. From the harsh sound of his voice, she doubted he would have appreciated her smile of approval.

"Where did she go?"

"Off looking for you, I imagine," Lady Edith said airily.

"But she has no idea where I am. Why in heaven's name didn't you keep her amused, as I asked?"

"Darling, I'm afraid your friend wasn't terribly interested in the kind of amusement I had to offer." This time Lady Edith's smile was broader.

"When did she leave?" Jonathan asked sharply. He was growing increasingly frustrated and irritated.

"First thing this morning. We did have a bit of breakfast together, though. Oh, and I hope you don't mind, but I offered her your little Austin to get about town in. I do hope she remembers to keep to the left. Americans, you know—"

"Where did she head?"

"She didn't say, Jonathan. Just that she was quite certain she'd find you before long. Just where are you, darling?"

"Look, if she phones, tell her—no, insist that she return home immediately and wait for me. Tell her I've promised to be back this evening. I'll be there no later than nine. Do you understand?"

"Well, yes, dear. But I can't say she'll call."

"If she does..."

"Wouldn't it be just as convenient for me to tell her exactly where to find you if she does telephone?"

Jonathan sighed. "No, Mother. It would not be more convenient," he said firmly.


"CAN I HELP YOU, MISS?"

"Is this where the tryouts for *Fanfare* are being held?"

"Yes, miss. But they don't begin until eleven." The assistant stage manager, a young man with skintight jeans, a tapered black shirt open halfway down his chest to reveal a slew of gold chains, stood at the stage door of the Garrick and gave Courtney a surprised look. "You trying out, then? A dancer is it?"

Courtney hesitated. Her expensive, sophisticated gray linen suit wasn't exactly what the everyday auditioning hoofer might wear. She smiled. "No, actually I was looking for someone."

"Who would that be?"

Courtney shrugged. "That's all right. I'll stop by after eleven. Thanks."

She turned from the stage door and headed up the alley. It was nine-fifty in the morning. Over an hour until the auditions. And when they started, then what? Would Jonathan be there? Or was this merely a wild-goose chase?

Jonathan hadn't exactly left a cache of clues lying about his bedroom at the mansion. In fact, the only lead, and a vague one at that, had been an ad circled in the back of the daily paper she'd spotted on his desk. The ad announced tryouts for the West End production of *Fanfare*, a new musical extravaganza. What connection a West End musical had with the Gorky manuscript, Marcus Lloyd and his kidnapper or her missing uncle, Courtney couldn't begin to imagine. But Jonathan must have had a reason for marking that ad.

By eleven-ten Courtney was back at the Garrick Theatre, twentieth in a line of leggy young dancers all there to audition. Courtney fit into the group just fine, having exchanged her linen suit, now folded up in a newly purchased duffel bag, for a black leotard and white tights. Butterflies were no longer fluttering in her stomach—they were making racing takeoffs and landings. She found herself remembering that phone conversation with her uncle when he'd inquired about the last time she'd gone dancing and she'd replied that she was a terrible disco dancer. Had she really had that conversation only four days ago? Was it possible?

The same assistant stage manager she'd spoken to earlier was walking down the line of dancers with forms for them to fill out. He didn't bat an eye of recognition when he came up to her. She'd not only changed her costume but now had her hair pulled back off her face in a ponytail, and she'd scrubbed her face clean of cosmetics, so that she looked closer to twenty than thirty. She was really quite pleased with her transformation.

Auditioning for the chorus was another story. She began praying as the line of dancers grew shorter that her four years of ballet and interpretive jazz as a teenager—Uncle Lou had insisted on those lessons, bless the man—would be enough for her not to make a fool of herself onstage. After all, it wasn't as though she hoped to land a part. Her only aspiration was to somehow spot Jonathan or have him spot her.

The choreographer was taking the women in groups of three, showing them a series of what looked to Courtney to be a complicated dance routine, running through it with them once, then having each of them in turn do the short number.

There were two groups ahead of her. She was close enough now to the stage to get a look around. The red velvet seats in the theater were empty save for five of them in the center of the orchestra area. There were three men sitting there, none of whom Courtney recognized, and two women. One of the women, a petite young redhead, got up and slipped past the other to get to the aisle, so it took a second or two for Courtney to focus on the woman still seated. When she did, she let out an involuntary gasp. It was the tall, dark-haired beauty she'd spotted watching the bookstore the other day. Courtney was certain of it. A cold prickle of alarm shot down her back.

And then a second prickle as she felt her arm gripped from behind.

"Phone call for you" came the gruff male voice, tugging her from the line. She opened her mouth to protest even before she turned to see who was pulling at her so forcefully.

But as soon as she turned, she clamped her mouth shut. Jonathan. As much changed as her and, at first glance, anyway, fitting into the group of male dancers as easily as she'd fit in with the women. He was dressed in a skintight black shirt and dancers' trousers and he'd taken a can of hair color and some mousse to his dark locks, giving himself a liberal blond streak and a modified punk hairdo. He, too, looked younger, and roguishly handsome in his new persona.

"What are you doing here?" he demanded after leading her to a secluded area backstage.

She grinned. "The same as you, it seems. Why Jonathan, you never told me you had aspirations to be a dancer."

"This is no time for humor," he said sharply.

"Believe me, I wasn't laughing when I discovered you'd walked out on me."

"Courtney, this isn't the time—"

"Katherine."

"What?"

"I'm auditioning under the name Katherine O'Malley."

"What happened to Harriet Oberchon? Oh, never mind. Listen, it's dangerous for you to be here."

"I know. I saw her."

"Saw who?"

"The dark-haired beauty. The one who was lurking about the bookshop in Boston. The one who was following you. She's here . . . sitting out front."

Jonathan sighed. "Yes, I know. It turns out she's in the show. One of the leads."

"So that's why you circled that newspaper ad."

Jonathan gave her a sharp look, but decided this was no time for a lecture about snooping. "She's not the only one here from Boston. Your Russian arson chums are around, too."

"Don't tell me they're trying out for the show?" she said with a grin.

"Hardly. But, then, I'm not exactly Baryshnikov myself."

"What is this all about, Jonathan? What is that actress's connection with the Gorky? Why does she want it?"

He looked back at the lines of male and female dancers, then glanced at Courtney. Frowning, he said, "I suppose you'll go on sticking your neck out no matter how great the risks."

Her eyes did not waver from his face. "I suppose so."

Anxiety darkened his features, and for a moment Courtney was sure he would say nothing more. But in the end he did take her into his confidence. Not as fully as she would have liked, but still, it was significant.

"I have reason to believe," he told her, "that the man who kidnapped Marcus is involved in this show. A major investor. His name is Daniel Emerson."

"Is he out there in the theater now?"

"I don't know. I have no description of him. No proof of any kind that he's the one, for that matter. And if he is, chances are slim that he'll make an appearance here."

"A long shot."

He smiled. "Very long."

"Perhaps," Courtney said conspiratorially, "we can shorten it a bit."

He regarded her with wariness. "Oh? How would we do that?"

"Well, love, we could double the odds of one of us making it to the chorus if we both try out."

Was there a glint of amusement in Jonathan's aquamarine eyes? If so, he managed to keep it out of his voice. "It's far too dangerous for you—"

"And not for you?" Before he could reply, she added, "But, then, you're used to danger, aren't you? Trouble seems to have followed you about London in the past just as it recently did in Boston."

"You've been having a chat with Mother, I see."

"She's a delightful woman."

He dug into his trouser pocket and pulled out a handful of change and a key. A hotel key, Courtney noted. The Savoy Hotel, room 643. He retrieved a coin and shoved the rest of the contents back in his pocket. "I'm going to phone my mother, whom you find so delightful, and tell her you'll be returning immediately. Once there, you're to stay put for a few days. Do you understand, Courtney?"

"'Katherine.'" She smiled.

"I'm afraid Katherine is to have a short-lived existence. My concern is that Courtney Blue manage a much longer one. I'm putting your risk taking on hold. Now—" He stopped, his eyes trailing her slender, wonderfully curved body, his insides starting to dissolve. Quickly he leveled his gaze at her face, only to find himself marveling at what an incredible, resourceful, remarkable woman she was, besides being so sensually appealing. And so very dangerous to his self-control.

"Now?" she echoed, smiling at him with shameless wantonness.

Yes, he thought, another danger was this woman's ability to read his mind. "Now get some clothes on while I telephone."

As he disappeared down the hall toward the phone near the stage-door exit, Courtney hesitated.

"Ellen Boone, Katherine O'Malley and Rebecca Finch. Stage center," the assistant choreographer called out.

With one quick glance in the direction Jonathan had gone, Courtney broke into a rather credible dancer's run as she headed for stage center. By the time Jonathan returned, she was already well into the dance routine, which really wasn't as complicated as she'd feared.

The women selected for the chorus line were chosen before the men began auditioning.

"Damn," Jonathan muttered as he heard the name Katherine O'Malley being called out. There was no holding Courtney Blue—or Katherine O'Malley—back. By whatever name she chose, she was utterly incorrigible...and beguiling. A faint smile softened his features. Well, at least he'd been spared from having to try out. And since Emerson's appearance here was such a long shot, having the lovely Miss Katherine O'Malley dancing in the chorus line of *Fanfare* might be just the thing to keep her from dogging his heels.

His brow creased. Katherine O'Malley. Hadn't she mentioned that name to him before?

Strolling over to a warm-up bar, Jonathan did a few bends, then flinched, gripping his ankle and muttering to the man warming up next to him that he'd gone and twisted his ankle and would have to drop out of the audition. His fellow hoofer attempted a sympathetic smile, no doubt gleefully thinking as he said "Gee, mate, that's too bad," that his odds of making it into the *Fanfare* chorus line had just improved.

Courtney jotted down the rehearsal schedule, then looked around for Jonathan. He was nowhere in sight. However, when she got to the stage door, the assistant manager with the blond hair and gold necklaces asked if she was Katherine O'Malley.

"Yes."

"One of the dancers left you a note."

"Thanks," she said, taking the folded-up slip of paper but waiting until she got into her car to read it.

The message was short and sweet. Well, not really sweet. Rather severe. Her orders were to return home and wait for Jonathan's call.

She rolled down the car window as a London bobby came strolling by. "Excuse me, Officer, can you give me directions to the Savoy Hotel?"

A minute later she was heading down Shaftesbury Avenue. Perhaps Jonathan didn't know that old American adage—home is where the heart is.

LOU VAUGHN STOPPED at the newsstand in the lobby of the Claridge and picked up copies of all the late-afternoon papers. He then stepped into the ornate elevator and got off at the fourteenth floor, heading down the hall to the lavish suite where Andrea Lambert awaited.

On his own he would definitely have selected a less distinguished hotel in a much less distinguished price range.

But Andrea Lambert, it seemed, always stayed at the Claridge when she was in London. And she'd insisted, since Lou was there at her bequest, that she foot the bill for all expenses. It wasn't that he worried she'd go broke on the deal—Andrea Lambert seemed to have no concerns about funds—but he never had let a woman pay his way before. Then again, he wasn't in any position at the moment to dish out the kind of money an indefinite stay at one of London's poshest hotels would cost. The few days he'd already spent at the Claridge were enough to sate his needs for luxury for months, but, then, he always did have rather simple wants. With the arrival of Andrea Lambert in his life, he was finding his wants growing more complex. And they could turn out to cost him more than he'd bargained for.

"Is the ad there?" Andrea immediately rose from the sofa as Lou entered the suite. She was wearing a vibrant gold satin dressing gown that set off her blond hair and showed her petite, graceful figure off to perfection. For a woman in her late forties she was in great shape.

It took Lou a few seconds to focus on her question. "I haven't checked yet. Let's see."

He walked over to the sofa. They sat down together, Lou stacking the three papers on the museum-quality neo-Gothic coffee table, then lifting the top one, riffling through the pages until he arrived at the personal columns.

As he scanned the rows of ads, Lou had difficulty concentrating on the task at hand. His eyes kept drifting over to Andrea's long, graceful fingers, their trimmed nails painted to match the soft peach sheen of her lips. The scent of her expensive floral perfume curled around him in a seductive embrace. The enticing scent, dab for dab, probably cost more than blood. That final observation did more than anything else to help him focus his attention back on the paper.

"Here it is," he said finally, doing his best to tune out the light but provocative pressure of Andrea's thigh pressing against his as she leaned forward to check the ad.

Her throaty voice held a little tremor as she read: "'Please notify me about the time and place of the next meeting of the Friends of Gorky. Most eager to attend. Will gladly pay full membership fees.'" Her eyes locked with Lou's. "If we're lucky there should be a response in tomorrow's paper. I suppose that in the meantime we'll...simply have to wait."

For all his years, Lou Vaughn's smile was surprisingly boyish. "I suppose so."

# CHAPTER TWELVE

COURTNEY'S TALENT at persuasion worked like a charm on the desk clerk of the Savoy Hotel.

"Didn't my husband remember to leave a key for me at the desk? Married only three weeks and already he's forgotten about me. Well, of course I did say I might arrive tomorrow. That's all right, though. Now I can surprise him. That is, if you don't mind giving me that extra key to room 643?"

The desk clerk wasn't able to recall whether Jonathan had returned to his room this afternoon. If he wasn't up there, Courtney had every intention of letting herself in to wait for him. There was a lot to talk about. While the message was certainly coming through loud and clear that Jonathan Madden had every intention of running the show and handling most of the details, she in turn had every intention of being an equal partner. After all, she was the one with the "in" at the Garrick Theater. Besides, hadn't Katherine O'Malley's stubborn refusal to remain on the sidelines saved Derek Colton's life?

*You need me, Jonathan,* she said to herself as she knocked on his hotel door. There was no response. She knocked again, waited, then slipped her key into the lock.

Jonathan's head was under the shower while Courtney was knocking on his door. Oblivious to her entry, he took his time soaping up, then letting the steamy hot jets of water vigorously attack the aching muscles in his back. Seven hours in a coffin, no matter how much attention was given to comfort, had not been easy on his body or his mind. And nothing that had happened since his arrival in London had done anything to alleviate the tension.

Only after he shut off the shower faucet did he have the disquieting feeling he was not alone in his hotel suite. Faint sounds in the next room gave his intruder away.

His gun. It was carelessly tucked away in his trouser pocket in the bedroom next door. Very likely the gun was now in the hands of the person lurking about in there.

Blasted to hell. Couldn't anything go right for him in this insane affair? He grabbed a towel, threw it around his waist and, still dripping wet, gingerly stepped out of the shower. His eyes focused on the unlocked door, the knob turning... slowly, cautiously.

Jonathan stepped behind the door, wishing he were wearing more than a mere towel. He felt exceedingly vulnerable in his near-naked state. And chilled. The Savoy's central heating wasn't working up to par. Or perhaps his chill had nothing to do with climate control.

The door slowly opened.

Surprise was a key element, he thought, and the only one in his favor at the moment. Just as the door was opening, Jonathan reached for the brass knob and gave it a fierce tug. The door flew back with surprising ease—a reassuring indication to Jonathan of the strength of the intruder—and a gray-clad figure came lunging into the bathroom, emitting a shocked cry of alarm.

Courtney instantly found herself facedown on the cold, wet bathroom floor, a knee digging sharply into her back, her shoulders pinned by powerful male hands. It was several tense moments before Jonathan recognized his hapless intruder.

"How the hell did you get in here?" Jonathan demanded as Courtney turned her head to the side, catching his eye. Immediately he slid off her, realizing only after seeing her eyes trail down his body, her smile enticing, that his towel had come off in the scuffle. He grabbed for it as he rose to his feet.

Meanwhile Courtney had rolled over onto her back on the wet tiled floor. She was slow to sit up. She could still feel the indentation of Jonathan's knee in her spine.

"I could have bloody well hurt you, you little fool."

"You did bloody well hurt me," she snapped back.

His expression softened as he gave her a hand up.

"You can't very well blame me, sneaking in like that. How did you get in, anyway?"

"Would you be impressed if I said I picked your lock?"

"Exceedingly."

She grinned, displaying the spare key. "The desk clerk thinks I'm your wife."

Jonathan scowled.

"Come on. Admit it. You're still impressed."

"You'd better lie down for a bit," he said.

"No, I'll be okay. By tomorrow I shall be dancing my little feet off, I promise."

He smiled. "I watched your tryout. You aren't bad. Quite good, really. Very graceful. Very talented all around, I must say."

"And the pay's not bad, especially for a woman recently unemployed." She grinned. "Although I've a feeling I won't be around for opening night."

"Let's bloody well hope not." He adjusted the towel more snugly around his waist. He wasn't chilled anymore; he was quite hot suddenly. But now he was certain it had nothing to do with climate control.

He saw the silent laughter on her lips, the bold study of her eyes. He felt a quickening of his heart even as he stepped back toward the open door.

"I'll go put something on and we'll...talk," he muttered.

She had come there to talk, to have it out with Jonathan. But seeing him now, standing at the door of the bathroom, looking so sexy, passion surged through, replacing any desire to talk.

The room was pulsing with a deep sensual heat. They could both feel it.

Courtney moved toward Jonathan. The air seemed lighter, and she felt almost dizzy. She feared he was a mirage, that this was all an illusion, that if she breathed too heavily he would dissipate like dust.

He didn't dissipate, but he did break the spell as he held up a hand in silent rejection. Then he turned and headed into the bedroom, moving directly to the chair where his clothes were strewn.

Courtney followed him. "Don't you want me, Jonathan?"

He heard the anguish in her voice, even as she worked hard to conceal it. She was an exceedingly good actress, he'd discovered, but there were some occasions when she couldn't quite carry off her role to perfection.

"It has nothing to do with wanting you." He couldn't turn to face her.

"What does it have to do with?"

"It's all getting quite complicated. My mind is in turmoil." He turned slowly to her then. "My entire life is in turmoil, Courtney. Nothing's going right. I need to be clearheaded. I don't know what's going to happen, Courtney. And now, on top of all my worries, I find myself desperately concerned about your safety. I shouldn't have brought you to London. I suppose I was a bloody fool to think you'd sit quietly at Mother's while I tried to straighten out this impossible business."

"I've sat quietly about since I can remember, Jonathan. I've only truly come to life since I met you. I don't know what's going to happen any more than you do. I'm not looking for guarantees. In your business, I know they're difficult to come by."

He gave her a cautious look. "My business?"

She let out a soft peel of laughter. "You really did look adorable as a punk dancer. I wonder what other clever disguises you've employed over the years?"

"Adorable was I? Not quite the most flattering of remarks. And what do you mean, other disguises?"

"Oh, Jonathan, you needn't play the innocent professor role any longer. It never was all that convincing, anyway."

"I am a professor. A rather good one, if I do say so myself."

"And before you were a professor, Professor?"

"I've lectured on Russian literature off and on for years."

"According to your mother—"

He cut her off. "My mother has a vivid imagination. It's no wonder the two of you hit it off so well. She is quite taken with you, you know."

"I'm quite taken with her." Courtney gave him a vampish smile. "I'm quite taken with her son, as well. Despite the fact that he keeps trying to elude me at every turn."

"I'm trying to protect you," he countered, slipping his trousers on discreetly, discarding the towel only after he'd done up the zipper.

"The best way to protect me is to keep a close watch on me. Anyway, you have to admit I've done quite well up to now. Go on, admit it."

"Okay. You're good. You're a whiz with disguises. You're clever, confident, you have all the right instincts." He came to a stop, focusing directly on her for the first time. "You're ... undressing."

She'd slipped off her shoes, removed her jacket and was unzipping her skirt by the time Jonathan had come to the realization.

She let the skirt slide down her hips. "It's a lovely suit, Jonathan. It must have cost you a pretty penny. As well as the rest of the outfits. You've been very generous." She was working on the little pearl buttons of her white silk blouse.

"Courtney, stop it. If this is an attempt at seduction on your part..."

"It *is* an attempt at seduction, Jonathan." She began to slip her blouse off her shoulders.

Jonathan got to her before the blouse came off. He took hold of the silky material in none too romantic a fashion. "Get dressed." The order wasn't sharp or angry, but definitely emphatic.

With a sinking sensation in her stomach, her fingers trembling, Courtney pulled the blouse closed. What a fool she was to think she could seduce him. She might pretend all she liked to be Katherine O'Malley, but it was simply that...pretense.

Jonathan had retrieved her skirt from the carpet and was handing it to her. She felt so embarrassed by her actions that she couldn't meet Jonathan's gaze as she hurriedly stepped into her skirt. Unfortunately she lost her balance in the process and began to sway. Jonathan's strong arms came around her waist to steady her.

"You are clever, love," he said in a low voice, refusing to release her, even though she attempted to pull away. "And confident, convincing. Oh, and yes, entrancing. But with all those assets, love, you have one infuriating, frustrating fault."

He was holding her very close against his lean, muscular, naked chest. She clenched her skirt somewhere mid-knee, Jonathan giving her no leave either to pull it fully up or let it drop. She was held suspended, a position that made her pulse flutter erratically.

"And what fault is that?" she asked, her voice tremulous.

"You never give me the opportunity to do the seducing first."

"I wasn't certain...I thought...I was afraid..." She did break away from him then, pulling the waist of her skirt up over her hips. "Damn you, Jonathan, you may be a pro when it comes to undercover work in the field, but in the bedroom...well, you could be a bit more convincing."

"Oh, is that what you think?"

"And you say I'm frustrating. You tell me you want me, but it's all too complicated. You tell me to give you a chance to do the seducing, but you behave as if seducing me is the last item on your agenda. If it's on there at all. I told you, Jonathan, I've sat about for years letting life pass me by, dreaming of excitement, passion, adventure. I want the real thing now. And as neither of us has the least notion how long it's going to last, I can't very well sit about waiting for—"

He pulled her roughly into his arms. "There you go again. I see I shall have to be more convincing at this—" he paused "—oh, yes, this 'undercover work' in the bedroom, as you so colorfully put it."

"What about all those complications you were so worried about?" she whispered.

His aquamarine eyes sparkled. No hero's eyes, real or imagined, could hold a candle to those incredible, mesmerizing eyes of Jonathan's.

"What's life without a few complications?" he said. "It does make for excitement. And perhaps it's excitement that we both crave, Courtney. Excitement and danger."

"And passion."

"And passion," he agreed, his mouth moving on hers, hot, moist, demanding.

Courtney's breath caught in her throat, waves of relief and yearning coursing through her body. She sagged against him, only to find herself being drawn fully back on her own two feet the next minute.

"What . . . ?"

"I have been accused by some of being in too much of a hurry. While there are occasions, love, when rushing about is necessary to get a deed done, this is one deed that deserves a great deal of time, effort and creativity."

As he spoke he did up the buttons of her blouse with the same degree of sensuality one might use in undoing them. He was equally provocative in his movements as he smoothed down her skirt.

He moved his hands to her hair, drawing the strands back from her face. He smiled beguilingly. "You looked adorable at those auditions. That skimpy leotard displaying your lovely body. Your features so young and innocent, yet your eyes so wanton and so fully grown up. I very much wanted to seduce you on the spot. It took great effort to control myself."

"Really. That surprises me. You always manage to appear so cool, so in control."

"Stick around," he murmured, touching her lips with a whispery kiss. "There are more surprises to come."

He left her standing on shaky legs in the middle of the bedroom as he moved to the telephone. Open to any and all surprises Jonathan Madden might whip up, Courtney smiled with delight as he ordered a bottle of Dom Perignon champagne and a big dish of strawberries from room service.

"And cream. Wonderful, thick, heavy English cream," she called out.

He smiled, adding cream to the order. When he hung up the phone he reached over to the bedside radio, twisting the dials until he found some dreamy mood music.

Courtney melted into his arms as they swayed to the soft strains. Jonathan might not be Baryshnikov, but he moved with an intoxicating rhythm, his hold on her firm. There was no issue as to who was doing the leading now. Jonathan was in charge, fully in charge. And Courtney burned with exquisite passivity. *Yes, my love, my hero,* she thought, *you're absolutely right. It is your turn. And you're doing ever so good a job of it.*

She was smiling as his lips found hers mid-twirl, catching her by surprise. But, then, Jonathan had promised to be full of surprises. And she had no doubt he was a man of his word.

A knock interrupted the progress of the kiss. Jonathan gave her one more Fred Astaire twirl and went to answer the door. He brought in the tray of champagne and strawberries and cream himself and set it on a table near the window. He uncorked the bottle, letting the effervescent spray escape into the air. He poured them each a glass, while Courtney continued to move dreamily to the music alone.

He handed her a bubbling, fluted goblet, then drew his unencumbered hand around her waist. They toasted and sipped as they danced, their movements slowing with each swallow.

"I've never gotten drunk in the afternoon," Courtney announced after a second refill. She closed her eyes, feeling a rush of warmth from the champagne and Jonathan's nearness spread through her body.

He allowed her one sip from the refill before taking the goblet from her hand.

"What are you doing?"

He smiled. "Drunk won't do, love. I can't very well prove my worth if you go and pass out on me."

"Am I allowed to get drunk on the strawberries, then?"

"They're very juicy. We wouldn't want you to stain that lovely silk blouse purchased by a man with such fine taste."

"And extravagance."

"I'm not often so extravagant."

"I'm glad."

He undid each button on her blouse, pausing to press a kiss to her newly exposed skin each time. Smiling, he drew the blouse from her shoulders.

To reward her loveliness, Jonathan fed her the plumpest strawberry dipped in cream. The juice from the fruit trickled down her chin. Jonathan caught it with his tongue. She laughed, the sensation erotic and ticklish at the same time. He fed her another strawberry, his other hand releasing the catch on her bra. And then, between strawberries, he removed the rest of her clothes.

Naked on the carpet of the Savoy Hotel in London, eating strawberries and drinking champagne with the hero of her dreams. Really it was quite extraordinary. Quite the most wonderful, magical experience Courtney Blue could imagine. Far more than she'd ever imagined. Jonathan was taking her beyond her dreams to uncharted worlds.

She stretched out on the carpet, smiling joyfully. Taking his hand, she kissed the palm, then closed her eyes as his lips met hers. The taste of the deliciously ripe cream-laced strawberries and the finest champagne was a most felicitous combination.

Jonathan rose on his knees, his mouth moving down her body, leaving a ribbon of fever across her belly, between her thighs. His hands cupped her full, high breasts, the point of his tongue flicking across the hard, hot buds. Then he moved his whole tongue across them in swift strokes that made Courtney cry out.

Electric surges whipped through her body as she entwined her legs around him in glorious abandon. Jonathan could feel his control evaporating as her thighs locked around his hips. Sensations rolled like thunder charges upward from his groin, engulfing him, the muscles quivering beneath his skin.

He maneuvered her on top of him, his large hands grasping her slender waist as she leaned back against his knees, her head falling back, neck arched, mouth open in soundless cries of passion. Their bodies trembled, straining for release. Perspiration dampened their skin as they dissolved into the timeless rhythm. Courtney felt herself expanding, mind, body, spirit, as she felt his fullness inside her. And when he emitted a deep, shuddering moan she experienced the breath of his pleasure, and answered with a shimmering golden sigh of her own.

"That was wonderful," he whispered. "You're wonderful. I've never met anyone like you."

Courtney thrilled to the admission. Her soft laughter mingled with a sigh of delight as his head moved and his lips lightly circled around one breast.

"Let's go to bed," he murmured, sharing one last strawberry from the bowl, which now rested on the carpet along with the nearly empty bottle of champagne.

She gazed at him coyly. "Isn't that offer a trifle anticlimactic?"

He laughed, pulling her up with him. "I can't get enough of you."

"Jonathan, would you really have left me to languish at your mother's?"

His laughter vanished. He met her gaze evenly. "Yes."

Her eyes widened. "Oh."

He buried his face in her soft, silken hair. "For your own protection, love." He moved his head back, tilting hers up, and kissed her tenderly.

"But now that I'm in *Fanfare* and I've infiltrated—"

He brushed her lips. "You must promise me one thing. That you will do nothing but observe and report back to me. Give me your word."

*I give you my love, Jonathan, will that do?* "Yes, Jonathan," she whispered.

*I do love him,* she thought as the words played over and over in her mind. Incredible, unrealistic, impossible...but true. *Jonathan knows. He knows and he doesn't want to hear.* She was sure of it. He was offering her excitement and passion. Not permanence. Wasn't that enough? She had to smile. Enough? It was more than she'd had in a lifetime.

"What's so amusing?" he asked, taken aback by her sudden shift of mood.

She drew her arms tightly around his neck, her eyes shining, her skin glistening with a moisture that was as much his as it was hers. "Let's go to bed."

THE FOLLOWING AFTERNOON, in various quarters in London, a number of people found a particular interest in a small ad in the personal column of the newspaper. It read: "Membership open to new Friends of Gorky. Fee negotiable. Next meeting—the Ambassador Club, nine tonight. Ask for button at door."

"WHEN DO WE STOP this irritating game of hide-and-seek, Daniel? I expected to see you at the Garrick." Christine gripped the telephone so tightly her knuckles were white. "And what's to happen to Marcus if Jonathan is telling the truth and the parcel has been stolen. I warn you, Daniel, if any harm comes to Marcus..."

"Darling Christine, you know very well that I abhor threats."

"Receiving them, anyway. You're quite amenable to making them."

Husky laughter traveled through the wire. "Ah, Christine, you are amusing. And quite accurate. What you must realize, though, my dear, is that when I make threats I carry them out. I always carry them out."

A cold shiver assaulted her spine. "Daniel, please..."

"That's better. Now as for Marcus, I assure you he's quite comfortable. And perhaps his unexpected vacation will soon be over."

The shiver turned into an icy chill. "What do you mean?"

Again the husky laugh rang out. "Not what you think, darling. I simply mean that the parcel may soon be mine, despite our professor having let us down."

"Who has it?"

"I haven't the vaguest idea."

"But you just said . . ."

"I want you to do me a favor, Christine. I want you to go out on the town tonight. Find yourself a nice young man to wine and dine you at the Ambassador Club. . . on me, of course. Oh, and when you go in, ask at the front desk for a club button. Display it on your gown. If all goes well, someone will come along wearing a matching button for identification and the two of you will go off to the terrace to begin negotiations for the parcel we both covet so dearly."

"And you?"

"Oh, I'll be close by, love. You need have no worry about that. Or any traitorous thoughts, either. Remember what I said about my threats, dear Christine. Cross me and your charming lover, Marcus Lloyd, will be taking a permanent vacation."

ZAKHAROV THOUGHT LONGINGLY of his samovar at home in Kiev as he swallowed the foul-tasting English coffee, then held the mug up for a refill. This was to be his last assignment in the field. Fifteen years of service, fifteen years away from his homeland, fifteen years of cunning, superior achievement, brilliant accomplishments. He was the best. This was his last assignment, and if he was not careful, it might be his first failure. Even after fifteen years of superb service, this failure could cost him everything he had hoped for, everything he had dreamed of. He swept his hand across the table in disgust, mindless of the mug he was holding. Coffee flew out onto Borofsky, who'd just finished pouring his own cup.

Borofsky cried out in pain as the steaming coffee splashed his shirt and the hot liquid burned his skin beneath. Zakharov seemed oblivious, his lips censorious, grim, full of distaste. He pounded his fist on the table. In another moment, Borofsky thought, perhaps he would remove his shoe and pound that.

Zakharov's cold eyes glittered with rage. Borofsky feared the worst. And the worst might well have occurred if Zakharov's henchman, Goncharov, hadn't entered the room at that moment. He had a newspaper in his hand and he was smiling. To see Goncharov smile, that was quite a sight.

"Isn't the Ambassador one of those private clubs?" Lou asked, looking up from the personal column.

Andrea smiled. "Yes, but all we need to do is pay a membership fee."

"A pretty hefty one, I bet."

"That's no problem."

Lou frowned. "It is to me. I'm beginning to feel like a kept man."

He saw the look of hurt on her face and was immediately sorry. He touched her cheek, a tender smile on his lips. "I've never been to a private London club before. How nice, after all these years, to be a member of the 'in' group."

Andrea pressed her hand over Lou's. "I'm growing very fond of you," she murmured.

Lou smiled, but a disquieting feeling lurked beneath the surface of that smile. He was out of his league here. Oh, he'd been out of his league before, but that was different. This was personal. This was dangerous. He found Andrea Lambert very appealing. Too appealing. Andrea Lambert, who could pay her way into any club, live lavishly at the Claridge, buy anything her little heart desired. In a way she had even bought him.

"Lou? What's wrong?"

"Nothing."

"We'd better go."

"Where? It's way too early."

"You'll need a tux for a place like the Ambassador."

"Oh. Well…I'll arrange with the desk clerk to rent one."

She smiled demurely. "Darling, no one wears rented tuxes at the Ambassador. You'll stick out like a sore thumb. And after all, if we're going to negotiate with that bastard, we must both look confident, well off. You know what I'm saying."

He nodded and answered quietly, "Yes, I know."


"JONATHAN, YOU HAVE TO take me to the Ambassador Club with you."

"Courtney, you have to be a member." As if such a weak excuse would deter her.

"Well, you're a member, right?"

"No. My mother is the member. Another perk she received from her divorce. I will be Mother's guest."

"I'm sure Lady Edith won't mind bringing along two guests."

"Courtney, you're dead, remember? If any of our chums spot you at the club they'll be on you like flypaper, since they might well think you've got the manuscript."

She raised one brow, her eyes sparkling. It was a look that made Jonathan uneasy.

"Courtney Blue may be dead, but Katherine O'Malley is alive and well."

"Whatever happened to Harriet Oberchon?"

"She's in mourning, the poor dear. Besides, I have more of an affinity for Katherine."

Jonathan emitted a low, weary sigh.

"I've never been to a private London club. You can't deny me the experience. You simply can't."

He stared at her in silence for a long moment. "What worries me, love, is that I don't seem able to deny you anything."

She grinned devilishly, slipping her arms around his neck. "Well, you haven't had reason to complain so far, have you?"

## CHAPTER THIRTEEN

"MY DEAR, YOU LOOK positively glorious. Like a fairy-tale queen." Little did Lady Edith know how influenced Courtney was by the stuff of fairy tales and novels of high romance and adventure.

"But there's one final touch...." Lady Edith opened a velvet-lined jewel box to reveal an exquisite jade necklace with a cluster of rose-cut diamonds in the center creating a flower effect.

Courtney emitted a little gasp as Lady Edith slipped it around her neck. "I couldn't.... It's far too valuable. I've never seen anything so lovely."

"It's the perfect finishing touch, my dear Katherine," Lady Edith said with a wink. "As for its value, it's well insured. You have nothing to worry about." She smiled. "I expect my son will be dazzled."

Courtney's eyes shone. "Will he?"

Lady Edith took several steps back and surveyed Courtney with a look that held both admiration and even a touch of envy. The transformation really was quite amazing. Before her stood a radiant young woman of grace and beauty.

Courtney had put a lot of effort and time into that transformation. She'd used some of her CIA funds that afternoon for a visit to one of London's poshest hair salons. She'd wanted something exotic and dazzling done with her drab sandy-blond locks, but the stylist had insisted understatement would ultimately be best. He gave her hair a rinse that didn't so much change the color as bring out the ash-blond strands and highlight the threads of gold. As for the style itself, the man drew her hair back much as she had done for the *Fanfare* audition, but instead of a ponytail, he'd created a chignon, letting tiny curls of hair escape in delicate wisps across her forehead and in front of her ears. While the style was simple, the effect was dramatic, especially when coupled with the teal-blue chiffon evening gown with a strapless bodice, whose soft material draped over her breasts.

"You look like an eighteenth-century beauty who might well have posed for Gainsborough," Lady Edith said.

"I do hope Jonathan will be dazzled." Courtney turned back to the full-length mirror in Lady Edith's sumptuous boudoir. Lady Edith looked on over her right shoulder, a faint frown marring her otherwise smooth brow.

"What is it? What's wrong? Have I overlooked something?" Courtney asked with true concern. She wanted to appear as perfect as possible for tonight, forgetting for the moment the danger and thinking only of the look of pleasure she hoped to see in Jonathan's eyes.

Lady Edith smiled quickly. "No, my dear. You haven't overlooked a thing."

"Then... what is it? What's worrying you?"

As Courtney turned to her, Lady Edith caught hold of both her hands gently. "I like you, Courtney. I think you're a rather splendid young woman. Full of spirit and fire." She paused, then her frown deepened. "And perhaps innocence."

Courtney smiled. "I'm not all that innocent, Lady Edith."

"I mean in the ways of the world. Of Jonathan's world," she added pointedly.

"Oh. Well... it's true I've led a pretty ordinary life." Courtney had lowered her voice, the lightness and expectation gone from it suddenly. "I suppose what you're saying is that I'm way out of my class. I suppose no amount of fine clothing, expensive jewels or fancy hairstyles can alter that. It's all pretense, isn't it? And after the masquerade ball is over, I'm Cinderella once again, aren't I? Not quite the match you'd hoped for Jonathan, I expect."

Lady Edith gripped Courtney's hands almost harshly now. "You silly child, you've completely misunderstood me. Why, you must think me an awful snob. That isn't at all what I meant. You don't know Jonathan very well."

"I'm getting to know him."

Lady Edith observed her closely. "You're very fond of him, aren't you?"

"Yes."

"And he of you?"

"I . . . hope so. I think so."

"Yes." Lady Edith smiled. "I imagine so."

"And that disturbs you?"

There was a long silence. "No, my dear. What disturbs me is that I truly don't want to see you hurt. And I believe my son could hurt you."

"Hurt me?" All the exuberance and excitement she'd been feeling was quickly evaporating.

"Courtney, my son has made an art of . . ." She paused. "I suppose detachment is the best word. He's never let himself get very close to any woman. Not that there haven't been those who have tried to persuade Jonathan otherwise."

Courtney swallowed. "Have there been many women?"

Lady Edith softly patted Courtney's shoulder. "Jonathan is very handsome, charming, quite well off as those things go. And, of course, there's that air of mystery about him. He has what you might call a magnetic appeal. But you know that as well as I."

A wry smile curved Courtney's lips. "If I read between the lines, Lady Edith, the fact is women are attracted to him like flies to flypaper."

"Jonathan likes women. He truly does. There's a respect and a tenderness there. And yet..." Again she paused. "He seems determined not to let any of them get too close. You, my dear Courtney, have gotten closer than most. Which is why I'm afraid you'll get more greatly hurt than most. That reason and also you seem the sensitive, passionate sort of woman. The kind of woman capable of a great love."

Courtney felt her cheeks warm. *Capable of a great love*... Yes, it was true. But what good was it to be capable of a great love if her hero was determined to reject it at all costs?

Lady Edith gave Courtney a light peck on the cheek. "We're very much alike, we two. I've had my passions, you know. I feel things very deeply. And my grief. I don't want to spoil the magical spell I can see you are under, my dear, but for your own sake, do keep it in perspective."

There was a firm rap on the bedroom door. "Are you two women ever going to be ready? It's one thing to be fashionably late..."

"We're quite ready, Jonathan," Lady Edith said after opening the door and sweeping past him.

"Good." He looked into the room and saw Courtney for the first time. Or it seemed to him it was the first time. "Hello, what's this?" he said, slowly stepping into the room and shutting the door, leaving Lady Edith to wait at the foot of the sweeping staircase, a smile on her face. Perhaps her son had finally met his Waterloo, she thought with a flicker of hope.

Courtney stood in the center of the room, frozen, as Jonathan surveyed her.

"Will I...do?" she whispered.

Jonathan continued his intense study, not answering.

"I mean... do I look different enough from Courtney Blue?"

As he stood there gazing at her, Jonathan was conscious of experiencing a strange feeling, one he couldn't quite identify. All he knew was that the feeling left him breathless and bedazzled, yet oddly disturbed at the same time.

"You are a true chameleon, Miss Courtney Blue," he finally murmured. "You take my breath away."

She smiled tremulously. Her pulse quickened. "I was hoping I would." In her anxiety about Jonathan's reaction to her appearance she'd been unable to focus on how splendid he looked in his beautifully tailored white tux jacket and black trousers. He was even more handsome, if that was possible, than ever before.

He moved across the room toward her. He had the rapid, graceful gait of a man in control wherever he found himself, Courtney thought. Little did she know how very out of control he really was feeling at the moment.

Without a word and with no regard at all for her careful grooming, he pulled her greedily into his arms, ravaging her mouth with an urgency he had never felt before. He had already possessed her body, but in that one fierce kiss he felt as if he were taking possession of her soul. And when she kissed him back with equal fire and sheer abandon, he thought, again with a flash of unease, that she was taking possession of his soul, as well.

He pulled away at last. *I'm no good at love,* he acknowledged with a wave of despair that showed with sharp clarity in his features.

Ironically, despite having seen that look of despair in Jonathan's face, Courtney felt buoyed. It was as if they had crossed an invisible barrier. In that instant Courtney felt changed forever. And no matter what eventually happened between them, she felt certain that Jonathan, too, was irrevocably changed.

As HE MILLED ABOUT the suavely dressed men and elegantly clothed women at the Ambassador Club, Jonathan made a concerted effort to focus his attention on the task at hand, which was to ferret out the "Friends of Gorky." *Negotiations are in the works,* he thought, *and I intend to be in on them.* But as he tried to charge himself up with the excitement he would normally have experienced, he was still reeling from those few moments with Courtney in his mother's bedroom.

Even as he tried to keep a distance from Courtney, who was being introduced around by his mother as the dear daughter of a close friend of hers from the States, he kept edging closer and closer to her without realizing it.

He was in a peculiar state of mind. As much as he concentrated on searching out the villains, his gaze kept drifting to Courtney, who looked utterly ravishing and was handling herself among this elite, cosmopolitan crowd as though she'd been born to it. Who was the real Courtney Blue, he wondered. As he'd suspected from the start, she was far more than an ordinary shop girl. Tonight she was far, very far, from that ordinary shop girl. Tonight she had stolen his heart.

His gaze drifted over to her again, this time catching a look from her that was filled with meaning. She made a faint motion with her head toward the dance floor. Clearly she wanted to have a word with him.

Jonathan hesitated. He thought of the last time they had danced together, in his suite at the Savoy, and a tremor of longing shot through him. He was almost afraid to dance with her now, fearing he'd lose control again.

Courtney's look turned insistent and he realized he was behaving like an absolute idiot. He strode purposefully over to her, took her formally by the hand and led her to the dance floor.

If Courtney sensed the difference in how he held her now, she didn't show it. She was far too excited by the news she had to impart. "Jonathan, I saw the two Russians over near the bar. And that dark-haired actress with the lead in *Fanfare*."

"Her name's Christine Dupré."

"French?"

He nodded. "Did any of them see you?"

Courtney's eyes sparkled. "They saw Katherine O'Malley. They saw her and didn't blink an eye of recognition."

"Well, it's best to keep your distance from them." He paused. "And perhaps it would be best to keep your distance from me, as well, while we're here. I'm certain Andrea Lambert will be showing up soon to work out a deal for the manuscript."

"And my uncle?"

He looked down at her with a solemn expression. "If, as we believe, she's holding him against his will, I doubt we'll be seeing him here tonight."

Her arm slipped higher around his neck, and despite his effort to keep a courtly distance between them as they danced, she moved close against him. "Thank you, Jonathan," she whispered in his ear. Then she kissed him fleetingly on the neck.

"Steady on," he said in a voice that made Courtney laugh. "What are you thanking me for?" he muttered, realizing that he was continuing to behave like an idiot.

"For saying, 'as we believe,'" she replied softly. "Do you mean that, Jonathan?" And then before he could answer, she went suddenly stiff in his arms, her feet frozen solidly in place.

Jonathan nearly lost his balance in the process. He gave her a baffled look, surprised to see her lovely rose-cheeked complexion almost ashen. Her eyes were wide with shock as she looked not at him, but over his shoulder toward the entrance of the club.

Jonathan managed with some effort to maneuver her a little to the right so that he could see what had caused her such upset.

There, stepping into the club, was the middle-aged Andrea Lambert, looking especially alluring, her slender, small frame encased in a very expensive black satin evening gown trimmed around the low-cut bodice with thin gold braid. But it was not the sight of Andrea Lambert that was disturbing Courtney, Jonathan saw. It was the man beside her. The man whose arm was draped quite affectionately over Andrea Lambert's shoulder. The man Andrea Lambert was regarding with obvious warmth. Courtney's uncle, Lou Vaughn. The man he had just told Courtney he believed was an innocent victim of circumstance. Well, Lou Vaughn did not look particularly innocent at the moment. And anything but a victim.

Courtney was trembling. Jonathan was afraid she would pass out on the spot.

"Steady on, love," he whispered, gripping her more firmly around the waist. "We've got to get you out of here. I'll have Mother take you home."

Courtney was too traumatized to protest, much to Jonathan's relief. Actually she was too traumatized to hear what Jonathan was saying.

He was guiding her off the dance floor, when a man approached from behind, his hands coming down on Jonathan's shoulders.

"Jonathan Madden, it's been bloody ages, old man."

Jonathan knew the voice without turning round. Avery Noble. Well, well, the major players were out on the town tonight.

Because Jonathan made no effort to face Noble, his one-time colleague was forced to move around to face him.

"Aren't you going to introduce me to your exquisite companion, Madden?"

Courtney stared numbly at the tall, balding man who, after giving her a rather thorough, appreciative and smiling once-over, had transferred his smile to Jonathan. His manner was smooth, but the smile held a hint of malice.

"Avery Noble, Katherine O'Malley. The daughter of one of Mother's close friends in the States." Jonathan had no idea which state his mother had chosen. Not that it mattered. Avery Noble knew very well Katherine's real identity.

Avery extended his right hand. When Courtney made no move, he merely caught hold of her upper arm lightly but persuasively and glanced over at Jonathan. "Perhaps I can steal your lovely companion away for one dance, Madden."

Jonathan's expression was cool, but beneath the surface he was seething. He knew Noble's game. The man wanted to get to know Courtney better now that Uncle Lou was making his move. Avery probably suspected she was involved in the operation.

"Miss O'Malley isn't feeling well," Jonathan said smoothly. "A headache, right, love?"

Forcing herself out of her numbed state, Courtney managed a vague nod. There was something immediately unappealing about this Mr. Noble. And it was plain to see that Jonathan disliked the man immensely.

Jonathan drew his arm around Courtney's waist. "Come on, darling," he said with a concern that was not fabricated. "Mother is waiting to take you home." He gave Avery a cold stare.

Typical of Noble, he let a few tense moments pass before removing his hold on Courtney. "Ah, you're staying with Lady Edith, then, Miss...O'Malley?" As he spoke his eyes drifted over her shoulder, his gaze cool and steady.

Instinctively Courtney knew Avery Noble was eyeing her
uncle. Just as she instinctively knew this man was a player
in the business at hand, even if she couldn't sort out exactly
what role he was playing. Or even what team he was on. If
Jonathan's response to the man was an indication, however, Courtney would bet he wasn't with the good guys. It
took all her willpower not to turn around and make contact
with her uncle—contact that would somehow warn him he
was in danger. Contact that would let him know she did not,
for one moment, despite the damning evidence, believe he
was guilty of any wrongdoing. Surely there was a good explanation.

Noble was staring at her expectantly. Only then did she
realize she hadn't answered his question. Just as she was
about to respond, Jonathan answered for her.

"Yes, Avery. She's my mother's guest for the next few
days."

"And then?" The man was nothing if not persistent.

"Miss O'Malley will be returning home very shortly."

Courtney shot Jonathan a quick look but said nothing.

Avery Noble's gaze kept shifting from Courtney and
Jonathan to other areas of the room. "Let's have a drink
after you see to Miss O'Malley, Jonathan. We can catch up
on current events." It wasn't an invitation but a command.

Jonathan made no indication one way or the other
whether he would show up as ordered. He merely started
off.

"Always a pleasure, Madden."

Avery Noble's farewell had a distinct bite to it.

So did Jonathan's silence.

At a safe distance from Noble, Courtney spoke as she
scanned the room for her uncle. Neither he nor the Lambert woman were anywhere to be found. "I'm not leaving,
Jonathan."

"This is not open for discussion, Courtney," Jonathan told her grimly.

" 'Katherine,' " she reminded him.

"As of now, Katherine is retired."

"Jonathan..."

He was already motioning to his mother, who, catching the tense expression on her son's face, immediately excused herself from her group of friends and came over to him.

"Courtney has a splitting headache, Mother. I'd very much appreciate your seeing her home, if you would."

"I do not have—" Jonathan gave her forearm a firm squeeze. She stopped speaking, aware this was one time she was not going to be able to persuade Jonathan to let her have her way.

Lady Edith's gaze swung from Jonathan to Courtney. "I'm so sorry you're not feeling well, my dear. We can leave immediately." She glanced over at Jonathan, whose face bore signs of relief. "Shall we call a cab and leave you the Bentley, dear?"

"No, I'll see to myself, Mother. You take the car. And do go straight home and see that our friend gets tucked in for the night."

He was still holding Courtney's arm, but more gently now. "It will be all right. Don't worry."

"Will I see you later?"

He nodded.

"You promise?"

He hesitated a moment. "I'll try my best."

"All right..." She sighed. "I won't rest until I do hear from you, though."

"You'll be okay."

"I'm not worried about myself," she said pointedly.

He kissed her lightly on the cheek. "I know." He motioned to his mother to escort Courtney from the club.

Once outside, waiting for the Bentley to be brought around Courtney took a few deep breaths, while Lady Edith looked on with both concern and curiosity.

"I do so hate being kept in the dark, my dear."

Courtney smiled softly. "I'm afraid it isn't much lighter where I'm standing."

A few minutes later, settled in the luxurious leather interior of the Bentley, Lady Edith behind the wheel, Courtney began to feel like her old self again. "Damn the man," she muttered.

Lady Edith drove the Bentley around Berkeley Square. Usually rather a hellion behind the wheel, her pace tonight was deliberately slow. "I take it you're referring to my son."

"Sorry."

"No, no. I've muttered the same myself upon occasion."

Courtney glanced over at Lady Edith and tried to smile. "I'm terribly worried," she admitted.

Steering toward the curb, Lady Edith brought the big car to a stop a moment later. "Tell me about it, my dear. You were clearly reluctant to leave the club. Why?" Lady Edith had obviously decided the time had come for a more forthright approach.

The approach proved effective. Courtney hesitated for only a moment before launching into a summarized version of the whole affair—omitting the more intimate details involving her and Jonathan. Details a woman as perceptive as Lady Edith did not need to have recounted.

"So you see," Courtney finished a scant ten minutes later, "why I didn't want to leave the club. I know there's a logical explanation as to why my uncle showed up arm in arm with that diabolical woman. I need to speak with him. I need to warn him. There are more dangerous characters at that club tonight than I care to count."

"Which is why," Lady Edith felt compelled to say, "Jonathan wanted you out of there."

Courtney sighed. "I've held my own so far." She hesitated. "This may come as somewhat of a shock, Lady Edith, but I'm quite convinced Jonathan is secretly an undercover agent with SIS. I believe Marcus Lloyd was his colleague, most likely his boss."

"I'm not the least bit shocked, my dear. I came to the same conclusion myself."

Courtney hesitated again.

"Yes, go on," the older woman encouraged.

"Well, I hope you won't be offended, Lady Edith, but I don't get the feeling that Jonathan is . . . well, that he's all that . . . adept at the work. I mean . . . he's rather mucked things up, as you might say."

Lady Edith laughed. "Yes, I might put it that way. Although my guess is real-life spies very likely muck up a great deal more than their fictional counterparts. I happen to be a great fan of spy novels and I do so admire the way those heroes always seem to come out on top of things." Her smile vanished. "I only hope Jonathan will manage to do the same."

"I wish he'd let me help him. He does need my help, Lady Edith. And so does my uncle. I'm good at this. Really I am. And yet I'm being sent off to bed like a child. It isn't fair. It simply isn't fair."

Lady Edith tapped her fingers on the mahogany steering wheel. "I do hate to ask this, my dear, but what if your uncle . . ."

"He isn't," Courtney said firmly.

Lady Edith nodded. Then after a moment she said, "It does seem rather unfair. After all, you have been involved from the start. Personally, when I begin a task I like to see it through to its end. And I imagine you feel the same."

"Oh, very much so."

"Yes," Lady Edith said. "Yes, of course you do."

"Then you'll drive me back to the club?"

Lady Edith took time to inspect Courtney thoroughly. "If Jonathan sees a beautiful blond in a teal-blue chiffon evening gown flitting about the club, I'm afraid there'll be hell to pay for both of us."

Courtney shifted position. "I've got rather a flare for disguise, if I do say so myself. Earlier this evening Jonathan said I was a chameleon."

Lady Edith nodded slowly, as if lost in thought. "Well, we haven't much time. There's no telling when the fireworks will begin. We shall return to the club immediately, but we'll enter through the rear entrance this time. Tell me, my dear, how are you at cocktail waitressing?"

Courtney grinned. "I've never done it in my life."

"Oh."

"But that shouldn't present any problems. You'd be surprised how quickly I learn."

Lady Edith cocked her head and laughed. "No, I don't think that would surprise me in the least, my dear."

# CHAPTER FOURTEEN

THE MANAGER of the Ambassador Club was not about to question the whim of one of his most prestigious patrons. Courtney was "hired" on the spot as a temporary waitress. She hurried through the kitchen to the employees' changing room, clutching her black uniform, white apron and cap. There, the exquisite gown was tossed aside, the jeweled necklace hidden by the high-collared severe black waitress dress. She exchanged the Cinderella slippers for a pair of serviceable black oxfords that were only a size too large, and the hairdo that had been so painstakingly styled was briskly combed out and frizzed. Courtney was nearly set. For a final touch she scrubbed her face clean of the subtly applied cosmetics she'd labored over earlier this evening, and borrowed dark eyeliner, red lipstick and rouge from one of the other waitresses, putting the new makeup on in a distinctly heavy-handed manner.

Checking herself in the mirror, even she was a bit startled by the striking change in her appearance. Her features had a purposefully hard edge to them. With the teased hairdo and the uniform, she had the look of a woman from the wrong side of London's tracks who'd seen plenty and knew plenty. Courtney was delighted with the effect.

Stepping out of the ladies' changing room, Courtney almost collided with another waitress, who was just picking up a tray of hors d'oeuvres from the kitchen.

"Sorry. I didn't—" Courtney stopped mid-sentence as the woman turned and gave her a bright smile.

"No problem, dearie. You must be new 'ere," the woman said with a broad wink and a thick cockney accent.

Courtney blinked several times. "Lady Edith . . . ?"

"Edie, love. Just Edie to me friends." She gave her black uniform, a copy of Courtney's, a little tug at the hips. "What do you think?"

Without thinking, however, Courtney gasped, "You're crazy."

Lady Edith laughed. "You didn't really expect that I'd elect to miss out on all the excitement."

"But . . . Jonathan . . ."

A slight shadow fell across Lady Edith's face. "I've already done a turn through the club and Jonathan didn't bat an eye. He's rather involved in—" she leaned a little closer and whispered conspiratorially "—spying."

Lady Edith picked up one tray and Courtney another. "Just to be on the safe side," Courtney said, "let's keep our distance from each other out front."

Balancing the tray quite adeptly on one upturned hand, Lady Edith gave a little salute with the other.

Courtney smiled. "You make an impressive waitress . . . Edie."

"More years back than I care to remember, I played a waitress in a parish players' production," Lady Edith explained. Then shifting back to her cockney accent she added, "I practiced for bloody hours doing this. Who would have imagined it would ever come in handy again?" She took off through the swinging door marked Out, leaving Courtney smiling.

Courtney's smile disappeared as soon as she stepped into the main room of the club and spotted Jonathan. Now she understood the faint look of consternation on "Edie's" face a few moments earlier. Jonathan was too busy to take much notice of a couple of waitresses, all right. His attentions were sharply focused on the dark-haired actress, Christine

Dupré. The two of them were dancing to a romantic little tune off to one side of the dance floor. Forcing her eyes off the cozy twosome, Courtney saw her uncle and Andrea Lambert dancing nearby. They looked pretty cozy themselves.

Courtney started walking along the perimeter of the dance floor, offering hors d'oeuvres to the club members in a distracted fashion. Her eyes kept straying back to Jonathan and Christine even as she searched for the two Russians, before finding them over at the bar. They both had clear liquid drinks in their hands, which Courtney guessed to be vodka. And from the slightly tilted way they were both standing, she concluded that they'd already tucked a few vodkas away.

"May I?"

Courtney turned as a male hand reached out toward the tray and plucked a cracker topped with pâté. She looked up to see Avery Noble scrutinizing her.

"Are you new here?"

Courtney gave a brief nod and started off. But Noble took a step after her. "I've been noticing you walking about."

Courtney stiffened as she continued walking, and Noble followed her. It took great effort to keep her eyes from drifting over to the dance floor where Jonathan and Christine were still entwined.

"You do look rather familiar," Noble went on. "Where did you work before coming here?"

Courtney was afraid she was going to have to try out a cockney accent herself, when she was saved by the wash of people leaving the dance floor as the song ended. She quickly scooted out of the way of several couples, hoping to dodge Noble in the process. She needn't have worried. He'd suddenly lost interest in her and was hurrying through the crowd in the direction of the terrace, where a number of couples were heading for a breath of air. Among them were

Jonathan and Christine and Andrea and Uncle Lou. Look-ing increasingly worse for wear, the two Russians bumped into several people as they, too, made their way across the club to the terrace.

Spotting Lady Edith about twenty yards away, Courtney gave her a subtle nod. The next moment, both of them were heading in the same direction as the others.

Courtney, however, didn't make it to her destination. Just as she was approaching the French doors, who should come walking back inside but Jonathan. She hurried to step out of his sight, but luck wasn't with her. Jonathan not only kept her in his line of vision but was moving directly, pur-posefully, toward her.

"Excuse me, miss. The bar's rather crowded and I'd like a glass of white wine for my lady friend. Would you bring one out to the terrace?"

Eyes downcast, Courtney gave a little nod and turned, letting out a low gasp of shock as she felt Jonathan pinch her buttock.

"Do be quick about it, if you would. That's a good girl," he whispered, adding insult to injury with a firm pat on the same spot that he'd pinched.

For a moment Courtney felt certain he'd seen through her disguise and was ribbing her. But as she shot him a quick look, she did not see the faintest glimmer of recognition in his dazzling aquamarine eyes. Steaming, she went off to get the drink for his "lady friend," contemplating an added dose of poison. Not only was she angry about his flirta-tious little moves with the enemy and the "help," but now she was forced to take a detour over to the bar. It would likely take several minutes to get that damn drink and by then . . . well, anything could happen.

A faint smile curved Jonathan's mouth as he stepped back out to the terrace. The smile deepened as he saw Christine Dupré furtively exiting the terrace via the stone steps that led down to the garden. Just as he had expected, she was not alone. Andrea Lambert and Lou Vaughn were accompanying her. Jonathan gave the threesome a small head start, then took off after them.

Courtney came to a sudden halt a few feet from the bar. She hadn't gone to all this trouble to miss out on the action. Swiping a temporarily abandoned full glass of wine off a nearby table, Courtney raced back over to the terrace doors.

Once outside, neither Jonathan nor her uncle were anywhere to be found, but she did spot the two Russians, who were also looking with bafflement around the terrace. Lady Edith hurried over to Courtney's side. "Jonathan took off a minute ago," she said, pointing to the steps.

Courtney handed her the wineglass. "How would you like a specific assignment, Edie?"

"Why, dearie, that would be ducky," Lady Edith quipped.

Courtney pointed out the Russians, who were crossing the terrace toward the stairs none too surefootedly. "Do you suppose you could come up with some way to head them off?"

Lady Edith took a fast swallow of the wine and nodded firmly. "I think I can manage that."

Courtney hurried away, beating the Russians to the stairs. Just as she started down them, she heard a loud shriek behind her.

"Why, of all the bloody cheek!" Lady Edith was shouting. "Just what kind of a girl do you think I am, you dirty old sot? Bloody cheek, I tell you. I'm a nice girl, I am. I've a good mind to see you tossed out on your ear for saying such things."

Courtney glanced back to see Lady Edith gripping the jacket of the Russian she was verbally attacking, while his comrade looked on with a helpless expression. Several patrons were gathering around for the show and before Courtney was out of earshot someone from management was rushing over to see what all the commotion was about.

Courtney laughed to herself as she went in search of Jonathan and her uncle. Unfortunately she had no idea in which direction they'd gone and she was forced to wander around the verdant grounds for a good ten minutes before having any luck.

It was the faint sound of voices that drew her to a shoulder-high hedgerow beyond which ran the Thames. The voices were coming from the far side of the hedge. As she drew closer, she recognized her uncle's voice, but she wasn't near enough to hear his words. A few steps farther and she was able to make out the shadowy image of three people. Her uncle was no longer talking. A female silhouette, her voice agitated, had broken in. Courtney was close enough now to hear what she was saying.

"Mr. Vaughn will make no such deal until our terms are met. You can tell whomever you're representing that we have what he wants, but he will not see it until we first have exactly what we want."

"Take it easy, Andrea." This came from Uncle Lou. "I'm sure the lady here is eager to resolve any differences. Let's keep a positive attitude."

Courtney took a few more steps, trying to keep hidden behind the hedgerow. Some twigs crackled beneath her feet and instantly the group on the other side was silent. Courtney dropped to her knees, breath held, as she pressed herself hard against the shrubs, attempting to blend into the greenery. The damp from the cool earth seeped through her uniform.

"I think we better continue our talk in a more private place."

This statement came from a third voice, throaty and very feminine. Courtney was pretty sure she knew what dark-haired beautiful stage star that voice belonged to.

"I have my car," Lou said. "Maybe the best bet is for us to follow you to your boss. I don't negotiate with underlings, even very attractive ones."

"I'll have to make a phone call" came the throaty reply.

"Do that. We'll meet you in the parking lot. I'd like to settle this affair as quickly as possible. As I'm sure your boss would, too."

My God, Courtney thought with mounting dismay, Uncle Lou certainly wasn't behaving like the poor innocent dupe she believed him to be. He seemed disturbingly savvy and very much in charge of the negotiations. Distress gave way to panic as she heard the three start to move toward the break in the hedge, just ten yards from where she was hiding. As soon as they came through that opening they'd surely spot her.

Scrambling on hands and feet, she went racing for a fair-sized flowering shrub and fell breathlessly behind it. Just as she was about to let out a relieved sigh, her breath once again caught in her throat as she felt a hand come over her mouth.

"Don't bellow" came a harsh but familiar voice as an arm encircled her waist tightly.

Didn't he realize she had no strength to bellow, she thought as she leaned against Jonathan limply.

Jonathan removed his hand from her mouth.

"They're leaving" she managed to gasp.

"I know." They could both hear the footsteps drawing closer and Jonathan made a gesture for her to remain perfectly still.

The threesome came frighteningly close to the shrub that just barely concealed her and Jonathan. Only when they'd moved past and were a safe enough distance away did

Courtney let go of the breath she didn't even know she'd been holding.

She started to rise, but Jonathan pulled her back down to her knees none too gently.

"Aren't we going after them?" she asked.

"'We' are not going anywhere. You're crazy, do you know that? Can't you listen to me just once?"

She smiled weakly. "No."

"I suppose the only way I can be assured of your remaining safely out of the fray is to tie you up and toss you deep into the nearest hedgerow."

"Jonathan, they're getting away. My uncle said something about—"

"I know what your uncle said."

"But if we don't hurry we'll never track them down."

"And how do you propose we chase after them? Mother has the car."

An impish smile lit up Courtney's face. "Lady Edith is here. The Bentley's in the lot. The employees' lot, that is. Did you know that your mother once played the role of a waitress in a local theater production?"

Jonathan sighed. "Mother...? Here? Serving tidbits to the guests? Will life ever again be normal and orderly?"

"I hope not," Courtney whispered as they scrambled to their feet. "This way," she said, but Jonathan tugged her in the opposite direction.

"There's a shortcut to the parking lot," he said. "If we hurry, we should beat them there. Christine will delay things a bit with her phone call."

"Christine, is it? How chummy," she said, racing to keep up with him, thankful for, if nothing else, the practical oxfords she was wearing. She wouldn't have gotten very far in the three-inch spiked heels she'd originally worn to the club.

The Bentley was parked in an ideal spot well away from the guest lot, allowing Jonathan and Courtney to slip into the vehicle unseen. Or so they thought. Just as Jonathan started the engine and flicked on his low beams, a tall male figure stepped into the light at the front of the car.

"Damn the man," Jonathan muttered as Avery Noble lifted his hand in a mock salute and came around to Jonathan's window.

"How about a lift, old man?"

Courtney gave Jonathan a dismayed look as Noble opened the rear door and climbed into the back seat with nary a word of consent from Jonathan.

Avery leaned forward. "Charming disguise, Miss O'Malley. Although perhaps you'll allow me to call you by your first name. 'Katherine,' right? Or do you prefer 'Courtney' just now?"

Jonathan let the supremely smooth Bentley lurch forward as he pulled out, forcing Noble to fall roughly back against the seat. "Steady on, old man. We don't want to give ourselves away at this juncture," Noble muttered.

This time Courtney's look in Jonathan's direction held equal amounts of dismay and puzzlement. "Is he working with us?"

Jonathan said nothing as he maneuvered the Bentley through the employees' lot, which connected at the east end to the guest parking.

"There's a car waiting over by the exit," Courtney said, pointing to a gray Austin.

"That will be Vaughn and Lambert," Noble stated. "I assume the Dupré woman has not yet completed her call."

Courtney turned in her seat. "So you overheard their whole conversation, too? But where were you hiding? And you, for that matter?" She directed the latter question at Jonathan.

"Ah," Noble said, "tricks of the trade."

"What trade?" she asked pointedly. "The spy trade?" She glanced from Noble to Jonathan. Neither man spoke up.

Courtney sighed. "Yes, yes, I know. It's not cricket to expose your cover. It would be rather foolish to go around announcing the nature of your profession. Quite dangerous. Besides, a good spy never trusts anyone. Isn't that right, Mr. Noble? You don't particularly trust me, do you? And neither one of you trusts my uncle, I'm certain of that. But you're wrong, both of you." She made every attempt to sound emphatic, but despite her effort, her voice held a distinct quaver of uncertainty.

"Besides," she went on, perhaps as determined to convince herself of her uncle's innocence as to convince the two men, "Uncle Lou may not be a wealthy man, but he's never been interested in material extravagances. He has everything he wants. A pleasant apartment, a lovely cottage on the shore, enough money to retire from the shop and travel. I can't believe he'd succumb to thievery just for money."

"Perhaps," Noble said, "it isn't only the money."

"What do you mean?"

"Did you know that your uncle was active at one time in certain organizations that were well infiltrated by Communists?" Noble asked.

"Communists? Never."

"Oh, it's quite true."

Courtney looked over at Jonathan. "Is he saying that he thinks my uncle is a Communist? That he's some kind of a...traitor? Is that what you think, too? That he's working with the Russians? That he's negotiating for them?" An angry flush spread across her face.

"Do be quiet, Noble," Jonathan said gruffly, looking at neither one of his passengers, keeping his eyes fixed on the car near the gate. "Back in the fifties, practically every service organization in the States was believed to be tainted by

Communist infiltration. As for Vaughn, the evidence of subversive activity in those organizations he'd joined was flimsy at best. You always did talk too much, Noble."

"Temper, temper, Jonathan. I am not making any direct accusations about anyone. I simply—" He stopped. "There's the Dupré woman coming out of the club now."

All three in the Bentley immediately put aside their discussion and focused their attention on Christine Dupré, watching her as she waved in the direction of the idling car near the gate before hurrying over to her own car, a sleek black Jaguar.

"My, my," Noble murmured, "our Christine is certainly doing all right for herself. I don't suppose Marcus gave her that little toy to get about town in."

"Marcus?" Courtney's ears perked up. "Marcus Lloyd? Christine Dupré is involved with Marcus Lloyd? But she's..."

"Double-crossing him?" Noble grinned. "It certainly looks that way. Poor Marc. He never did have great luck with the ladies."

"One more word, Noble," Jonathan snapped, "and you'll be following on foot."

"We do have the same interests at heart, old man. Do remember that."

Jonathan gave a sharp laugh as he let first the Jaguar, then Vaughn's Austin get a good head start. Just before pulling out himself, he turned back to Noble. "My only interest in this excursion is in rescuing Marc. Once he's safe, the bloody manuscript be damned. The whole miserable business be damned. I want no part of it."

Noble leaned forward and rested a hand on Courtney's shoulder. "Don't believe a word of it, my dear. He thrives on the excitement of the chase. He's merely sulking because of all the mishaps and distractions."

Courtney turned around to level a steady gaze on Avery Noble. "It seems to me you're doing your best to compound those distractions, Mr. Noble. I wonder why."

Jonathan let out a hearty laugh. "I do adore you, Miss Blue, and that despite all the distractions you may cause."

Noble gave a little snort but remained silent, for which both Courtney and Jonathan were grateful.

They were following the Embankment Road heading south in the direction of Battersea Park. In the silence Jonathan drove with skilled concentration, staying two or three cars behind the Austin at all times. For a short while Courtney allowed her overworked, agitated mind a respite as she watched the twinkling city lights reflected on the Thames.

It was Jonathan who lifted her from her brief reverie. "I don't like this," he commented. "They're heading directly into Battersea Park."

Courtney could feel Jonathan's tension and it quickly became her own. Only Noble seemed undisturbed. "I doubt they'd call a meeting at the boss's own home. A park is a rather commonplace meeting ground for business transactions such as this. We need only be cautious. As soon as we see the Austin slow, I suggest we tuck the Bentley out of sight and proceed on foot. Miss Blue, you will remain in the car."

She noted with amusement his switch to a more formal address. "I see no reason to take orders from you, Mr. Noble."

"Ah, then I propose you give the order, Jonathan."

Jonathan laughed. "I'm afraid Miss Blue doesn't take well to orders from anyone, Noble."

"I must insist."

Jonathan shrugged off Noble's demand. "The Austin's pulling over to the curb up ahead." Immediately Jonathan slowed and took a sharp right off the narrow park road, driving onto a wooded knoll that would provide good cover should any other cars come along. Cutting the engine, he watched in tense silence to be certain both the Jaguar and the Austin had arrived at their designated spots.

Noble leaned forward. "We'll circle round from either side, shall we?"

Jonathan nodded.

"You will remember, Jonathan, that we don't merely want the small fry. We want the big fish. Which means above all else we don't want to behave rashly."

Courtney gripped Jonathan's arm. "Above all else we want to make sure my uncle doesn't get hurt, Jonathan. My uncle and the manuscript, that's all we need to worry about. You said yourself the rest isn't your affair." Her throat was dry and she swallowed with difficulty.

"I'll head west. You head east," Noble said firmly. "We'd better get a move on. As for you, Miss Blue..."

Jonathan reached across and squeezed Courtney's hand. "I want you to stay put, love. And before you argue, just consider that if anything does go wrong, we shall need someone at the wheel to help us make a clean getaway."

As much as she longed to go with Jonathan, at least to see that the unpleasant Mr. Noble in no way harmed her uncle, Courtney had to admit that Jonathan was right. She agreed reluctantly, sliding behind the wheel as Jonathan got out. He lowered his head and gave her a quick kiss before shutting the door very quietly.

Courtney watched both men head off, Jonathan circling east, Noble west. Her anxiety mounted as they disappeared from view. She turned her attention to the Austin, which was parked too far away to distinguish the two figures inside. As for Christine Dupré, she'd parked her Jaguar just around the bend from the Austin, and Courtney could see no more than the sports car's rear bumper. There was no sign of the double-crossing femme fetale herself. Courtney was left to assume Christine was remaining in her car until the arrival of her nefarious boss.

The park was eerily silent, all the players fixed in their positions, all waiting. Courtney wondered if the waiting was wearing on the others as it was on her. Her fingers curled tightly around the steering wheel. Jonathan's words echoed in her head. *If anything does go wrong . . .*

Why wouldn't something go wrong? she thought with despair. Hadn't something gone wrong for them every step of the way so far?

IN ANOTHER SECLUDED SPOT in Battersea Park, the two tipsy but fast-sobering Russians, Borofsky and Petrenko, sat meekly in the back seat of the rented English Ford. Up front was a very sober Zakharov and his henchman, Goncharov. The henchman wore a sardonic smile on his face, but Zakharov's features looked to be etched in steel, except for the liquid fire burning in the dark pools of his narrowed eyes.

"I can be a ruthless man," Zakharov said in a low fierce voice, removing a Turkish cigarette from a gold case.

Goncharov quickly, expertly produced a lighter even before his superior brought the cigarette to his lips.

"All right, Yevgenni," Zakharov went on after taking a long drag, "we shall forget all that has transpired and make a successful showing this evening. Do I make myself clear?"

Both men in the rear nodded in rapid succession. Up front, Goncharov merely broadened his sardonic smile.

"These, then, are my orders, Comrades," Zakharov said, forcing composure. He prided himself on calculated ruthlessness, not weak, emotional outbursts of temper. "We want the manuscript without delay. I have received confirmation that the book dealer, Louis Vaughn, and his companion, Mrs. Lambert, are now in possession of that manuscript. Need I remind you that they will not relinquish the parcel to us willingly. And the others here tonight will do everything in their power to abort our mission. They will all have to be dealt with. Do I make myself clear, Comrades?''

Petrenko muttered, ''You want us to kill them all, yes?''

For the first time Zakharov smiled.

''Even . . .'' Borofsky began.

''All'' came Zakharov's sharp reply. ''I rely on the three of you to see that my orders are carried out precisely. Seize the manuscript and tidy up the mess.''

''What if the book dealer and his woman friend haven't brought the manuscript with them?'' Borofsky asked timidly, knowing very well that his superior did not want to hear of any further problems.

Zakharov's fingers leaped across the back of his seat and clutched Borofsky's thick neck. Those fingers were cold as ice and strong as a vise.

''In such a case, Yevgenni, you will bring them to me. I am certain I can convince them to tell me what I need to know. Don't you agree, Yevgenni?''

Choking and gasping for air as Zakharov released him, Borofsky could manage no more than a nod.


THE CAR PHONE RANG only once before Christine nervously grabbed for it.

''Where are you, Daniel?''

''Don't fret, darling. I'm close by. I want you to proceed to the Austin and get our friends to step out of their car. I shall take it from there.''

''You aren't going to . . .''

''I have no interest in harming anyone, dear Christine. I simply want the manuscript.''

''You intend to meet their demands?''

''If they are reasonable.''

''I have the impression there is more involved here than money.''

"Do you? What more is there?"

"You tell me, Daniel."

"I shall have to think about that, my dear Christine. Now be off."

"LOU, I'M SCARED."

"Don't worry, Andrea. They aren't going to do anything to us as long as we hold the winning card, and that card is safely tucked away. If they attempt to use force, they will never get their hands on the manuscript."

"Do you think Emerson will actually show up? He could send anyone in his stead and we'd never know. That photo of him my sister sent was too blurry to get any real sense of what the man looks like."

"I'll bet he's growing very impatient. I believe he'll come. And his impatience could very well work in our favor."

Andrea cast him a curious look. "You're very different from what I first thought, Lou."

"How's that?"

"You're stronger, more confident. As if you've done this sort of thing before. That's crazy, isn't it, Lou?"

CLOUDS WERE GATHERING, making the dark sky even darker. Courtney's worry was being powerfully supplanted by her newfound impatience. No harm, she thought, in just getting a better look of the area where her uncle's car was parked. If there were going to be any problems, she'd spot them more easily from a better vantage point. Pulling off the white cap from her hair and the white apron from her black uniform to prevent accidental detection, she carefully opened the car door.

She was about twenty yards from the car and feeling quite pleased with her clear view, when she heard footsteps approaching from the direction of the woods. Her heart pounded loudly in her chest as the sounds grew sharper and closer.

She glanced across at the Bentley. No, she'd never make it in time. On the other hand, there was little cover where she was standing. Run or stay put? Neither choice was very promising.

She could hear voices now. Two men speaking in hushed tones. Speaking Russian. And then she saw the slender thread of light from the flashlight one of the men was carrying run along the ground, heading right toward her feet.

Terror gripped her as she realized the futility of her situation. In the next instant the light flashed on her shoes. Then slowly rose to her face.

Courtney grimaced in fear, certain this was the end for her.

And then something extraordinary happened. At the sight of her, the Russians gasped in abject terror. The flashlight fell to the ground, it's light bouncing off their stricken faces, revealing the men clutching each other in quivering fear. As if they were seeing a ghost. And they were—the black shrouded ghost of a woman who had burned to death in a bookstore fire thousands of miles away.

Courtney silently blessed her luck, as the reason for their terror quickly dawned on her. To bring home the frightening effect she let out one low, bloodcurdling hiss and took off for the woods, flapping her arms like a spectral wraith.

## CHAPTER FIFTEEN

RACING THROUGH the night shadows past a stand of trees bordered by thorny shrubs, Courtney managed to come within fifteen yards of the Austin. Crouching low to the ground, she could see her uncle and Andrea Lambert standing just outside the car on the roadside. She had all but decided to make contact with Uncle Lou, warn him that the park was filled with dangerous enemies and spies, when she heard the sound of an automobile coming down the narrow park road. The next moment she saw the car, a large black limousine, slow as it approached the Austin.

As Courtney watched the dark limousine, she felt a premonition that something terrible was about to happen. She could not explain it. Perhaps it was all the years of reading thrillers, feeling the tension rise to a fever pitch, sensing, just as the heroine seemed always to sense, that moment—that fateful moment—when catastrophe was going to strike.

Catastrophe did strike, but it all happened so fast Courtney had no time to react. The screech of tires, the muffled reports, the black limo racing away in a cloud of dust, a second later the Austin following, then the Jaguar. And then another car went roaring after them, a gray Ford sedan. Dazed, Courtney forced herself to shake off the shock, then she started toward the road. A few yards away, she halted abruptly, her mouth opening wide in horror. To her right, a man's body was stretched facedown on the road.

*Oh, my God . . . Uncle Lou . . .*

There was a cry of anguish. Her own. And then she began to run toward the still body.

She was grabbed roughly by familiar hands before she got there. Jonathan spun her around to face him, holding her fast.

"What's . . . happening? Uncle Lou . . . I've got to get to him . . . please, please let me go, Jonathan."

"They grabbed the woman." He gripped her shoulders. "But your uncle . . ."

"No. No."

"Listen." He shook her. "That's not him. That's not your uncle over there."

The words were slow to penetrate. "It's not." Again she looked over at the body. Avery Noble was approaching the limp figure. He rolled the man over. In the darkness, Courtney couldn't make out the features, but she saw the man's head loll to one side. There was no motion at all. Noble glanced up, gave a thumbs-down sign.

Jonathan nodded, then returned his full attention to Courtney. "Your uncle took off in the Austin," Jonathan told her. "He's chasing after the limo, but he'll never succeed in that car of his." He rubbed his face. "Everything's gone haywire. What else is new?" He looked at her, his expression weary. "What happened to the Bentley?"

Tears slid down Courtney's cheeks. "It's . . . still in the woods. I . . . ran into a little trouble. Or I should say trouble ran into me." Remembering the blanched faces of the Russians made her smile faintly. The smile didn't last long. "I wanted to help. And I've done nothing but botch things up tonight. We'll never track them down now. First Marcus, now Andrea Lambert. If she has the manuscript on her . . . they're both done for, aren't they?"

He put his arm around her. "Come on. There's nothing more we can do here."

Noble wandered over to them. "I'll stick around. Call the department for me, will you? Have them send some men over."

Jonathan nodded.

"Who is he?" Courtney asked Noble. "The man in the road?"

Avery Noble raised his eyebrows and looked from Jonathan to Courtney. "Russian thug named Goncharov. I've had a run-in with him before. I shan't miss having future opportunities."

"Then . . . he's dead."

Jonathan felt her shiver and he held her closer.

"I never thought about that part of it," she whispered. "Real death. It separates the fact from the fiction quite vividly, doesn't it?" She swallowed hard as she stared at Avery. "It's not an easy job, is it?"

Noble smiled sardonically. "If it was going to be easy, I'd get the missus to do it," he said with a sneer.

Totally drained, Courtney was slow thinking up a retort. Jonathan ended the matter, taking her firmly in hand and steering her away.

"We'll be in touch," Noble called out.

Jonathan glanced back at Noble, then looked sideways at Courtney. It was Courtney who called back, "Right."

Once they'd driven out of the park, Jonathan stopped at a phone booth. From the car Courtney could see that he'd made two calls.

Together the calls took less than a minute. When he slid back behind the wheel, Jonathan said, "I called in for Noble and then phoned my mother. I told her we'd be staying at the hotel in town. I thought you might prefer it."

Courtney nodded. Lady Edith was a dear, but she'd be sure to be filled with endless questions about the adventure tonight, and Courtney was feeling too exhausted to answer them. Besides, she had some questions of her own. The time had come for Jonathan to provide some answers.

She waited impatiently with her inquiry until he had settled her in the adjoining room of his hotel suite.

"Shall I order up some cocktails?" he asked, his voice tender.

Courtney sat down on the edge of the bed. "No. Perhaps some answers, though."

Jonathan locked eyes with her. Slowly he walked over to an armchair, pulled it up across from her. He leaned forward, pressing the palms of his hands together, his elbows resting on his knees.

"You have such glamorous notions about the intelligence business," he said in a low voice.

"Not as much now," she admitted. "But it is exciting. The danger is thrilling. You are a secret agent, aren't you, Jonathan?"

"The idea of spying did fascinate me once upon a time. It was Marcus who stimulated much of that fascination. I had met Marcus through a mutual friend. I knew he was with the government, but his work was very hush-hush. It was a short while later that he told me he was with British intelligence. We got rather chummy. Soon after he was made head of the department he would occasionally ask me to authenticate some papers for him, do some translating. I began doing more and more of it." He smiled at her. "It was all rather mundane paperwork. Absolutely nothing glamorous about it."

"I had the impression from Noble that you did more than push papers around."

"I'm coming to that." He sighed. "I find it difficult to talk about."

She reached out for his hand, a tender smile on her face. "If it was easy, you'd get the missus to tell it."

They laughed. Jonathan relaxed a little.

"I'm afraid I've led you on a bit. I didn't mean to initially. I had no desire in the world at first to have you know I'd ever been in the spy trade. Back when we first met under those extraordinary circumstances, I was ruing the fact that I was getting caught up in the game. But you seemed so taken with the notion that I was this dashing cloak-and-dagger hero, clever, daring, mysterious. And I found myself wanting to...be that fellow for you. But, love, the truth is, I'm no James Bond. Far from it."

"You fit the part for me."

"I admit, I had dreams of being 007. You see, we're not all that different, you and I. I was caught up in my imagination, too."

"But you did something about it. You took action."

"I was bitten by the bug. I remember the day quite vividly when I walked into Marcus's office, set a document I'd reviewed for him on his desk and told him I'd rather do some fieldwork. I wanted an assignment. Something I could really sink my teeth into."

"What did Marcus think of the idea?"

"I'm afraid that while Marcus was fond of me, he felt I'd led a rather sheltered and privileged life, and that things might get too messy for a man of the aristocracy. But I was determined to convince him otherwise. I wanted to be a part of the danger and excitement. I longed for the thrill of it all." His startling aquamarine eyes trailed her face. "The passion of it all. Do you understand?"

"Do I understand!" Her eyes sparkled.

He smiled at her, thinking she was the loveliest woman he had ever known and that much of that loveliness flowed from within.

"And did you find danger, excitement...passion?" she asked softly.

He rubbed his eyes and fought back a yawn. It was nearly two in the morning. He was tense, exhausted, depressed at how the night had gone.

She leaned forward, touched his cheek. "Come. Lie down." She moved onto the center of the bed, tugging her funny black uniform demurely over her knees.

He hesitated for a moment, then rose from the chair and stretched out on his side on the bed, his elbow resting on a pillow, his head in his hand.

"Tell me about it," she whispered.

He gave her a long, solemn stare. "I did manage to convince Marcus to give me a try. I was paired with Noble on my first assignment. We didn't hit it off very well. I thought him plodding, out of date, far too cautious."

"And he thought you ..."

Jonathan laughed dryly. "He thought I was wet behind the ears. Which of course I was. He also thought I was hotheaded, too eager to get into the action, willing to take foolish risks."

"Which of course you were?"

He grinned. "Which of course I was."

"What was the assignment?"

"I can't give you the details. It's still classified. But it was a mission that required infiltration of the iron curtain and the removal of certain information."

"How did it go?" she asked, her own exhaustion evaporating as her curiosity mounted.

He gave her a rueful smile. "Not as well as it might have. At the last minute we had to abort the mission. Needless to say Noble got quite upset when his plan didn't work."

"Maybe it was a bad plan."

"I don't like the fellow, but I can't put the blame wholly on him. I didn't exactly follow orders. And I should have. Noble had the experience. He was in charge. I honestly don't think his plan would have worked, but I didn't give it a fair shot. I tried a plan of my own, which failed badly. It was a rather humbling experience."

"What was your friend Marcus's reaction?"

"Oh, he was none too pleased. Then again, he was never what one might call a fan of Avery Noble. Nor was Noble a fan of him. Avery was quite bitter about Marcus getting the nod for chief of service. He felt he deserved that position himself, and, I think, was devious and determined enough to do something about it. Sometimes I suspect Noble was scheming from the first and intentionally played me for a fool when we were on that assignment."

Courtney looked puzzled. "What do you mean?"

"Well, Noble knew I wasn't very keen on his plan. I think he might also have known I'd venture a few moves of my own. Perhaps he purposely set something up that I would question. Which would lead me to go off half-cocked and muck up the works. I'd end up looking the fool and Marcus would end up with egg on his face, having backed me as he did."

"Not a very nice man, that Mr. Noble," Courtney concluded, stretching out beside Jonathan on the bed, her head resting against the headboard. "Was that your first and last assignment?"

"Ah, no. I admit I was humbled, but it didn't last very long. I wanted a chance to redeem myself. And I think Marcus wanted a chance to redeem himself, as well. Noble's gloating did not please Marcus or me. However, to be on the safe side, Marcus decided that he and I would team up together on the next assignment."

"Again classified?"

He smiled. "You're a fast study, love. Yes, classified. This time we were dealing with a delicate and intricate matter of subterfuge. It required that I go under deep cover, with Marcus remaining in the background as my control. Unlike my partnership with Noble, Marcus and I were on the same wavelength. Things were going swimmingly. The assignment was tremendously exciting. I was flying high, feeling...well, it was an exhilarating feeling. I'd never experienced anything like it.''

Courtney smiled. Since she'd met Jonathan she, too, had experienced unique feelings, extraordinary feelings.

"Then you did both redeem yourselves?" Courtney asked.

He shook his head. "You see, love, it isn't at all like it is in novels or cinema. There aren't always happy endings, with all the pieces neatly tied up, the bad guys brought to justice, the heroes victorious.''

"What happened? What went wrong?"

"I don't know," he said. "I wish I did. Everything was going fine. And then everything went wrong. There was a third agent involved. His cover was essential to seeing the operation through. Somehow that cover got blown. It was airtight, Courtney. Except for Marcus I was the only other person who knew.''

"But surely Marcus wouldn't..."

"Of course not. Any more than I would blow it. But we were the only two around to be blamed. Oh, Noble had a field day with that one. He didn't go after Marcus. That would have been too indiscreet. But I was a great target for his wrath. He claimed I was careless, that I rushed things, moved too impulsively. And that inadvertently I'd blown the other agent's cover.''

"I don't believe that for a minute."

He looked at her steadily. "Perhaps I did. I thought I'd been careful, but Noble could have been right. I had to do some serious soul-searching after that blunder. And I admit I began feeling unsure of myself, unsure of whether I had what it takes." He glanced at her. "I suppose that disappoints you. A hero without confidence isn't much of a hero.''

"Nonsense," Courtney argued. "You're only human And I believe the cleverest heroes are the ones who are aware of their fallibility. Even the best fictional heroes have that awareness. Anyway, what did Marcus think?"

"He thought I ought to get quickly back on the horse or I might never ride again."

"And did you get right back on?" she asked.

"In a way. Shortly after that terrible fiasco, Marcus grew concerned that there might be some internal funny business going on at the service. He began missing certain papers. They'd inevitably turn up, usually misfiled somewhere. Nothing top secret. Financial statements, expense account sheets, that sort of thing. Marcus didn't worry much about it at first. But he did need someone he could trust to look into the matter. When he put me on the assignment ... well, I had the feeling he thought a safe pony ride might be in order before I went galloping off again on a race horse out in the field."

Jonathan grew silent, his expression hard. "It turned out not to be a pony ride at all. All of a sudden I found myself on a fierce steed in the middle of a polo match. And in the end, a fine man's career was ruined."

Courtney remembered what Lady Edith had told her about the hint of scandal involving Marcus and his abrupt resignation. She told Jonathan about the conversation.

"Marcus was completely innocent," Jonathan said. "He was being set up by someone in the department. I was certain of it. Certain that documents were being doctored to make it look as if Marcus might be abusing his administrative powers, using government money for personal interests." A muscle twitched in his jaw. "And I became a pawn, a very useful pawn, in the affair. As Marcus's friend and protégé, it looked as though he might be using me to cover up his supposed hanky-panky. I was being used all right. But not by Marcus."

Courtney sat up. "Noble? You think he set you both up?"

"Obviously I've no proof of that, or Noble would not now be sitting in Marcus's swivel chair behind Marcus's old desk in the head office."

"But it seems so obvious."

"Noble covered his tracks well. And let's face it, Marcus's leadership record in the service was shaky, thanks mainly to me."

"That's unfair. You've no cause to be so hard on yourself. Noble had to be pulling the strings."

"Ah, easy to put the blame elsewhere, love. But had I been as smart, as clever as I'd believed, I might have better protected myself. Men like Noble are all part of the game. They become the winners unless someone comes along who's wilier than them. I wasn't and neither was Marcus. When the scandal at the service threatened to break wide open, it was made clear to Marcus that his choices were either to resign quietly, with no undue embarrassment either to himself or the service . . . or face a most unpleasant list of charges. Even if acquitted, the publicity would likely have ruined his career. As it was, some word leaked out." His eyes narrowed. "I have my theory as to how and why that happened."

"Of course," Courtney broke in. "Noble wasn't going to take any chances that Marcus might fight back." She gripped Jonathan's hand. "Noble can't be allowed to get away with all this."

"It wouldn't do to go accusing the head of the service with no proof of any kind. When Marcus resigned, I was disgusted and angry. And frustrated. But I was tempted to stay. I thought I might be able to get to the bottom of the plot against Marcus."

"Why didn't you?"

"Noble was in charge. And Noble wanted me out. I merely resigned before he had the pleasure of firing me. I could have tried to hang on, make a stink, but I had no stomach for serving under Noble. I would have stayed had Marcus wanted me to. But the whole ugly business had taken its toll on Marcus. He urged me to leave things be. He appeared to withdraw into a shell. It was so unlike him. I was quite worried. But he finally convinced me he was happily retired and content leading a quiet life. He was very much for my decision to leave London altogether to take the teaching post in Boston. I heard from him infrequently in the States until the problem with the Gorky manuscript arose."

"And suddenly you were back in business again."

"Marcus obtained the Gorky through a contact in Moscow. State secrets were alleged to be hidden in the manuscript. Out of his old spy instincts Marcus tested the waters with discreet feelers. Interest was immediate and intense. One dealer, Daniel Emerson, was especially eager to buy. Then, of course, there were the Russians, who wanted to get their hands back on the manuscript."

Courtney was a little perturbed. "Were there any secrets hidden in the manuscript?"

"I never got the chance to find out. But we do know that the KGB, the CIA and certainly SIS all have their fingers in the pie. Then Marcus was kidnapped. And who snatched him? I'll wager it's Emerson. But we still don't know if he wants the manuscript because it's a rare Gorky work or for its spy secrets."

Courtney thought for a moment. "And what about Andrea Lambert and my uncle? Where do they fit in? I still refuse to believe that Uncle Lou is a common thief or, worse, a traitor. But I must admit I don't understand his actions. Or what his relationship is with Andrea Lambert. Then there's that Mata Hari, Christine Dupré. Is she really Marcus's lover?''

''So Noble says.''

''He could be lying.''

''No, it would be too easy to verify. Noble is too clever to lie about something like that. She must have been involved with Marcus. She very likely helped set him up for the kidnapping. She's one of our most valuable links.''

''Is that why you were dancing with her at the club?''

He caught the hint of jealousy in Courtney's voice and smiled. ''I thought it about time we make direct contact. Although knowing I hadn't the manuscript limited her interest in me.''

''And were you disappointed?''

He grinned. ''I was disappointed at sensing she'd be a difficult nut to crack.'' He sighed. ''Once again it's all gotten rather out of hand. So many puzzle pieces that I can't fit into place. I'm afraid I'm no more successful as a spy today than I was before I left the service.'' He gazed up at her. ''Not exactly James Bond, love. Perhaps you should have stuck with fantasy.''

''No,'' Courtney said emphatically. ''Maybe I have gotten the two mixed up on occasion. Maybe I did make you into something more than flesh and blood. I did have a little difficulty separating reality from fantasy early on. But, Jonathan, it's you in the flesh and blood that excites me. I don't want James Bond, love. Besides,'' she said, smiling, ''Bond's had his own share of troubles on the job. More than a few times a woman's had to come to his rescue, if I recall.''

''You're remarkable, Courtney Blue.''

Her hazel eyes sparkled. ''I'm only flesh and blood, Jonathan.'' She leaned closer to him, lips parted, half smiling. ''Really I am.''

Her hair tumbled forward as she pressed her lips to his
Their lips met and held. But Courtney was aware of th
subtle tension emanating from Jonathan, the faint resis
tance to her advance.

She drew back, stared deep into his eyes.

Jonathan looked away. "My life is in a jumble right now
I've a great deal of sorting out to do." He was silent fo
several moments. Finally he gazed at her. "I'm afraid you'r
not helping the matter any. Indeed, love, you add greatly t
my confusion. I don't know what I want, Courtney. I don'
know what I'm after. But . . . it isn't teaching at a college i
Boston. It's taken a while for me to realize I wasn't runnin
from the service or from London. I was running from my
self. And one can't do that, love, and find any peace."

"I think you want to go back into the service."

"I'm not sure. And then there's Noble. I couldn't wor
under him, even if he'd have me back. Right now I mus
concentrate on one thing only, and that's fitting the piece
of the puzzle together."

"I intend to continue helping with that puzzle, Jona
than. Don't forget, my uncle is one of those pieces."

"Yes. I know." He gently kissed her cheek. "You'd bet
ter get some sleep. You do start rehearsal tomorrow fo
*Fanfare*. It's still our best lead."

She'd almost forgotten.

He started to rise, but she caught hold of his hand. "W
won't bungle this operation, Jonathan. We do have a pretty
solid partnership, don't you think?"

He smiled tenderly, but he didn't answer her question
Instead he said, "I can't afford to bungle this one, Court
ney. Marcus was always there for me, and I must be there for
him now. Once this is settled . . ." He paused.

Again Courtney's expression held anticipation. "Yes?"

"I just may try to convince Marcus to let me help him
clear his name, regain his rightful position in the service."

Courtney felt a tightness in her throat. "A noble cause."

He grinned. "Pun intended, I hope."

She smiled wryly. "Right."

They stared silently at each other, each acutely aware of their unspoken agenda.

"Well, I'll let you get some sleep, then." Slowly he rose, this time unhampered.

"We have been having quite a time," she whispered. She longed to reach out to him, but she didn't.

"Yes, it's the most extraordinary adventure I've ever had." He ran a hand through his thick, dark hair. The air seemed to sizzle with electricity. He walked to the door, stopped, turned back to her. "It isn't over yet."

A tentative smile crossed her lips. "Not by a long shot."

## CHAPTER SIXTEEN

CHRISTINE DUPRÉ WIPED the sweat from her face with the edge of the towel hanging around her neck, as she spoke into the phone. Her voice was breathless from having put in a good two hours of rehearsal.

"Daniel? It's about time. I've been trying to get you at every break. Just what was that madness about last night? You said you—"

"Where are you phoning from?"

"My dressing room at the theater. I've been at rehearsal. I just finished running through my first act routines with the head choreographer."

"I told you never to call me from the theater. There are too many people—"

"The only others here today are the chorus dancers, and they're all onstage. We must speak, Daniel. I don't understand what's happening. You promised this would be a quick, clean deal. Get the manuscript, sell it and divvy up the take. I never dreamed there'd be so many people involved, so much chaos. And...shooting. Daniel, I saw a man..."

"Never mind him. That wasn't my doing."

"But the abduction of that woman was your doing. Why did you grab her and drag her into your car? Did she have the manuscript on her? I swear I shall go mad before this thing is over. I don't know how much more I can take."

"You don't have to take anything at all, my dear Christine."

"Daniel..."

"Settle down, Christine. You do go on so. My little maneuver will work out greatly to our advantage. If Vaughn wants to see his lady friend again, he'll hand over the manuscript without any fuss, and with no expense to me. So you see, my dear, things are moving along quite nicely."

"Oh, very nicely. I'm now an accessory to the kidnapping of two people—one of whom I happen to care about, as much as that seems to amuse you—there's no bloody manuscript and I've got Jonathan Madden breathing down my neck, not to mention a few Russians."

"I realize that we must wrap this up quickly. London is getting too crowded. Madden and the Russians have been joined by the British secret service. And I wouldn't be surprised if some American agents aren't lurking about. I shall have to pull up stakes."

"Where will you go? How will I get in touch with you?" There was an edge of panic to her voice. "And what about Marcus? Are you taking him with you? Is he still...all right?"

"I shall be in touch with you, Christine. Just sit tight. I've left word for Mr. Vaughn at his hotel that he can reach me through you at the theater. Tomorrow afternoon. I have made it clear that he is to show you the manuscript, and once you have verified that he has it, you will have word from me as to where the exchange is to take place."

"What if Vaughn doesn't show up here? What if he decides to keep the manuscript and make his own deals?"

"And have the demise of Mrs. Lambert on his conscience? I tend to doubt that."

Christine scowled. "And what about your conscience, Daniel?"

He laughed sharply. The sound sent a chill down Christine Dupré's spine. It was a pointless question. She already knew that Daniel Emerson had no conscience to speak of. What she needed to examine was whether she had one.

THE ASSISTANT CHOREOGRAPHER, Lennie Aarons clapped his hands sharply. "Okay, boys and girls, we're ready to try the routine one more time. Now you all will try to remember your left feet from your right, won't you? Please take your positions— Hold on, where's the blond . . . what's her name . . . O'Malley? The one who's third from the left?"

A redhead with a pixie hairdo, who was tightening the laces on one of her ballet shoes called out, "She had a bad blister on her foot. She went to find a bandage for it about five minutes ago. Maybe she had to run over to the chemist's shop across the street. She said she'd hurry back."

Aarons scowled. "I thought I made it clear no one was to leave this stage until break. We can't have some prima donna mucking up the schedule. All right, we'll start without her. If she doesn't show within the next minute she can consider herself out. And let that be fair warning to all of you. This isn't nursery school, boys and girls. You can't go about whining over every little ache and pain."

He motioned to the pretty brunette piano player, tapped the beat during the run-in, then shouted, "And begin . . ."

Forty-eight seconds later, Courtney, flushed and elated, ran back onstage and hurried over to her place. She struggled to pick up the routine, but she was too distracted, too intent on finishing up for the morning and racing back to the hotel to relate her news to Jonathan. Her brief little sojourn had paid off in spades.

JONATHAN was just hanging up the phone when Courtney came flying into the suite.

"Wait until I tell you—" she began, but Jonathan cut her off.

"That was Noble. We're to come right down to his office. Your uncle is there."

"My uncle is with Avery Noble? He went to see him? To explain?"

"Well, not exactly. Avery had him detained."

"Detained? Because of the manuscript? But he didn't steal it. It was the Lambert woman. I know what Noble thinks, but he has no evidence, no proof..."

Jonathan was at Courtney's side. "It's got nothing to do with the manuscript."

"I...don't understand. How can he be held against his will if there's no charge?"

"I'm afraid there is a charge." Jonathan glanced down at her leotard, over which she'd thrown a pair of jeans and a denim jacket. "You'd better go and change."

"Jonathan, what charge? Why was my uncle picked up?"

For a moment Jonathan's eyes flickered away. But he forced them back on Courtney's face. "He's being questioned for...murder."

Courtney stared at him, thrown completely off balance. "Murder?" she said, then said again, "Murder?"

He saw her start to sway, and reached out for her. "You'd better have a drink."

But she pulled away. "Who is Noble saying he murdered?" she demanded.

He knit his brows. "The man you saw last night on the road beside your uncle's car. The Russian. Goncharov. He was with the KGB. He worked directly under a man by the name of Zakharov. British secret service has been trying for years to track Zakharov down. He keeps eluding them."

Courtney didn't give a damn about this Zakharov at the moment. "If my uncle did kill Goncharov, it was an act of self-defense. The Russians were after him. Noble knows that. Besides, this man was a Russian agent. Surely there are certain considerations, certain..."

"Take it easy. I don't think Noble intends to press charges. He simply wanted to bring your uncle in, no doubt put some pressure on him in order to obtain some answers."

She breathed a bit easier. "What are we waiting for? Let's get down there. Poor Uncle Lou. Does he know that I'm...alive? Has Noble said anything to him?"

"I don't know. Rare as it is for the man, he said very little on the phone."

Courtney was already at the door.

"Don't you want to change?"

"No. I want to get down there." She started to open the door, then closed it again, leaning against it for support. "Oh, my God, I almost forgot about Christine and Daniel."

"Daniel?"

"Christine was speaking to him on the phone. She was very upset. And angry. It seems things aren't going the way she planned." Quickly Courtney recounted Christine's end of the conversation. She could see the excitement rise on Jonathan's face. "Did I do good, then?"

He smiled ruefully. "I'm afraid to ask how you managed to overhear that call. But yes, you did remarkably well, love." He came over to her. A flicker of a smile remained, but there was a brooding look in his eyes. "It seems I can't manage without you."

She knew Jonathan didn't mean that as a compliment. Jonathan prided himself on not needing anyone. Hadn't his mother told her he'd been a loner since he was a boy? Still, she allowed a faint smile to give her pleasure away. She wanted him to need her. "It seems we need each other," she whispered. Jonathan's smile deepened, but the brooding look didn't vanish from her hero's eyes.

And then, as they were walking rapidly to the elevator, he said, "I have to know. How in heaven's name did you manage to overhear Christine's phone conversation?"

Courtney cast him an impish glance. "I was under her day bed. Searching for a Band-Aid," she said with a grin.

AVERY NOBLE GAVE COURTNEY a kindly look. "I'm sorry about all this, my dear. I know how upset you must be." He produced a sympathetic smile. Courtney took both the look and the smile for what it was worth. Very little.

"Where is my uncle, Mr. Noble? I'd like to see him. I'd like to speak to him. In private."

Noble glanced at Jonathan, then at her. "Well, now, I think under the circumstances it might be best to have someone with you...."

Courtney gave him a challenging glare. "This whole business is ludicrous. You can't still believe my uncle is in any way involved with the Russians. Not when you claim he shot one of them."

"Well—" Noble leaned back in his chair "—he might have been angling for a better position. After all, this Goncharov was Zakharov's right-hand man."

Jonathan, who had remained silent up to now, spit out, "This is bloody nonsense, Noble. Your theory is full of holes. And the manuscript, what about that? Does Vaughn even have it? Or was he set up by the Lambert woman? Did our Mr. Daniel Emerson really abduct her, or was that all part of the plan?"

Noble crossed his legs and considered Jonathan's words. "I never thought of that."

Neither had Courtney. "Why would Andrea Lambert bring him with her if she meant all along to take off?"

Both men focused their eyes on her, but it was Noble who spoke. "Perhaps he had overplayed his usefulness and she decided to double-cross him in the end. As it turned out he was more clever than she expected, since it appears he's the one who has ended up with the Gorky.''

"You think they were in this together from the start? That's a ridiculous theory," she snapped.

Noble merely shrugged. "There are others. Your uncle knew a good thing when he saw it and put on the charm in order to induce Mrs. Lambert to bring him along, hoping, perhaps, to get in on the profits. Or your uncle allowed himself to get set up initially per orders of the KGB. Or—"

"Or," Courtney cut him off sharply, "he was dragged off by the Lambert woman, who then somehow convinced him she was in trouble and in need of his help, her subsequent abduction by Emerson confirming that fact."

Jonathan smiled wryly. "As good an explanation as the rest, Avery. Wouldn't you agree?"

But before Noble could respond, Courtney said, "Why not ask my uncle which theory is correct?"

Noble smiled indulgently. "What would he say under the circumstances? What would anyone in his precarious position say under the circumstances?"

Jonathan saw Courtney stiffen, and he hastily put his hand on her shoulder in an effort to keep her from losing her temper. He knew that Noble was purposefully egging her on. And he guessed Noble's intent—to see if Courtney, as well as her uncle, was involved in the treachery. Noble was hoping to pound away at her defenses until he'd wrung out a confession. Jonathan knew that was not going to happen, but he didn't put it past Courtney to storm over to Noble and give him a good, solid punch in the jaw. Under other circumstances he would have taken great pleasure in that attack, but right now Noble was in the driver's seat and it wouldn't do to alienate the man.

"What has Vaughn told you so far?" Jonathan asked, his voice calm, his hand remaining on Courtney's shoulder.

His touch and the even tone of his voice seemed to settle her a bit.

"The man has been mum. Were he military I'd at least have gotten rank and serial number as well as a name. As it is, I merely get shrugs, a few sighs and blank looks."

Courtney couldn't help smiling. "All the more reason to let me talk with him. Does he know that I'm here? Does he know that the story about my death was a lie?"

"Oh, he did respond when I told him that. Very relieved, he was. Only I got the distinct feeling he wasn't as surprised as he pretended. When I confronted him on that issue, he merely said he never could accept the fact that you had perished."

Noble leveled an unpleasant stare at Courtney. "Perhaps because he knew all along that you were all right. Perhaps because the two of you—"

"Enough, Noble." Jonathan was fast losing patience. In another moment he wouldn't have to worry about Courtney throwing that punch. He'd be throwing it himself. "Bring the man in. Let his niece have a few words with him."

Noble clearly did not like to take orders. Especially from civilians who had supposedly resigned from his service. Courtney and Jonathan both could see that. So, when he agreed rather glibly to the reunion of uncle and niece, they both assumed the meeting would not be private. Courtney's eyes strayed to a large mirror on one wall of the office and then she looked at Jonathan. Yes, she thought, a one-way mirror. Jonathan's faint nod confirmed that he had read her mind and agreed with her conclusion.

"While they're meeting," Jonathan said to Noble, "I'll tell you about an interesting phone conversation between Christine Dupré and Daniel Emerson. You might decide, after hearing about it, that it isn't in your best interest to keep holding Lou Vaughn here."

Noble smiled with an air of superiority. "I already know what you're going to say, though I admit some curiosity about how you found out. As to our methods, we merely intercepted a message left for Mr. Vaughn at his hotel. Mr. Vaughn has been ordered to meet with Miss Dupré tomorrow afternoon, Gorky in hand. We have every intention of him keeping his 'date' with Miss Dupré. But, I'm afraid, if he does not produce the manuscript, that meeting will not be very productive."

Noble turned his gaze on Courtney. "I think you can impress upon your uncle how important it is for him to produce that manuscript. In fact, that is the primary reason I called you down here. As long as you agree to that request, I shall have your uncle brought in and the two of you can have your little reunion."

"She'll tell him," Jonathan said. "Call him in."

Noble hesitated for a moment, to get a reading on Courtney. She gave a faint nod. He pressed a buzzer on his desk.

Jonathan and Noble left the room immediately, and Courtney sat alone in the office, waiting for her uncle to arrive. She felt a rise of tension and anticipation, and breathed a heavy sigh of relief when her uncle walked into the room, a bright smile on his face, his step confident. He drew her affectionately into his arms and she found all her dread ebb. She clung to him.

"A pretty mess, this is," he said, but his tone was light, almost amused. "And here I thought we both led mundane lives." He drew her gently back and gave her a quick examination. "Well, you certainly don't look any the worse for wear. Why, you look . . . quite fantastic."

She felt her cheeks redden. "Perfectly pleasant looking, as you've told me."

He shook his head. "No, no. More than that. You've never looked more vibrant, more enchanting."

She smiled. "You look pretty damn good yourself. Quite a surprise under the circumstances."

"All a misunderstanding. It will get ironed out." He looked at her meaningfully. "I haven't done anything wrong. You must believe that, Courtney."

She threw her arms around him. "Of course, I believe that." Slowly she pulled back, a rueful smile curving her lips. "But I don't understand any of it."

"I'm afraid I don't understand a lot if it, either."

Courtney shot a surreptitious glance over at the one-way mirror, then looked back at her uncle. She was sure he got her message.

He smoothed back her hair. "Hey, I like the color."

"Uncle Lou, you do intend to cooperate with the authorities, don't you?"

He ignored her anxious question. "When I read about that fire in the shop, I nearly went out of my mind. But something told me—no, convinced me—that you were all right. And then at the Ambassador Club..." He grinned. "I couldn't believe my eyes at first, but that was you there in that waitress outfit, wasn't it?"

She laughed, a feeling of relief also surfacing. That explained why her uncle hadn't seemed all that surprised when Noble had told him about her being alive. "Yes, it was me. Just one of my recent incarnations."

"You amaze me, Courtney. How in heaven's name did you get so deeply involved in this messy business?"

"How did you?"

He grinned. "Something tells me we were both seduced, me by a damsel in distress and you by a tall, dark and handsome stranger."

Courtney's eyes once again flitted over to the mirror. Was Jonathan standing on the other side, watching, along with Noble? She turned back to her uncle. "I'm afraid I did a bit of seducing myself. Until your arrest, I've been having...the time of my life.''

"Ah. I see.''

A shadow crossed her face. "A once-in-a-lifetime adventure,'' she murmured. "And while it's certainly been fantastic, it's not a fantasy. It's very real. Far more exciting and intense than any intrigue I've ever conjured up.'' She hesitated. "And far more dangerous.''

He gave her a solemn look. "I know the time has long past to be giving you advice, Courtney, but I think this adventure is turning ugly and you'd best be out of it. Don't you agree?''

"I don't know what to think any more, Uncle Lou. Everything works out so well in fantasy. But this...this is so complex. I can't sort any of this out at all.'' Her gaze was steady as she looked at her uncle. "But I intend to see it through. And I'm going to do everything I can to make sure you are released. Even if you did shoot that dreadful KGB man.''

He took firm hold of her shoulders. "Don't worry about me, Courtney. I'll straighten all this out, I promise. But...you can do me a favor.''

"Anything, Uncle Lou.''

"It may sound silly to you under the circumstances, but I need you to call my broker back home for me.''

"Your broker? You mean your stockbroker? Carpenter, isn't it?''

"Right. You met him over at my place once. Anyway, he's got me rather heavily invested in gold right now. And what with gold having gone down so drastically recently, I want him to pull out some of my money and reinvest it elsewhere. Tell him I'd have liked to call myself, but I'm...tied up at the moment. He'll take care of the matter.''

"Uncle Lou, your financial investments are the least of your problems right now. What about the murder charge?

What about the manuscript? Do you have it? Mr. Noble wants you to bring it to that Dupré woman you spoke with last night. You're to show it to her and presumably she'll set up a meeting with you and Daniel Emerson. I suppose Emerson will want to make a trade. The manuscript in exchange for Andrea Lambert. But the secret service will be on hand. Hopefully they'll rescue both her and Marcus Lloyd. And take possession of the manuscript. And round up all the bad guys."

He stared at her in amazement. "Good heavens, child. You certainly know a lot about this affair. What's this about—what did you say his name was—Marcus Lloyd?"

"We believe Emerson kidnapped Marcus to get his hands on the Gorky. Jonathan—my tall, dark and very handsome stranger—was in Boston authenticating the manuscript. The manuscript was to be ransomed for Marcus. Then everything went haywire, and that awful woman, Andrea Lambert, ended up with the booty."

He smiled indulgently. "Andrea needed it for a similar reason as your friend."

"You mean for Marcus Lloyd?"

"No, for her sister. It's a complicated story. We planned our own exchange with Emerson. He's married to Andrea's sister, Denise."

"Her sister?"

"Yes. Denise disappeared recently and Andrea feels certain Emerson is involved somehow. Andrea's desperate to find out what happened to Denise. She learned through her sister that Emerson coveted the Gorky and she believed her only hope of finding her sister was to get her hands on it first."

"And where do you fit in?"

Lou smiled sheepishly. "I'm just being a Good Samaritan." He shrugged. "Anyway, I was about to negotiate with Emerson last night. Only he pulled a dirty trick and snatched Andrea. He probably thought she had the Gorky. Still, the odds are far more in his favor, as he's holding all the top cards—Andrea, her sister and Marcus Lloyd."

"But you're holding the Gorky. You could say we've got the trump card."

There was a long pause. "Well, I'm not exactly holding it."

Courtney could imagine the dismayed sighs of both Jonathan and Noble on the other side of the mirror. She sighed herself.

"What do you mean, Uncle Lou?" she asked, her voice fretful.

"It's . . . en route, you might say."

"En route to where?"

He gave a little shrug. "I can't say just yet."

"But Uncle Lou . . ."

"Please, Courtney, don't worry. I should have it by tomorrow."

She breathed another sigh, this one of relief. "Oh, that's all right, then."

"Now you'd better be off." He glanced over at the mirror and smiled. "I imagine they'll want to question me further." He put his arm through hers and walked her to the door. "Oh, you won't forget about that call to Carpenter for me? I intend to get out of this mess, and when I do, I'd like my little nest egg intact. So be sure to tell him I insist he pull my money out of the gold market and invest in something that promises more security. Tell him I plan to retire fully. The next shop I open up will be solely for you, Courtney. Not as manager, but owner. If that's still something you want to do."

Her gaze drifted from her uncle over to the one-way mirror. "I suppose," she said slowly, "I'll need something to occupy me when this adventure is over." But she knew, even as she spoke, that no involvement, professional or personal, would ever fully occupy her again. Jonathan and all they'd been through together, all the danger and the passion, would forever hold a portion of her heart and mind captive.

# CHAPTER SEVENTEEN

JONATHAN DROPPED COURTNEY off at his mother's estate that afternoon. Courtney had the manor to herself, as Lady Edith was off doing charitable works and Jonathan was off doing…doing what? Doing a good job of proving he could carry on without her, that's what.

It was nearly dinnertime when he made an appearance. He wasn't alone.

"Uncle Lou." Temporarily putting aside her frustration at being left out in the cold, Courtney ran across the hall and threw her arms around her uncle. "What are you doing here? Has Noble let you go?"

He gave her a comforting squeeze. "As far as the leash will stretch."

"Oh, I see." Courtney shot Jonathan a narrow look. "Are you in charge of him, then?" Her frustration came back with added measure.

"I didn't think you'd prefer having your uncle spend the night in custody."

"I'll tell you what I'd prefer. I'd prefer the ridiculous charges against him were dropped. Then he wouldn't need a watchdog."

"I'm afraid that's Noble's decision, not mine. I'm not even on his payroll."

"Not yet, anyway."

Lou grinned at Jonathan. "She's got a sharp tongue, this niece of mine."

Uncle Lou was adding to Courtney's frustration. "I don't see why you aren't angrier, Uncle Lou. You don't seem the least bit upset by what's been happening. Why, you'd think Jonathan was your best pal instead of your keeper."

"Madden here is only looking after his interests, as I'm looking after mine," Uncle Lou said soothingly.

"She's out of sorts because I've left her cooling her heels at home," Jonathan said. "Quite an adventuress, this niece of yours."

Courtney glared at both of them. "I don't find either one of you amusing. I don't find anything that's happened amusing. And what about your damsel in distress, Uncle Lou? Aren't you worried about Andrea Lambert?"

"She'll be all right as long as I have what her kidnapper wants."

Courtney glanced at Jonathan before leveling her gaze back at her uncle. "But you don't have it."

She saw from the bland expression on Jonathan's face that he already knew that, which only confirmed that he had been listening along with Noble behind that one-way mirror.

Uncle Lou smiled equanimously. "But I will have it."

She caught a quick exchange of looks between the two men. More and more, she was sensing the budding of a conspiracy, one from which she was intentionally being excluded. She felt both puzzled and irritated.

If either man was aware her annoyance he gave no hint of it. Uncle Lou made a sweeping gesture with his hand as they stood in the grand marble-floored hallway. "Quite a place, Madden. There must be a library with a bar around here somewhere, am I right?"

Jonathan grinned. "Absolutely. Just at the end of the hall on the left. I'll lead the way."

"Sure, go on ahead, and mix me a bourbon and soda, would you? I just want a word with my niece."

Jonathan hesitated for a moment, then nodded and took off.

"Thanks for putting in that call to Carpenter for me," Lou said when Jonathan had gone. "I was worried he might not get the message straight, but he did."

Courtney frowned. "You've heard from him? How did he reach you? I didn't tell him where you were."

"Once Noble agreed to release me, I was able to phone him. He told me you'd already conveyed my message."

"He sounded a bit put off on the phone. I had the feeling he was unhappy about your decision to pull out of the gold market."

Lou rubbed his jaw. "Yes, well, you know stockbrokers. They like to run the show. Always think they know what's best."

"But he agreed to do as you asked." She observed him closely, a curious expression on her face. "Another thing. He laughed when I told him you were retiring. He said a funny thing to me."

"What's that?"

"He said, 'What? Again?' Now what did he mean by that? You've never retired before. Slowed down, maybe, but until the shop burned down—"

"You probably misunderstood. I'm always telling Carpenter I'm going to retire and he never believes me, that's all. The only thing that matters is he's taking care of business as I want."

"I still don't understand why you seem more worried about your investments than you do about the manuscript, Uncle Lou. You aren't in on some imminent world collapse, are you?"

"I'm just looking after things, that's all."

"And what about the meeting with Christine Dupré tomorrow? Unless you bring that manuscript with you, you won't get anywhere."

"Come on, let's go to the library. You can have a drink with me. You're tense."

"Of course I'm tense. And I'm feeling more and more in the dark. Have you and Jonathan talked further about the situation? What does he think? Why is he following Noble's orders? I believe he's trying to ease me out of the operation."

Lou frowned at her paternally. "This is dangerous business, Courtney, not a fantasy. You can't simply dream up a safe and happy little ending, you know. Real life doesn't work that way."

"Tell me about it."

Lou's eyebrow arched. "Have it bad, do you?"

"Does it show?"

"You've never looked so radiant. So lovely. Yes," he said quietly, then smiled. "Being in love agrees with you."

She laughed dryly. "You're wrong there. It doesn't agree with me at all."

"I see."

"Do you?"

He took hold of her hand. "I've known men like Madden. I think I understand them. Hell, I'm one of them myself. Never did want to get tied down."

"I tied you down."

He smiled. "Not in the same way. Some men just can't handle too much intimacy. Or they think they can't. Every now and then, one of them finds out maybe he was wrong."

"If and when he does, it might be too late."

"True enough." Lou leveled a steady gaze at his niece. "You've really gotten yourself into quite a fix, sweetheart."

Courtney managed a smile. "I'm holding my own. It isn't over yet."

He was watching her intently. "I think it is, Courtney."

Her eyes narrowed. "What do you mean?"

"Go back home, Courtney. You've already had enough adventure to last a lifetime."

She could feel her fury rising. "I'll be the judge of that."

"Courtney, if it's because of Madden that you're sticking around..."

"Yes...go on, say it. I'm wasting my time. Is that what you were going to say? What would a handsome, clever, aristocratic British secret agent ever want with the likes of me, right?"

He gripped her arm. "Take it easy. That wasn't what I was going to say. The thing is, it might work out better for you if you gave the man a little breathing space, that's all. Give him time to sort out how much you mean to him. Anyway, what good are hopes for a happy ending if something terrible happens to you?"

"I've done okay so far," she said stubbornly.

"According to Madden, you've been extremely lucky so far. But luck has a way of running out."

"Luck, is it?" She swung abruptly away from her uncle and marched down the hall to the library. She strode across the thick gray carpet up to Jonathan. "Is that what you've told my uncle? That I've been *lucky*? I don't suppose you told him how I saved your life, risked my own on more than one occasion, found out information you'd otherwise have never obtained. I don't suppose you told him you've admitted needing me on this operation, as distasteful as you find that realization."

Jonathan sighed and cast a glance over Courtney's shoulder at Lou Vaughn. A smile curved his lips. "Headstrong, my mother calls her."

"Damn it, Jonathan, be serious," she snapped. "I haven't come this far not to see it through."

He erased his smile. "I am being serious. Look, you came to London to find your uncle. Well, now you've found him and I promise he's in good hands. His story about the

Lambert woman's sister checks out. Denise Lambert and Daniel Emerson were married a few months ago. Noble's people have verified it." Jonathan handed Lou his drink, and their eyes met for a moment.

Again Courtney caught the shared look between the two men. "What is it I'm not being told?"

Amazing how innocently both men smiled. "Nothing," they said, practically in unison.

Lady Edith arrived as Lou was polishing off his second bourbon. After a few minutes of tense chitchat, Lady Edith suggested showing Lou around the estate. Jonathan and Courtney stayed in the library.

Jonathan glanced at Courtney's untouched glass of sherry. "Would you prefer something else?"

There were many things she'd prefer, but they had nothing to do with alcoholic beverages. "You and my uncle have gotten very chummy."

"You don't seem pleased."

"Why are you pushing me out, Jonathan?"

He emitted a long sigh. "Listen to me, Courtney. You are a clever, courageous, wonderful woman. But..."

"But you don't need me anymore."

Smoothing his expression to cool granite, he said, "I'm afraid that's the way it is."

Her obvious pain at his cold words spread to him. A part of him longed to take them back. At least to soften the words by telling her what she had come to mean to him, how very much he did care. But to tell her that implied a promise of some kind of future. It meant asking her to wait. It meant accepting responsibility for embarking on a relationship. And he was not ready for that responsibility. His mind was once again filled with daring, dangerous adventures. In his heart he'd never really left the service, and now that he was so close to seeing this one to a successful end, he envisioned endless new adventures to come. It was only fair to Courtney to break clean now.

Feeling at a loss for what else to say, he merely turned and poured himself a stiff glass of scotch, straight up.

He could feel her watching him, and finally faced her. She was only a few feet away, her lovely face taut, her eyes burning into his.

"Did I imagine it all?" she whispered hoarsely. "Did I only imagine you . . . loved me just a little?"

She looked confused, angry, bewildered.

Her eyes left his face. "I'm sorry. That wasn't fair. From the moment you stumbled into the back room of my shop, I've been pushing my way into your life, trying foolishly to make my fantasy yours."

"You've most assuredly gotten under my skin, Courtney Blue," he said gently, trying to lessen her pain. "I shall never forget how incredible you are. But let's face it, love, you want strings. Permanent strings. We both know that. And . . . I'm just not ready for strings."

She wanted to argue, but she didn't. He was right, even though she'd never said a word about strings. She loved Jonathan and she wanted a happy-ever-after ending.

"I've arranged for you to fly back to Boston in the morning, Courtney."

She stuffed her hands into her jeans pockets. As much as Jonathan was trying to convince her it was over she just could not let go. "And if I refuse to leave?"

"Courtney . . . be sensible. Your uncle will see Christine. She'll arrange the meeting with Emerson. We'll be there when that meeting takes place, and the whole mess will be straightened out even before you're settled back home."

"And the Russians? What about them? What about Zakharov?" she asked calmly, while inside her heart was pounding, aching with the pressure.

"We hope Zakharov will show up, too. We want to get him, as well."

"The final showdown. Yes, we need the final showdown."

He knew her flippancy was an attempt to mask her hurt. "Let's hope it's quick and final, and that none of our people get hurt in the process. You do realize that's why you must return home now. I don't want you to get hurt."

"Isn't it a bit late to worry about that?" Her flippancy had turned to cool irony.

"I knew from the start I was going to end up falling a little in love with you despite my best efforts," he whispered. He set down his glass without even having touched the refill, and reached out to her.

It would have been so easy to let him hold her. Easy even now to pretend his loving her truly meant more to him than it did, that her safety was his sole motivation for sending her away. Part of her wanted to believe that. But that was a fantasy, and she no longer wanted fantasy. Never again would fantasy hold the same joy or magic for her.

She pushed him away even as she argued with herself to take what he had to offer and be satisfied. "I'll leave, Jonathan. But not until after the showdown. Not until I can board that plane for Boston with my uncle. I must know that he's all right. This plan he's to carry out puts him in terrible danger."

"Your uncle will do splendidly. Really, he can handle this."

She looked at him curiously. "You sound very confident."

He shied away from her gaze. "Well, I've met him, gotten to know him a bit. He seems able. And his story holds. So I agree he's honest. And he does want to see Andrea Lambert safely out of Emerson's clutches. So there's strong motivation."

"Do you think she means something to him?"

"He hasn't said anything, but I get the feeling he's not the sort to get too wrapped up in a woman. Especially one he hardly knows."

Courtney flashed Jonathan a wry smile. "Yes, she rather forced herself on my uncle just as I forced myself on you. You and my uncle share that in common. Perhaps that's why the two of you hit it off so well," she said with a sharp laugh.

"That's better," Uncle Lou said from the open door. "Good to hear you laughing again, Courtney." He sauntered into the library. "Your mother's a most charming woman, Madden. She's gone to arrange for dinner. I was wondering if you could lend me something a bit more formal to wear." He looked down at his wrinkled shirt and trousers. "I won't have time to scoot back to the hotel for a change."

"No problem," Jonathan said, clearly relieved by the interruption.

Lou looked over at his niece. Her laugh hadn't really fooled him for one instant. "Everything all right?"

"No," she said bluntly, "everything isn't all right. The two of you have been conspiring to get rid of me. Jonathan is filled with confidence about your ability to handle things with him from here on out. Just why he thinks you're any more equipped—" She stopped abruptly. Slowly she ran her index finger across her lips, her expression thoughtful. Her eyes narrowed on her uncle. "Wait a minute." She stared more closely at him. "I've got all the pieces here. I just need to fit them into place," she said. "My mind's been in such a fog. So much has been happening." She found herself recalling the conversation with her uncle in Noble's office that afternoon. All that talk about investments...about gold.

"Gold," she said out loud. "Les Sharp...he talked about gold, too."

Uncle Lou shot a quick look at Jonathan. "Funny name, Les Sharp."

"Yes...yes, that's what I thought. A funny little man with a funny name." She could picture with absolute clarity that first meeting with Mr. Les Sharp, CIA agent, at the ersatz colonial restaurant in Cohasset. She recreated it all, her clever disguise, poor Les Sharp's discomfort thinking Jonathan was involved with another man. And she remembered what Sharp had told her, something she'd forgotten until now. Sharp had said there would be a CIA deep-cover operative on the case. A very highly respected man. A superspy who went by the code name Gold.

"Gold," she repeated aloud.

Lou smiled slowly, awkwardly. It was a telling smile that spoke more than words.

She stared at her uncle in stunned silence. Finally she said, "It's you. You're Gold. That message to your broker...all that business about selling gold. It didn't make sense, but I was so relieved to see you and I've had so many other concerns..." She kept her eyes riveted on her uncle. "Still, it isn't the most obvious thing to think your uncle...a man you've known all your life...the man who raised you for over fifteen years...a man who seemed to be a perfectly ordinary book dealer...has in truth been leading a double life. My uncle...a deep-cover intelligence agent for the CIA. It seems so...incredible."

Both men remained silent.

"But, then, there were all those trips to Russia. And other places. Well, rare book dealers travel a lot. Who would imagine you were really off on dangerous missions for the government?" She paused, her eyes widening, a chill going through her. "They were dangerous, weren't they?"

Lou said nothing.

She turned to Jonathan. "And you aren't his watchdog. You're his partner. No wonder you're so confident. You don't have to rely on an amateur any longer. You have yourself a real pro now.''

Again her eyes shifted to her uncle. ''This is your official assignment, isn't it? Not just getting the manuscript, but getting Emerson. And you're probably after Zakharov, the Russian agent. American agents are always after Russian agents and vice versa. It's part of the game. But there's still something I can't figure out. Was the kidnapping a hoax? Was Andrea Lambert working with you the whole time? Is she CIA, too? Was I out of my mind with worry about your safety for no reason at all?''

Lou smiled awkwardly. ''No. There was no hoax. Andrea Lambert isn't a secret agent. I told you, she's just a desperate woman trying to track down her sister. This whole business all sort of fell in my lap, in no small measure due to you, Courtney. There I was, a happily retired intelligence agent, when you dropped that Gorky bomb in my lap. Old habits die hard. I phoned into headquarters at Langley. They pulled me out of retirement. Hell, this is one profession it isn't easy to walk away from.''

Courtney met Jonathan's eyes for a moment and nodded. ''Yes, my view, as well,'' she said in a low voice.

''Anyway,'' Lou went on, ''word had already filtered through to Langley about the Gorky manuscript. Rumor was that a noted Russian scientist working on a new submarine detection device had smuggled the plans out in the Gorky. I was directed to send the manuscript off to headquarters pronto.''

Jonathan grinned. ''And beat our boys to the glory.''

Lou winked. ''Call it friendly rivalry. We're all working for truth, justice and...well, skip the rest. Anyway, Andrea Lambert got in the way of the plan.'' He shrugged. ''Later, when she told me her sad story, I decided to help her.''

Jonathan grinned. "And hopefully track down Zakharov in the process. I'm sure Langley would be very pleased to have that elusive KGB agent out of the picture."

"I also got to keep my mitts on the Gorky," Lou continued. "I agreed to help Andrea Lambert. But first I told her she had to prove she was on the level. She could have been making up the whole story about her sister. So, to show she was straight arrow, she gave me the manuscript, and I locked it in a box at Heathrow and pocketed the key. I have a feeling she meant to pick it up later. I found the key hidden away in her purse. But I beat her to it, slipped back there and shipped the Gorky off to Langley before she even knew the key was missing." He grinned. "After this, I'm going to have a hard time convincing the boys at Langley that I really am serious about retirement."

Courtney walked over to the library table. Ignoring her sherry, she lifted Jonathan's glass of scotch and took a sip. "And the message to Carpenter?"

"I needed the manuscript back. And in order to get Noble off my case, I needed Langley to verify my identity."

Courtney took a longer swallow of scotch. "It really is quite incredible," she said, sputtering from the burning sensation the alcohol left in her throat. "My uncle a secret agent." She turned and leveled her gaze on Jonathan. "A man who pretends to be an ordinary professor...a secret agent. And I imagined I lived a sort of double life." She laughed sharply. "Am I the only one around who isn't a spy? Next you'll be telling me Lady Edith is a secret agent, as well."

Jonathan smiled tenderly. "Not to my knowledge." He grinned in Lou's direction. "Not one of your recruits, is she?"

Lou chuckled.

But Courtney was not the least bit amused and told them so. "You've both lied to me...made every effort to trick me each step of the way. Neither of you ever had any intention of telling me the truth. It's only that I was smarter than you gave me credit for. And determined to get answers... honest answers." She gave them both hard stares. "You don't play fair, either one of you."

"This isn't a game, Courtney," Jonathan said firmly. "And it isn't a matter of fairness. In this business you never reveal more than is absolutely necessary. It's one of the cardinal rules."

"Yes, I know about that rule. As Derek Colton says, 'One gives out information on a need-to-know basis only.' And it seems that as far as the two of you are concerned, I don't need to know very much. Well, shall I tell you what I think?"

Both men shared a look that acknowledged she'd tell them whether they wanted to know or not.

"I think you're every bit as confused by what's real and what's fantasy as I am. That's what I think." And with that pronouncement she wheeled around and made her exit.

Both men watched in silence as she left. Then Lou cast Jonathan a puzzled look. "Who's Derek Colton?"

Jonathan scowled. "I haven't the foggiest."

Lou smiled wryly. "Better watch it, Madden. That man might be your competition."

# CHAPTER EIGHTEEN

"WE WORK FOR A GOVERNMENT that does not tolerate failure," Zakharov said.

Borofsky and Petrenko nodded nervously. Failure. They'd known nothing but failure. After this, even Siberia might not look so bad.

"Fortunately I maintain certain...connections." Zakharov sneered. Or perhaps it was a smile. Sometimes it was difficult to distinguish. "Connections that shall help us turn failure into triumph. And now I want that triumph not only for my country, but for a valued comrade who lost his life attempting to bring us honor."

A moment of silence for the slain Goncharov ensued. Borofsky and Petrenko wore very sorrowful expressions, but when Zakharov's back was turned the two comrades shared a quick smile. Neither man would ever dream of mentioning that the bullet that had downed Comrade Goncharov had been one of theirs. Neither was sure which of them had actually hit the mark. It was just as well. It made the unspoken vow of silence between them less of a worry. Besides, it wasn't as if they'd gone out of their way to gun down their comrade, although they would have been fools to have many regrets. Goncharov had not exactly endeared himself to them.

Actually they'd been gunning for the American book dealer, Lou Vaughn. Of course, Zakharov would not have been any more thrilled if they'd killed Vaughn. Zakharov's orders had been to capture Vaughn and Lambert. Dead people, after all, didn't talk. And if they didn't have the manuscript on them, they would certainly need to talk.

No, Zakharov would not have been pleased if they'd murdered Vaughn. But they'd been so spooked, seeing that ghost of a woman in the woods the way they had. Then, when they'd made their approach to the Austin sedan, they'd caught the gun in Vaughn's hand. Reflex. That's what it had been. Reflex and nerves. That explained their misguided aim. And the inadvertent loss of a comrade.

The moment of silence was over. The mourning period for Comrade Goncharov had come to a close. It was now time for Zakharov to finish his job.

And it was time for Borofsky and Petrenko to redeem themselves. This was likely to be the last chance they'd get.

"I DON'T CARE how far you've come on this, Jonathan," Noble said tightly. "This is where you step aside. I have far too much riding on this mission to risk a hotshot novice making another mistake. Your record in the trade, old man, isn't exactly unblemished."

Jonathan's mouth twitched. "Neither is yours, Noble."

Noble ignored the insult and turned his attention to Lou Vaughn. "I won't have the CIA mucking up the works, either, Vaughn. You're to follow orders. I've had a few words with your superiors in Virginia."

Lou Vaughn grinned. "Don't tell me my record in the trade isn't so hot."

Noble smiled with polite derision. "Oh, they say you generally manage to come out of operations with the goods, as they put it, but they also say your methods are frequently unorthodox. You are a man who likes to follow his instincts. Like Jonathan here. I don't trust instinct. Instincts can be misguided. I am a man who believes in being disciplined, thoughtful and careful. In the end, my approach will ultimately prove the more durable."

Lou Vaughn was standing behind a chair in Avery Noble's office. He gripped the back of it, leaning over a little. "Well, I guess we'll find out which approach proves the best this time around."

Noble's eyes narrowed. "Your superiors in Langley have made it clear you are to cooperate fully with British intelligence. You did quite well this afternoon at your meeting with Miss Dupré. Your next step is to use the airline ticket she gave you and board that plane for Paris. We'll arrange to have a car for you there. Emerson seems more than eager to make the trade—the Gorky manuscript in exchange for the three people he is holding, the wife, Andrea Lambert and Lloyd. You are to act as if the man is honorable. Show up, present the manuscript and leave the rest to my people."

Lou's eyes narrowed. "I suppose you realize the Russians are likely to be on the scene, as well. Emerson, the Russians, a delicate rescue operation, keeping the manuscript from falling into the wrong hands. That's a big order for your people."

"I will have my best team on the job. Men who follow orders, not instincts. Whatever transpires, you can trust them to do what needs to be done to successfully complete this mission."

Jonathan stood by the window, observing Noble with an icy stare. He crossed his arms over his chest. "Tell me something, Noble. Just what does success mean to you? Saving the lives of three people, or advancing your career another notch by getting your hands on that new submarine detection device?"

"We don't yet know whether that information was smuggled out in the Gorky. Langley only had the manuscript for a few hours. They didn't have time to check the work thoroughly."

"And you weren't eager for me to take a look at it either."

"There wasn't time."

"Langley had the manuscript here in your office at eleven this morning. Lou didn't take it over to the Dupré woman until three. There was time, Noble."

"I had one of my people going over it. And when I get it back he shall study it in more detail. The manuscript is only the bait, though. You seem to forget that."

Jonathan strode over to Noble's desk. He would have liked nothing better than to punch the bastard, but he controlled his impulse, slamming his fist down on the top of the desk, instead. "I'm not forgetting that, Noble. Nor am I forgetting that Marcus Lloyd's life is on the line. As are the lives of two innocent women. But that's not what you mean by bait, is it, Noble? No, you don't give a damn about Lloyd. And you probably consider those two poor women expendable."

Noble rose angrily from his chair. "I think you had better leave, Jonathan. I refuse to listen to such unfounded accusations. You forget who I am."

"My memory is functioning just fine." Jonathan was seething. "I know exactly who you are, Noble. You're a cutthroat, greedy, small-minded man motivated solely by self-interest. And to achieve your goals you'd do just about anything. All you want is the glory. The glory of the big catch. Trophies, Noble. And a big pat on the back from the prime minister for bringing down Emerson and Zakharov. That's who the bait is for. And anyone caught in the cross fire be damned." He leaned forward across the desk so that he was practically nose to nose with Noble. "Or maybe I'm being overly generous, old man. Maybe this operation provides you with the perfect and final resolution to an old problem. The problem of Marcus Lloyd."

"Just what the hell are you implying?" Noble demanded.

Lou Vaughn put a calming hand on Jonathan's shoulder. "Jonathan just wants to make sure his buddy and former boss doesn't get caught in the cross fire, Noble. But I think that a man as disciplined and orderly and cautious as you wouldn't be fool enough to let that happen." He gave Noble a long, steady look, then patted Jonathan on the shoulder. "Come on. Let's get out of here. I've got some packing to do. And I have to contend with my overenthusiastic and very stubborn niece back at that high-class OK corral of yours."

Noble was having a hard job controlling his temper. "And that's another thing," he shouted as the two men turned to leave. "If I see one sign of Courtney Blue in Paris, or you, Madden, I just might follow *my* instincts this one time. That's fair warning, Jonathan."

Lou opened the office door, making a sweeping gesture with his arm for Jonathan to precede him.

"Do you hear me, Madden?" Noble's voice was shrill with fury. "Damn it, Madden, you stay out of this. I mean it. Do you hear me, Madden?"

Whether or not Jonathan heard, there was no doubt that every person on the fourteenth floor did.

"LOOK," JONATHAN SAID, "you can't come with us. If anything goes wrong, your uncle and I will have enough to worry about without worrying about you." He saw Courtney's mouth start to open. "I won't have any argument this time. You must stay put. You'll only be in the way."

"In the way?" Courtney snapped. "Is that what I've been so far? Merely in the way?"

"Courtney, be reasonable," Uncle Lou interjected. "You aren't equipped to cope with a situation like this. You could

get hurt...or worse." He stood by the bar, pouring him
self a bourbon and soda.

Lady Edith was sitting beside Courtney on the couch
"I'll have a sherry, if you don't mind, Mr. Vaughn," sh
called out.

"The name's 'Lou.' And I don't mind at all...Edie."

Courtney looked over at Lady Edith, momentarily di
tracted. "You told my uncle about the Ambassador Clu
episode?"

Lou smiled. "We spent a couple of hours shooting th
breeze last night. The incident at the Ambassador Club di
come up. And hey," he said, "I was very impressed."

Courtney's brow arched. "If you're so impressed, let m
come with you. I won't do anything foolish. I haven't ye
have I? We're coming to the most exciting part. I am n
going to sit here, cooling my jets while the two of you hav
all the fun."

Jonathan sighed wearily as he ran his fingers through hi
hair. "Fun? That's what I mean." He came over, leane
down toward her, hands on her shoulders. "Fantasy is fur
maybe. But this...this is real, Courtney."

"I know the difference, Jonathan," she said tightly.

He stared deeply into her eyes. "Do you?"

Lou brought the sherry over to Lady Edith and sat dow
across from her.

"This is not only real," Lou joined in, "it's getting rea
ugly. I smell something rank going on and I've got a reli
able sniffer."

"I can tell you where that foul odor is coming from,"
Jonathan said in a low, angry voice. "From Avery Noble."

"You've got a good sniffer, too, Jonathan." Lou winked

"What about my sniffer?" Courtney demanded, tap
ping her nose angrily.

Jonathan smiled as he sat down beside her on the couch
"You've got the prettiest little sniffer I've ever seen."

"Don't you dare patronize me, Jonathan Madden."

"I agree with Courtney, dear," Lady Edith said, her tone scolding. "From everything she's told me about this madcap escapade, she's been an asset to you every step of the way." She raised a nicely shaped brow. "I haven't done badly, either, if I do say so myself."

Jonathan gave Lou a look of abject frustration. "Most families, should they discover a loved one's in the spy business, fear for their loved one's safety. But not your niece or my mother. They find out there's a spy in the family and all they want is to get in on the act. Fun and games. That's what it is to them."

"You're twisting my words, Jonathan," Courtney argued. "I'm fully aware of the danger and the risks. But I'm also aware of the excitement, the exhilaration...yes, the fun. Tell me, either one of you, that you don't feel the same way."

Her uncle threw a "she's got us there" shrug in Jonathan's direction. Jonathan merely sighed, then glanced at his watch. Lou's plane was departing from Heathrow in an hour. And Jonathan had a stop to make before getting to the airport. But he couldn't leave until he made certain that the ever-resourceful Courtney Blue did not don some new disguise and take off after him.

Lou saw Jonathan check his watch. "We'd better get a move on." He rose from his chair and reached out his hand to Lady Edith. She took it and smiled demurely when he gallantly gave her hand a chivalrous kiss.

"A pleasure to meet you, Mr.—Lou."

"The pleasure's all mine...Edie."

Jonathan rose, too. With his outstretched hand he helped Courtney up from the couch. "I'll see you in the car, Lou. I want a few words with Courtney first."

"Come, Lou. I'll walk you out," Lady Edith offered. "I'm driving into the city to meet some friends for dinner."

She glanced back at Courtney. "You're sure you won't come along?"

Courtney smiled innocently. "Yes, thanks, anyway. I have a few other matters to attend to tonight."

"Listen to me, Courtney," Jonathan said earnestly when the other two had left the room, "There's something I want to say to you before I go."

"If you're about to give me further reasons I should stay put—"

"One reason," he broke in. "Only one." He drew her into his arms, feeling her body stiffen in protest, even though she made no effort to pull away. He lowered his mouth and kissed her very gently, very tenderly. He didn't stop raining light, provocative kisses on her lips until he felt her resistance ebb. Only when she'd responded fully did he ease her away, his gaze holding hers.

"I love you, Courtney," he said quietly. "That's the reason I want you to stay here, out of harm's way. It's the best reason."

Courtney felt a tremor shoot through her. She had not anticipated that—those three words she'd so longed to hear her hero utter, spoken without prodding or hesitation. She would have been lying if she'd told herself those words had no effect on her. She could feel her defenses start to slip. Still, her instincts kept flashing beware signs in her head. She tilted her head back and observed him closely.

"How do I know you're not trying to manipulate me, Jonathan? You've guarded your feelings so well up to this point. Only now that you're about to run out on me do you tell me you love me. And what about those strings you were so worried about? What happens when you come back?" She felt a cold chill snake down her spine. "Or are you thinking you might not make it back, so I won't be able to hold you accountable."

"Damn it, Courtney, you can be bloody impossible at times. I'm telling you I love you because I do love you. I didn't plan on it, God knows. And I admit I didn't want it to happen. But it did. As for what happens when I get back, we'll have to deal with it then." He put his hand under her chin and raised her face. "One thing I guarantee, I will be back. This is one assignment I won't muck up."

She threw her arms around him suddenly and kissed him hotly on the lips, then just as suddenly drew back, a smile on her face, a cautious smile. "Is that a promise?"

Their eyes met and held.

"First promise me something," he said. "Give me your solemn word you will not follow us to Paris. Promise me you will stay here, safely out of trouble."

They had reached an impasse and they both knew it. "You'd better hurry," she said quietly. "My uncle is waiting."

He couldn't help smiling, any more than he could help admiring her. Or, for that matter, loving her. He did love her. Even if he continued to find the feeling a decidedly unsettling one.

His smile turned rueful. "You are incorrigible, love. But I don't suppose I'd have you any other way. And when I do return—" he pressed his lips against her hair "—we shall both have to separate the reality from the fantasy. I'm no more certain than you are exactly which is which. As my mother observed, life has been rather madcap since we met. What happens, I wonder, when the adventure is over? When we are both just . . . well, ordinary people again? How will either of us feel then?" He smiled at her.

She eyed him searchingly. "There is nothing ordinary about you, Jonathan." A feeling of despair swept over her. She could not say the same about herself. Okay, so she'd played out some of her wildest and most exciting fantasies these past few days. But when the adventure was over . . .

She clutched the front of his shirt. "Jonathan, you've got to let me come along. You must. We've been lucky together. It isn't smart to mess with that luck."

"You won't give up, will you?" He sighed, sliding his hands along her arms, his fingers coming to rest at her wrists, circling them, drawing them first down to her sides and then behind her back.

Before she fully comprehended what he was up to, she felt more than his strong, masculine fingers entwining her wrists.

She felt a rope being coiled around them.

"Jonathan, are you mad? What are you doing? Stop it. You can't do this to me."

He worked quickly, effectively, the bindings firm but not tight enough to do any damage.

"I'm sorry, love. But it's the only way I can be sure you won't follow me to Paris."

She struggled in earnest as he began tying her ankles together, but she was no match for him.

"I swear, Jonathan, I'll never forgive you for this. I'm not some damn chicken you can truss up. Ouch. You're hurting me."

"Then stop fighting me. My mother will be home in a couple of hours and she'll untie you. Really, love, I just can't have you showing up on the plane disguised as a stewardess. Or popping up in Paris dressed in a gendarme's uniform."

"Look, I give you my word..." She paused, knitting her brows. "You don't trust me, is that it?"

Jonathan almost broke into laughter. He cast her a wry look and resumed his task. When he was quite certain she was secured, he swung her over his shoulder, fireman-fashion, and set her down in an armchair.

She glared at him in silence.

He smiled. "Oh, by the way, I gave the staff the night off." He grinned. "So I won't have to tape shut that lovely mouth of yours."

Her eyes glinted fire.

"You'll thank me one day."

He started to tie her to the chair itself to be on the safe side, but the car horn tooted—Vaughn warning him to hurry. Jonathan gave her one last look. Well, the bindings would suffice.

He leaned over to kiss her. She turned her face away.

He laughed softly. "I said that before this was over I was going to fall head over heels in love with you. Instinct told me. And I do have a bad habit of following my instincts. Even when they land me in a good deal of trouble."

BOROFSKY SNEEZED for the fourth time as he hid in the shrubbery outside Lady Edith's mansion. He was coming down with another of his spring colds. The damp London climate wasn't helping any. He felt irritable. The weather in Paris would be better. Why couldn't Zakharov order him to follow Madden, leaving Petrenko to stay here to observe the ghost? Well, not a ghost, it turned out. The lady shopkeeper was very much alive. Still, this was a waste of time. Madden and Vaughn had left several minutes ago. As had the mother earlier in the evening. Courtney Blue had not come out. Borofsky did not think she was going anywhere. It was going to be a long, boring night.

But go tell that to Zakharov. His superior was convinced the Blue woman was no innocent shopkeeper. Ever since Zakharov's contact here in London had informed him of the real identity of Lou Vaughn, Zakharov was convinced that the niece, too, was working for the American government. He was certain she was a high-ranking CIA agent, perhaps even higher than the uncle. Perhaps even the mastermind behind the whole operation.

MINUTES AFTER JOHNATHAN departed, the telephone started ringing. Courtney stared wanly across a space of a good twenty feet to where the phone sat on the bar. If only she could get to it before it stopped ringing....

She rolled off the armchair onto the floor with a painful thump.

The phone rang for the third time.

Chin resting square on the carpet, she drew her knees up to her chest, then dove forward as best she could, propelling herself in the direction of the bar.

She counted rings as she maneuvered across the room. The phone was on its sixth ring when she finally reached the bar. She still had to get back up on her feet to reach the phone.

She managed it in two more rings. Then, with her chin, she nudged the receiver from the cradle.

"Hello. Hello? Jonathan? Courtney? Hello?"

Courtney was just about to answer, when she saw the closed library doors start to open.

Jonathan had given the staff the night off. It couldn't be Lady Edith. Courtney was alone in the house. That is, she was supposed to be alone.

"Hello? Can you hear me?" the caller said.

Courtney's eyes were fixed on the library doors, which were parting like the Red Sea. Her whole trussed-up body broke into a panicky sweat. She silently cursed Jonathan for putting her in this terrifying position.

Rousing herself from terror for one brief instant before the intruder appeared, Courtney lowered her head to the receiver and whispered, "Help."

When she looked over at the library doors again, her eyes fell first on the gleaming blue black pistol pointed in her direction, then on the hand holding it. A hand with exquisitely manicured red lacquered nails.

Courtney was trembling too hard to notice that Christine Dupré's gun hand wasn't all that steady, either.

"What's going on? What's happening?" came the voice on the phone.

Christine Dupré looked over at the receiver, then at Courtney. She started to motion her to hang up the phone, but saw that that would be quite a feat, considering Courtney's bound state. A look of surprise altered her grim features as she crossed the room and hung the phone up herself.

Courtney sighed in despair. Her lifeline had just been yanked.

"Where's Madden?" Christine demanded.

"You're too late," Courtney responded tartly. She might be shaking like a leaf, but she wasn't about to give the Dupré woman the satisfaction of hearing her whimper.

"He's ... gone, then?"

Courtney saw Christine's gun hand drop to her side.

Wait a sec. This wasn't the way the scene was supposed to go. "Why do you want Jonathan?" Courtney asked cautiously.

Christine Dupré closed her eyes and swayed a little. "I've made such a mess of everything. It's gotten utterly out of hand." She opened her eyes.

Courtney was stunned to see tears trickle from the temptress's long-lashed blue eyes. "It's not too late," Courtney said softly. She hobbled closer to the bar for support.

Christine stared at her in silence for several moments, then asked, "Who tied you up? The Russian who was snooping around outside?" A faint smile curved her ruby-red lips. "He won't be bothering you again for a while."

Courtney didn't bother to correct her assumption. "Will you untie me?"

Christine shook her head. "It wouldn't be wise. You'd have the police after me in no time. I've got to get away. Far away. It's over for me. One ought never to make a deal with the Devil."

"You mean Emerson?" Courtney asked.

"I suppose no one will believe now that I do love Marcus. Daniel had me so convinced I'd lose him. It was only a matter of time. I thought having a great deal of money would cushion the blow when he eventually left me. I never knew Daniel meant to kidnap Marcus. Even afterward, I kept trying to deny that Daniel would harm him. But I know deep down that Daniel never leaves loose ends. He means to . . . finish Marcus off. To finish them all off, no doubt."

"The women, too?"

"You mean his wife, Denise?"

"And her sister, Andrea," Courtney added.

"Sister?"

"Andrea Lambert, the woman you spoke to at the Ambassador Club. The one with my uncle."

Christine laughed sharply. "Is that who she told you she was?"

"What do you mean?"

"Denise has no twin sister as far as I now. That was Daniel's wife, Denise. She walked out on him a week ago. After she found out he planned to obtain and sell the Gorky manuscript, then run off with—"

"With you?" Courtney broke in.

"Me? I see. You think Daniel and I are lovers." She made a brittle sound that was a poor imitation of a laugh. "No, we've never been lovers. Daniel doesn't like to mix business with pleasure. Our relationship has always been . . . professional. We share certain interests." She paused, her expression downcast. "And greed."

Courtney's head was spinning. Was absolutely no one who they said they were? "Andrea is Denise Emerson," she repeated slowly.

"Daniel married her a few months ago. I never did see what he saw in her. Apparently he didn't see it for very long. Unfortunately for Daniel, Denise overheard him one evening telling me about his amorous plans. He said he was leaving Denise for the pianist in *Fanfare*. And Denise overheard him tell me about the manuscript being in Madden's possession. I was to fly to Boston and retrieve it. The next morning when Denise cleaned out one of their joint bank accounts, then turned up in Boston, as well, Daniel realized she'd been eavesdropping. Denise meant to make Daniel pay through the nose for the manuscript and for his infidelity. A very vindictive woman, Denise Lambert Emerson. And a very foolish one to think she was any match for her husband."

Just as Courtney was nodding slowly at Christine, her eye caught a glimpse of black fabric at the edge of the open library door. Then a head popped out for an instant. It took a masterful piece of acting for Courtney not to reveal her surprise.

It was Lady Edith. Her arrival was unexpected enough, but it was Lady Edith's getup that really got Courtney. Lady Edith playing Edie the waitress was nothing compared to Lady Edith playing... Sister Edith.

The "nun" moved swiftly and silently across the room while Courtney kept Christine's attention focused straight ahead by pleading with the woman to untie her.

It wasn't a Bible in the Sister's hand that rose up behind Christine Dupré. It was a vase. Probably a very expensive vase at that. And like Humpty-Dumpty, after it crashed down on Christine's head it wasn't likely to be put together again.

Lady Edith seemed unperturbed by the loss of her objet d'art, although she expressed dismay at having had to clobber the woman.

There was little time, however, for regrets. Quickly she ran to Courtney and untied her, then withdrew a second habit from under her own robes.

"The Garden Club is doing their musical review next week. These are a couple of the costumes," Lady Edith said, helping Courtney into the habit. "I called you from town to have you meet me at the airport. When I heard you whisper help..."

Courtney threw her arms around Lady Edith. "Sister," she said with a grin, "you're bloody terrific."

Lady Edith smiled with delight. "I couldn't very well sit back cooling my jets any more than you could, Sister Courtney." She gave the young "novice" a quick, affectionate hug. "We'd better hurry if we want to get to Heathrow before Lou's plane takes off." She allowed a moment for a quick sigh. "Poor Lou. I'm afraid he's going to be quite upset when he finds out Andrea Lambert is really Denise Emerson. He did mention her to me last evening and I had the feeling he rather liked her."

Courtney smiled at Lady Edith. She'd seen sparks between Uncle Lou and Jonathan's mother. And she was certain it wasn't her imagination. "I wouldn't worry about it. I think he'll get over her very quickly. Once he sees that their relationship was based solely on illusion, each of them pretending to be someone else." A faint shadow passed over her face. Wasn't the same true for her and Jonathan? Where did illusion end and reality begin for the two of them?

# CHAPTER NINETEEN

COURTNEY AND LADY EDITH boarded the plane for Paris with only minutes to spare. Both of them breathless from having run along endless corridors, they straightened their habits and started down the aisle. When they spotted a priest wearing a black mac and a matching hat sitting on an aisle seat, they donned pious expressions.

"Father," the two nuns murmured.

"Sisters," the priest responded.

Five rows farther down the aisle, the two nuns stopped in their tracks and shot each other startled glances.

"Here, Sisters," a burly gentleman said, misinterpreting their dismayed looks and quickly moving over to the window seat, "you can sit together now."

Courtney and Lady Edith gave distracted nods of thanks as they slid into their seats. Immediately Courtney leaned close to Lady Edith and whispered anxiously, "That wasn't who I think it was . . . was it?"

Lady Edith knit her brows. "Jonathan must have had the same idea as us. He knew about the Garden Club review. In fact, I'd only recently asked him if he might fill in for our ailing dentist, Mr. Alperthorn."

Courtney closed her eyes. "And Mr. Alperthorn was to play a priest."

"Precisely."

Courtney sighed. "Do you think Jonathan realized who we really . . . ?" She did not have the opportunity—or the need—to complete her sentence.

"Excuse me, Sisters, might I have a word with you?" The priest addressed them politely, hands clasped in front of him, and then looked solemnly over at the bruiser of a man in the far seat. "Would you be ever so kind, sir, as to exchange seats with me? I'm just a few rows up the aisle. There are certain...church matters...I need to discuss with the Sisters."

The burly gentleman gave the priest a pious look and rose immediately. "Certainly, Father. No problem at all."

Once the passenger had made his way to the vacated seat a few rows up, Jonathan leaned down and in a cool, low voice muttered to Courtney, "Tell Mother Superior to move over a seat, will you, Sister?"

Courtney's perfunctory nod in Lady Edith's direction got the message across. Jonathan subjected Courtney's toes to quite a crush as he squeezed past her to take the empty seat in the middle. Courtney was convinced Jonathan's clumsiness was deliberate. And, she had to admit, understandable.

With a weary movement, he lowered himself into the seat between the two "nuns," leaned his head back against the padded cushion, reverently pressed his palms together in prayer and closed his eyes.

"Sisters, Sisters, Sisters," Jonathan intoned. "Whatever shall we do about this disturbing situation?"

Courtney leaned a little closer to Jonathan. "We had to come. Wait until you hear what we've found out. Oh, but first, you needn't worry about our multi-talented actress, Christine Dupré, for a while. Your mother's seen to her."

"My mother...?"

"But not before Christine saw to one of the Russians," Courtney hurried on. "So that takes two people out of the game—temporarily, anyway. As for that middle-aged siren Andrea Lambert...well, that's quite another story altogether."

Jonathan's eyes glazed over. "I truly don't believe this. What a fool I was to think tying you up would in any way hinder you. And now you've managed to recruit my mother, as well."

"I was not recruited. I was a volunteer," said the "Mother Superior." "And if it hadn't been for my arrival home in the nick of time, one doesn't even want to imagine what might have happened to Courtney. That awful Miss Dupré was holding a gun on her. And Courtney, poor girl, wrapped up like a parcel... was utterly defenseless. Really, Jonathan, I was most shocked to learn that was your doing. It isn't like you at all." She came to an abrupt stop and scrutinized her son. "Or is it? I wonder if I know you at all."

"I wonder," mused Courtney, "if any of us really knows anyone very deeply. Even the ones we love. Perhaps especially the ones we love."


"WHAT ARE WE WAITING FOR? Shouldn't we be following them?" Courtney asked impatiently as they walked out of Charles de Gaulle Airport and she saw her uncle pulling off in his rented Renault, keeping just behind a sleek black sedan.

"Yes," Lady Edith agreed. "Shouldn't we, Jonathan?"

He cast them both dark looks. "I wish the two of you would just stick to prayer."

"They're getting away," the women exclaimed, practically in unison.

With an ambling gait that Courtney and Lady Edith found frustratingly slow, Jonathan headed for a white Mercedes parked along the curb of the arrival area. He paused for a long moment and surveyed the two anxious-looking nuns.

"All right, Sisters. In the back. Be quick about it."

Courtney shared a winning smile with Lady Edith. "Yes, Father," they said in perfect unison, hurrying into the rear seat, their habits slowing them up only a trifle.

"Now what?" Courtney asked as she slammed the back door shut.

Jonathan pulled out and headed for the *autoroute* leading into Paris.

Courtney leaned forward. "Do you know where they were heading? I thought Uncle Lou wasn't told—"

"Silent prayer would be most appropriate at the moment, Sister."

"Come on, Jonathan. You're not playing fair. Didn't I tell you on the plane what I found out about Andrea Lambert? Without me you would never have known she was really Denise Emerson. Not quite the innocent my uncle or you imagined. I for one never trusted her. Now I've given you key information here. I think I deserve some credit. And some of your confidence."

"Here, here," piped in Lady Edith.

Jonathan pulled off sharply at the approaching exit.

"You aren't thinking of leaving us at the side of the road somewhere?" Courtney asked anxiously.

He gave her a fast glance over his shoulder. "Nothing would please me more. But you'd only hitch a ride and somehow, someway, manage to track me down."

Courtney frowned. "So where are we going?"

After a long pause he relented. "About forty kilometers southwest of Paris is a little village called Dampierre. Mostly a valley of orchards and vineyards. One of those vineyards happens to be owned by an English gentleman."

"Emerson?"

Jonathan nodded.

"But how did you find out? Emerson's covered his tracks so thoroughly up to now."

Jonathan didn't answer right away. When he did, his voice sounded both troubled and guarded. "I still have a few friends at intelligence. One of them contacted me last night with some interesting information. There's a special file on Emerson that Noble keeps with his private papers. It seems Noble knows a great deal more about our elusive Mr. Emerson than he's led us to believe."

Jonathan unconsciously pressed harder on the accelerator. "Someone's been keeping Noble quite well informed."

"Was there any mention of Andrea Lambert in that file?" Courtney asked. "Did Noble know that her real name was Denise Emerson?"

"It was mentioned."

Courtney scowled. "So then you knew... Well, why'd you let me go on about it during the flight?"

He smiled for the first time. "You seemed so bloody pleased with your findings, I didn't have the heart to say anything."

"Does my uncle know about Andrea—Denise—too?"

"He took it quite well."

Courtney glanced over to her right to see a pleased smile on Lady Edith's face. Focusing back on Jonathan, she asked, "Who do you suppose is feeding Noble word on Emerson?"

"In this business we all have our informants. I'd be curious to know who Noble's is myself. Not that Noble would confide such vital information to me. He's made it quite clear that he doesn't want me involved in the denouement. So I doubt he'd even hint at where it was to take place."

Courtney smiled. "Isn't he going to be surprised, then, when we show up for the denouement, anyway?"

THE DRIVE TO DAMPIERRE took very little time. Jonathan slowed down as he pulled into the outskirts of the town, coming to a full stop across from a quaint little stone church.

"Why are we stopping here?" Courtney asked cautiously.

Jonathan gave her a stern look. "The Emerson place is just down the road. I'm going to park off the street and head the rest of the way on foot." He took hold of Courtney's hands. "Courage and cleverness are to be respected, love. But so is caution and good sense. I've never tied up a pair of nuns before." He paused for effect. "Now please, Courtney, go over to the church with my mother, as befits your station, and wait for me."

"But you can't go there all alone," Courtney protested.

"I won't be alone. I told you, I have some friends at intelligence, friends who are still loyal to Marcus Lloyd. They're already in position at the vineyard and will step into action if any funny business ensues."

"If Noble spots you, he isn't going to be very pleased."

"That's his problem. I'm here to make certain Marcus doesn't get caught in any cross fire. Noble is only interested in grabbing Emerson and retrieving the manuscript. And I'm sure he's counting on nabbing Zakharov, as well. My guess—and I'm certain Noble's—is that once Emerson has his hands on the Gorky, he'll turn right around and negotiate a quick sale to Zakharov. Emerson is nothing if not shrewd. The Russians will not only pay top dollar, they might throw future business his way as well."

Jonathan helped both women from the car. Then he pulled Courtney aside. "If not for my sake, then my mother's safety, Courtney, you must stay here at the church. Events will move swiftly from here on out. If all goes well, your uncle and I will have Marcus—and Emerson's wife, if she's being held against her will—safely away from the vineyard while Noble and his boys round up the Gorky, Emerson and Zakharov."

"If all goes well," Courtney echoed with a worried look.

Jonathan discarded his priestly garb and gave her a tender smile. "Prayer really might help, love." He didn't say another word, merely held her captive a moment longer with those incredible aquamarine eyes of his. Suddenly Courtney was beset by the alarming thought that she might never see those wondrous eyes again.

JONATHAN HURRIED down the narrow dirt path at the west end of the Emerson vineyards. This affair had turned out to be one surprise after another, and he was certain the surprises were not over yet. As he rounded the bend he could make out a two-story white farmhouse off to the right. Lou's Renault was parked out front.

Jonathan slipped into a wooded area, heading toward the western end of the house. Then he cupped his hands over his mouth and emitted a low, warbling birdcall. A moment later he received an answering call from a point deeper within the vineyard. Good, he thought, his agents were in place.

As he worked his way stealthily toward the farmhouse, Jonathan could make out a white barn just behind the main building. He decided to check the barn first on the faint chance that Marcus was being kept there while Emerson examined the parcel Lou had brought as ransom.

As he approached the barn from the rear, Jonathan could no longer hold back the question that had haunted him for days. Was his dear friend Marcus Lloyd still alive? Emerson and Lou Vaughn had spoken by telephone at Christine Dupré's dressing room yesterday afternoon and Emerson had sworn Marcus was in good health. Not that either Jonathan or Lou Vaughn were prepared to take Emerson at his word. That was one of the reasons they were going in with professional backup.

The wooden door at the back of the barn was ajar. Jonathan peered in cautiously, then slid the door open a few more inches and slipped inside. The air in the barn was cool and damp. The place itself was empty save for some farm machinery that looked as if it had been left idle for a long while.

But the barn had been occupied recently, Jonathan was pleased to note. A makeshift straw bed stood off to one corner with a rumpled blanket on it; paper cups lay strewn about, and the smell of stale coffee and tobacco hung in the air. Not only had the barn been recently inhabited but whoever had holed up there had done so for some time by the look of things.

Jonathan stole out of the barn and made his way to the rear of the farmhouse, ducking behind trees and shrubs. Crawling now, he rose for an instant at each window and glanced inside. One room after another was empty, until he got to a small rear bedroom window at the far end of the house.

Jonathan ducked back down quickly and let out a sigh of relief. Then, concealing himself behind a large shrub, he reached for the automatic stuck in the waistband of his trousers and pulled it out slowly.

ZAKHAROV ENTERED the stone church in Dampierre, Petrenko following behind him.

"Stay here," Zakharov sharply ordered his underling.

Petrenko shrugged and came to a stop just inside the wooden doors, then pointed to the two nuns kneeling at the first pew.

Zakharov frowned. He stubbed out his cigarette on the old, worn wooden floor. He'd been told this would be a safe, private place for a rendezvous, since the church had not been used for nearly ten years. Once again he cursed his bad luck as he stared at the backs of the two kneeling nuns. Neither one of them turned. They both seemed deep in prayer.

Zakharov listened as another car pulled up. Petrenko turned and cracked open the door to have a look. He swiveled back and nodded.

Moments later, the man Zakharov was to meet entered the church. Zakharov motioned in the direction of the two nuns in prayer.

The other man frowned. "Out back. In the graveyard," the new arrival muttered.

Zakharov followed the man outside, whispering an order in Russian to Petrenko.

When the two nuns rose, Petrenko slid into a back pew and pretended to be praying. The Sisters passed the pew, giving the kneeling man surreptitious glances.

Once outside, Courtney grabbed Lady Edith's hand. "Russians. I heard one of them speak. And the one sitting in the pew I recognized from Boston. I wonder who came in after them? Both cars are still here. The men must be close by. I'm going to have a look behind the church."

"I'll go with you." Lady Edith did not sound enthusiastic.

"No, two of us might be conspicuous. Look, there's a little café up the street." She pointed. "Wait for me there."

Lady Edith clutched Courtney's hands. "I'm not sure you should go snooping about."

Courtney gave her a quick hug. "Don't worry about me. I'm quite good at this. You will sit tight at the café?"

"I suppose I really have no choice."

Courtney watched Lady Edith start off up the street, then quickly plucked a few marigolds from a small flower bed at the side of the church. Forcing herself to walk slowly, she headed for the graveyard behind the church.

The two men were there—as she'd suspected. Head lowered, she moved to a gravestone about thirty yards from an elm tree under which the men were conferring. Her movements were silent, but one of the men must have caught sight of her in his peripheral vision. He glanced nervously over in her direction just as she was kneeling on the ground, pretending to say a prayer before placing the flowers on the grave.

Courtney's eyes met his for the briefest of moments, and when they did, she felt such a shock that it took all her effort to fight back a gasp of surprise.

Her knees shaking, her heart pounding, Courtney wanted to bolt. But she forced herself to stay put, praying in earnest that the recognition hadn't been two-way.

Her prayers must have been answered, because the man didn't glance back at her again but merely concluded his talk quickly thereafter. Then both men headed down a narrow dirt path that led west toward the nearby vineyard.

Hesitating only a moment, Courtney hurried back around the church, following the path Jonathan had taken to the vineyard. And once again she was praying—this time that the path she'd picked would get her to Emerson's place quicker than the route chosen by the two men from the graveyard. To help her prayers along, she hoisted her habit and broke into a run.

JONATHAN TOOK A LAST LOOK around before forcing open the window as noiselessly as possible and slipping inside. As he stepped down the floorboards squeaked, and he cursed silently. He stood still, apprehensively watching the closed door that led into the hall, but there were no sounds. Jonathan turned his attention to the huddled form on the narrow metal bed.

He approached slowly. The Spartan room, furnished with only one bed, a wooden chair and a rickety table, was dim, musty and still.

The man on the bed lay as motionless as a statue. His face was to the wall, his hands bound behind him, his legs roped at the ankles.

At first Jonathan thought he was dead. With trepidation, he touched the man's hand, fully expecting it to be cold as ice. But the skin was warm, and the man's fingers moved faintly at Jonathan's touch.

"Marcus." Jonathan leaned over, whispering in the man's ear. He did not get a response, nor did he wait for one before quickly untying his friend's wrists and ankles.

Only when Jonathan started to lift him did Marcus's eyes flicker open.

"Jonathan? Is...that...you?" Marcus Lloyd's voice was hoarse.

"Yes. It's all right. I've come to free you."

"They drugged me..."

"You're coming round. Just lean against me. I'm getting you out of here." As soon as he had safely delivered Marcus into an agent's care, he'd come back and help Lou Vaughn contend with Emerson.

Jonathan had gotten the tall, solidly built Marcus to within a few feet of the window, when he heard footsteps approaching from out in the hall. Quickly Jonathan half dragged Marcus back to the bed, hastily twining some rope around his wrists and ankles. He barely had time himself to crawl under the bed before the door opened.

"There. Have a look for yourself. He's just had a bit of sleeping sedative."

Lou Vaughn raised a brow at Emerson, then crossed the room to the bed, spotting immediately that Lloyd had been untied. He turned quickly back to Emerson. "Okay. Looks like we have a deal."

"Fine. The manuscript, then," Emerson said impatiently.

"What about your wife?"

"Denise has behaved very foolishly, and she's admitted it to me. Jealousy can make a woman do strange things, Mr. Vaughn. We had a nice long chat, and who knows...perhaps we'll mend some bridges. Sorry, old chap, if you had other ideas."

Lou shook his head in wonderment as he stared at the short, slightly built, remarkably ordinary-looking man with the thinning brown hair, overly broad nose and narrow lips. Lou had pictured Emerson as tall, powerfully built, exceedingly handsome and charismatic. As for Emerson's cheery view of his marriage, Lou decided to let it ride for now. There'd be time after Emerson had been dealt with to check up on the woman he still thought of as "Andrea."

"We're wasting time, Mr. Vaughn. The manuscript, please. Then you and Lloyd here can be on your way."

Lou slipped the parcel from his inside jacket pocket, his eyes never leaving Emerson's. "No funny business now. I wasn't fool enough to come without protection."

He crossed over to Emerson and handed him the manuscript. Emerson's dark eyes gleamed. Lou went back for Marcus.

That was where Lou made his big mistake. Just as he leaned over to help the drugged man up, he took his eyes off Emerson for a split second. That was all Emerson needed to pull out the gun from his pocket.

Lou caught the blue-black glint of the weapon out of the corner of his eye. "Don't be an idiot, Emerson. We've got the place covered. You won't get ten yards."

"Sorry, old chap," Emerson said, taking aim. "By the time your friends outside realize something is wrong, I'll have concluded our business and vanished."

"You have the manuscript. Why complicate your life?"

But it seemed Emerson wasn't worried about complications. Or he wasn't until he spotted the figure in black at the window. Instinct and self-preservation took over. Emerson swerved abruptly, directing the barrel of the gun at the window as he squeezed the trigger. The black figure ducked just as the bullet pierced the glass, shattering it.

Still under the bed, Jonathan had no idea what had distracted Emerson, causing him to alter his target, and he couldn't have cared less at the moment. The diversion was all he needed to get off a clean shot of his own. Emerson cried out, as much in surprise as in pain, as the bullet from Jonathan's gun ripped into his shoulder. Emerson's pistol thudded to the ground, followed by the manuscript. Emerson came tumbling down right after, passing out cold. Lou grabbed for the weapon and the parcel just as Jonathan scooted out from under the bed.

"Great timing," Lou said, grinning.

Jonathan was about to say thanks, when his eyes were drawn to the window, where a very familiar-looking nun was peering in. It seemed that once again the inimitable Courtney Blue had managed to save the day.

Or so he thought... until a second figure appeared behind Courtney, a tall, gaunt man. Jonathan, Lou and a still-woozy Marcus froze as they watched the fellow place a gun to Courtney's temple.

In a heavy Russian accent, the man known as Zakharov ordered Jonathan and Lou to drop their weapons, then commanded all three men to climb out the shattered window.

Courtney stared wanly at Jonathan and her uncle after they'd managed to help Marcus outside.

"Jonathan, I'm sorry. I only meant to warn you—"

"Silence," Zakharov ordered, the barrel of the gun making an indentation in her temple. "In my entire career I have never dealt with such an infuriating group." He dragged Courtney a little closer to the men. "Take the manuscript from your uncle, Miss Blue."

All three pairs of eyes were glued on her. Courtney's muscles were taut, screaming with tension, but she swore she would not make it easy for the Russian. She might not have much experience at this game, but she had done all right so far on instinct alone. She'd take it as far as she could. Ther really weren't any other viable options, anyway.

It all happened with lightning speed. Courtney had n sooner taken hold of the manuscript from her uncle than sh flung it with all her might right into Zakharov's face. In th same instant she stomped on his foot with as much force a she could muster. Zakharov cried out more in outrage tha in pain, but his momentary surprise caused him to loosen hi grip on her waist. Courtney dropped hard to the ground jus as her uncle and Jonathan took running leaps at the Ru sian.

That was when Noble appeared. Courtney didn't see hir at first, but Jonathan did. She heard him call out to Nobl for assistance as he and Lou wrestled with Zakharov.

"No," Courtney screamed to Jonathan. "Noble's wit them. He's with the Russians."

But the warning came too late.

Noble smiled at Courtney as he trained the gun on her. " had the oddest feeling that was you in the graveyard. B Zakharov had assured me one of his men was keeping close eye on you in London."

Noble turned his attention to the three men on th ground. With a wave of his gun he motioned Jonathan an Lou off Zakharov. "It's tidying-up time. I never doubte for a moment that you would show up, Madden. You neve were one for taking orders. It's just as well. You've mucke up once again, old chap. We can all rest easier knowing thi will be your last faux pas."

Jonathan sneered at Noble.

"Oh, if you're thinking your friends out in the vineyar will come to your rescue, I wouldn't hold my breath, Mad den. I have my special handpicked crew out there taking car of them. You must take me for a fool."

"The problem is, I didn't take you for a big enough fool." Jonathan glared at both Noble and Zakharov disdainfully

Noble merely seemed amused. He looked over at Courtney, his smile deepening. "You are good, Miss Blue. I will say that. Quite a flair with disguises. But I'm afraid this will be your last one."

Sadly Courtney believed him. Nor were her spirits in any way lifted when she noticed the Russian whom she'd earlier seen in the church ambling over, gun in hand.

Zakharov motioned the lumbering Petrenko to hurry up. "Take them all to the barn, tie them up and set the place on fire." He might have been ordering a barbecue dinner.

Petrenko nodded, motioning all of them to precede him. Lou took charge of the still dazed and woozy Marcus, while Jonathan kept a firm arm around Courtney. As soon as they passed Zakharov and Noble, Jonathan gave Courtney a bright smile. She in turn gave him a baffled look, finding not the slightest reason for such cheeriness. But if she was baffled by the smile, it was nothing compared to her utter confusion when, just after they stepped into the barn, the stocky, balding Russian who went by the name of Petrenko, drew two more guns from his deep pockets and tossed one to Lou and one to Jonathan.

"What the...?" Her mouth hung open in shock.

Jonathan kissed her quickly. "You see, none of us really are whom we pretend to be. It's the nature of the business. Meet Ian Powell. We studied Russian together at Oxford."

Petrenko slipped off the fake gold caps on his front teeth and grinned. "I'm pleased to meet you...Sister," he said in perfect upper-crust English.

"I suppose I shouldn't even be surprised at this point," Courtney muttered.

Minutes later it was all over. Noble, the double agent, Zakharov, the KGB man, and Emerson, the kidnapper, were all quickly rounded up and led away by Jonathan's men. The agents Noble had thought "taken care of" had actually been busy turning the tables on Noble's handpicked

crew. With a swiftness that left Courtney reeling, the wild
fantastic adventure was suddenly and finally over and done.

Well...not quite.

It remained for a worried "Sister" Edith to bring things
to a close. She was hurrying to the farmhouse when she
nearly tripped over a little package that had been dropped
earlier. She retrieved the prize and with a flourish presented the much-sought-after Gorky manuscript to her son,
while Courtney gave her a well-earned pat on the shoulder.

As Jonathan stared down at the manuscript, Marcus
Lloyd, now quite recovered, came over and grinned.
"Well," Marcus said, "we can chuck that bit of nonsense
out now."

Courtney and Lady Edith looked over at the former chief
of intelligence as though he'd truly lost his marbles. Even
Uncle Lou shook his head with wonder.

It was Lou who found his voice first. "What's he talking
about, Jonathan?"

"Well, tell them, man," Marcus encouraged. "It was
your brilliant plan, after all. And with the help of our man
in Moscow—" he grinned at Powell alias Petrenko "—you
pulled it off."

"With a few snags along the way," Jonathan muttered,
his aquamarine eyes holding Courtney's, then moving rest-
lessly away.

"Yes, I'll grant you we didn't cover all bases," Marcus
admitted. "Still, we got that traitor Noble in the end, and
that's what counts."

"Yes," Jonathan said slowly. "That's what counts." He
found it easier to look at Lou than Courtney. "Marcus and
I have suspected for quite a while that Noble was a double
agent. But we had no proof, so we had to force his hand.
And—" he shot Courtney a glance "—the plan had to be
utterly convincing." He focused back on Lou. "Even the
CIA had to be misled. The key was to persuade everyone

nvolved that the manuscript was valuable. Most important, Noble and the Russians were convinced the Gorky was not only a rare Russian treasure, but that it concealed a top-secret plan for a submarine detection device smuggled out by a leading Russian scientist. Noble and Zakharov had to get it back. And chances were they would make every effort to get rid of Marcus and me permanently once they got their hands on the goods."

There was absolute silence around Jonathan. He looked over at Courtney. Her confusion and anger at his ultimate subterfuge was evident. He quickly went on and finished his tale. "We hadn't planned on Emerson getting in on the act. Certainly not on him kidnapping Marcus and holding him for ransom. We hadn't planned on a lot of things that happened."

Marcus flung an arm around Jonathan's shoulder. "We needn't bother with any of that now. We return victorious, my boy. That was the goal. Wipe the slate clean. I have big plans for you, Jonathan. You've got what it takes to go straight to the top. And I'm going to help you get there."

It was Lady Edith who discreetly ushered Lou, Marcus and Powell off to the Renault, giving Jonathan and Courtney a moment to themselves.

Courtney stood looking at Jonathan silently, all energy spent.

"I'm sorry, Courtney. In this business subterfuge is sometimes all there is between life and death. I simply couldn't risk—"

"It's a perfect ending, really. Nothing, absolutely nothing was what it seemed to be." Her voice was devoid of inflection, but a mix of emotions fluttered across her face. "Marcus is right, Jonathan. Getting your man is all that counts. And that glory, of course."

She started off. Jonathan called out to her to stop, but she kept walking. He caught up with her at the car. "Things are going to be chaotic for a while at intelligence. But when the dust settles a bit . . ."

"It will be time to face reality. I suddenly find myself too old for dreams and fairy-tale fantasies."

"We made some of those fantasies come true," he said quietly.

"Yes," she whispered. "For a short while . . . we did." She gave him a forced, fragile, but dismissive smile and stepped into the car.

## EPILOGUE

"I THOUGHT YOU WOULD WAIT for me," he said softly.

She turned slowly toward him, meeting those extraordinary aquamarine eyes once again. He had walked in so silently she hadn't realized anyone was there until she heard his voice—a voice that instantly, as always, sent shivers down her spine.

"The adventure was over. There was no point...I couldn't see any sort of a future...I assumed you'd be very involved...that you'd very likely forget about me in time...." Nervously she swept her fingers through her hair.

He smiled, shaking his head slowly. "I could never forget about you. I could never forget what we shared."

"That was yesterday." She was trying desperately to hold on to some semblance of control. She loved him now more than ever, but she had known the rules of the game from the start. He had set them and she had agreed to them. If the rules were going to change it must be his doing.

He sighed deeply. She was going to make this difficult for him. But he knew this was difficult for her, too. He could see into her soul. He could feel her tension, her desire, her fear, as if they were his own. They were his own.

"Our yesterdays were wonderful, love." His blue-green eyes smoldered as he stepped toward her. His voice was low as his face moved closer to hers. "But our tomorrows will be even more exciting. The adventure isn't over, love. It's only just begun." And then, before she could say a word, he swept her into his arms and kissed her fiercely, greedily, fit-

ting her body against his until they were molded together
one.

"Oh, my sweet, stubborn, dearest love. Marry me,"
urged. "You must marry me." His look was so earnest,
filled with tenderness, so vulnerable beneath that han
some, rugged facade, that he erased all the pain and dou
from her mind.

Tears of joy escaped her eyes as she threw her arr
around the man of her dreams, the man to whom she ha
sworn true and undying love right from the very start. "Ye
my darling. Yes, I'll marry you."

Once again Derek Colton swept the irrepressible Kathe
ine O'Malley into his arms, the soft breeze whistling throug
her shimmering red hair, the sky melodious with the soun
of gulls, this moment the most exciting—

"EXCUSE ME. I wonder if you carry any first editions o
*Reminiscences.* It's by Gorky."

The book fell from Courtney's hand as she heard h
voice. She did not look up immediately. Her heart quick
ened. Oh, no, she thought in a panic, the fantasies wer
getting out of hand again. *This is a daydream. You've bee
wishing so hard all these weeks . . .*

He was on his knees, lifting her romantic adventure nove
His head was lowered. He was skimming the last page she'
just been reading. With an almost intolerable blend c
trepidation and excitement, she let herself gaze at his thick
dark hair.

Slowly he lifted his head, those wondrous, magical aqua
marine eyes meeting hers. "I see your friends Kate an
Derek had a happy ending."

She swallowed hard. "They often do . . . in novels."

His eyes trailed over her face. "You ran out on me."
There was a hurt note in his voice.

She was having trouble breathing. "The adventure was over. I . . . had to get on . . . with my life."

He surveyed the little bookshop on Newberry Street in Boston deprecatingly. "This is no life for someone like you."

"Someone like me?" Her voice sharpened. "Who am I, Jonathan? Just a foolish shopkeeper who, for a brief moment in time, pretended to be a daring, beautiful femme fatale. It feels now that what happened was even more of a fantasy than all the others I've had since childhood." She stopped and stared deeply into Jonathan's magnificent aquamarine eyes. "No, I'm wrong. It wasn't a fantasy. I could have controlled the ending if it had been. The problem was, it was real life, and I was forced to face the harsh realities."

Jonathan was about to argue, when a woman walked in. Courtney rushed over to assist the customer, hoping the distraction would help her to calm down. But the woman only wanted directions to the subway. Courtney walked her to the door and pointed the way. She remained there after the woman had gone.

"I saw your uncle before I left London."

Courtney turned to Jonathan. "I thought he was somewhere in Berlin." She quirked a brow. "Purchasing a rare work."

Jonathan smiled. "I doubted he'd actually retire. But he finished his 'purchase' quickly and stopped in London to visit my mother."

Despite her tension, she smiled. "I'm glad."

"She's quite smitten with him, you know."

"And he with her."

Jonathan crossed the shop to Courtney. He still had the Hilary Bennett thriller in his hand. "See, some happy endings occur in real life, as well."

"I don't suppose the ending was very happy for Chris tine Dupré or Andrea—I mean Denise Emerson."

"Denise did get to see her husband punished for hi crimes, even if her own plan backfired. Sweet revenge in fashion, but she wound up broke and alone in the end. And Christine Dupré made out even worse. She lost her man and her career. Instead of star billing in a West End produc tion, she earned an extended run behind bars."

"How did your friend Marcus take the news of her de ceit?"

"Despite everything, I think he still feels rather los without her." Jonathan looked into Courtney's eyes. " understand how he feels." His gaze was so filled with ten derness she found herself trembling. And fantasizing.

"I told Marcus all about your participation in his rescue the downfall of Noble and the safeguarding of the manu script," Jonathan went on.

She threw him a wry glance. "Yes, the precious manu script. He must have had a good chuckle over that."

Jonathan smiled gently. "Marcus didn't laugh. He wa terribly impressed with you. He thought you were quit brilliant. A real natural, as they say over here." He move a few paces closer. "As for the Gorky, it was precious. Jus not for the reasons you believed. More precious even than realized at the time."

She remained silent, but her eyes did not waver from his

"If it hadn't been for that manuscript," he said slowly, a faint tremor in his voice, "we would never have met."

"And you might not have gone back to your true calling as a secret agent." A smile lit her face. "And I wouldn' have had the adventure of a lifetime," she admitted softly "Or," she added, not knowing where the courage came from, "fallen in love with the hero of my dreams."

"Every hero needs a heroine, love." Jonathan's eye smoldered with tenderness and passion. "Every good spy needs a good partner." He stood very close to her, but he didn't touch her yet. "Did you really think I could forget you, Courtney Blue alias Katherine O'Malley?"

She lost her courage. Inside her was a whirlpool of anticipation and wild speculation. She stood frozen in place, afraid to move.

"Don't you know, my beautiful, passionate, stubborn and irrepressible Miss Blue, that you are unforgettable." His eyes floated down to the Bennett thriller. He scanned the last page. Then slowly he raised his eyes once again to Courtney's lovely face. His hand moved to her hair, and, smiling, he undid the clasp on the tortoiseshell barrette. " 'The adventure isn't over, love. It's only just begun,' " he quoted, his eyes warming her with a mixture of candor, sensuality and tenderness. "I love you, Courtney. That is the reality—the only reality that matters to me. And nothing ever again will be real for me unless you marry me. You must marry me, Courtney."

Her heart was pounding madly. Here he was, the hero of her fantasies, brave, incredibly handsome, everything she had ever dreamed of... telling her he loved her and wanted to marry her. Could such an offer ruffle the unflappable Courtney Blue?

"Must I?" she answered with remarkable cool. But Jonathan knew her so very well by now. He knew her passion, her daring, her vulnerabilities. And he could feel, now more than ever, the power and intensity of her love.

He gazed deeply into her eyes and smiled a breathtaking hero's smile. "Yes, my love. You must."

And then, because she was so brave, so beautiful, and because it was what he longed to do most, he swept her into his arms and kissed her hotly, passionately... a kiss that convinced Courtney Blue once and for all time that indeed the adventure had only just begun.

# *Harlequin Superromance.*

## COMING NEXT MONTH

**#366 UNTIL OCTOBER • Margaret Chittenden**
Maddy Scott knew Dr. Nate Ludlow's type—fun-
loving, footloose, no commitments. But between
holding down a full-time job and caring for her
sister's kids, she welcomed some fun in her life.
Their relationship wouldn't last . . . unless Nate had a
change of heart.

**#367 THURSDAY'S CHILD • Nancy Elliott**
Sheltered since birth, Elise St. James knew nothing
about the world . . . or about men. Then Logan
Hunter became her bodyguard. Attorney by trade,
adventurer by inclination, Logan proved to be a
good teacher. Maybe too good. Soon Elise was
deeply in love, yet she could tell him nothing about
her past. . . .

**#368 HONOR BOUND • Shirley Larson**
The last time Shelly Armstrong had seen stunt pilot
Justin Corbett, she'd been overwhelmed by his good
looks and opulent life-style. She'd been a tongue-tied
teenager then. Now she was an accomplished pilot
with her own flight school, and equal to Justin in all
respects but one—she was still a novice at loving.

**#369 CANDLE IN THE WINDOW • Suzanne Ellison**
Gary Reid was imprisoned in a notorious California
correctional institution for a crime he refused to name
as such. Still, he refused to commit to fire
fighter and conservationist Carly Winston while he
had nothing to offer. And Carly had her own doubts.
Did Gary love her, or was she just his candle in
the window?

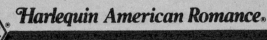

*Gull Cottage*

The sun, the surf, the sand...

One relaxing month by the sea was all Zoe, Diana and Gracie ever expected from their four-week stay at Gull Cottage, the luxurious East Hampton mansion. They never thought that what they found at the beach would change their lives forever.

Join Zoe, Diana and Gracie for the summer of their lives. Don't miss the GULL COTTAGE trilogy in Harlequin American Romance: #301 CHARMED CIRCLE by Robin Francis (July 1989); #305 MOTHER KNOWS BEST by Barbara Bretton (August 1989); and #309 SAVING GRACE by Anne McAllister (September 1989).

GULL COTTAGE—because one month can be the start of forever...

# Your favorite stories have a brand-new look!

American Romance is greeting the new decade with a new design, marked by a contemporary, sophisticated cover. As you've come to expect, each American Romance is still a modern love story with real-life characters and believable conflicts. Only now they look more true-to-life than ever before.

Look for American Romance's bold new cover where Harlequin books are sold.

NOUNCING . . .

Harlequin
Romance
#3000

# *The Lost Moon Flower*
## *by Bethany Campbell*

Look for it this August
wherever Harlequins are sold

HR 3000-1